OTHER BOOKS by KASSANDRA LAMB

The Kate Huntington Mysteries
Psychotherapist Kate Huntington helps others cope with trauma, but she has led a charmed life...until a killer rips it apart. (10 novels) ~ Plus the **Kate on Vacation Mysteries** (4 novellas)

The C.o.P. on the Scene Mysteries
Eight days into her new job as Chief of Police in a small Florida city, Judith Anderson finds herself one step behind a serial killer. (spinoff from the Kate Huntington series; 6 stories—more to come)

The Marcia Banks and Buddy Cozy Mysteries
Marcia Banks trains service dogs for veterans, and solves crimes on the side, with the help of her Black Lab, Buddy. (13 novels/novellas)

The Unintended Consequences Trilogy
writing as Jessica Dale ~ A sweet romance combined with three chilling mysteries, and a couple of ghosts. (3 stories)

FOUNDERS KEEPERS

a C.o.P. on the Scene Mystery
Kassandra Lamb

a mistero press publication

Published by **misterio press LLC**

Cover art by Melinda VanLone, Book Cover Corner; Background photo credit: ©
Lunamarina | Dreamstime.com (purchased right to use)

CHAPTER ONE

I do not normally wish my life away. But today...

I was wishing it was tomorrow. The day *after* Founders Day.

The annual celebration of the incorporation of Starling, Florida was described by one of my officers as "a second Fourth of July, only with even more drunk and disorderlies."

And domestic violence calls, when some of those drunks went home and got disorderly with their families. And lost children. We'd reconnected three minors, ranging from four to ten years old, with their parents.

I took off my hat, ran fingers through my short dark hair—now soaked with sweat—then pulled at the neck of my navy uniform shirt. Mid-August in Florida was not the best time to be decked out in one's dress blues. Nonetheless, I'd ordered everyone, even my detectives, to wear their uniforms, to make our presence as obvious as possible. Hopefully to deter problems, but also to make it easier for folks *with* problems to spot us in the crowd.

The sun was now setting, but it seemed to be getting hotter, or at least muggier.

However, dusk settling over the city signaled that the parade of boats was about to start. Thank heavens. As the final fanfare of the celebration, local boat owners sailed slowly along the Sofki River, their boats alight with decorations, mostly patriotic displays of flags and eagles.

And the city's entire population of eleven thousand, four hundred and thirty-two souls—according to the 2020 census taken a couple of years ago—were now crowding onto the riverwalk to watch the flotilla. Plus several hundred tourists.

Replacing my hat on my head, I keyed my radio. "Armstrong, Bradley, make sure your people are watching for pickpockets."

Sergeant Armstrong was my newly promoted Chief of Patrol, overseeing the other watch commanders and all the uniformed officers. And Lieutenant Bradley was my second in command and Chief of Detectives.

The latter materialized, stepping out of the crowd. He looked almost as dapper in his dress uniform as he normally did in his well-tailored suits. Light brown, slightly-too-long hair bracketed a boyish face. He was one of the handsomest men I'd ever met.

Thank heavens he's gay. I silently chastised myself for that spontaneous but rather non-PC thought. It was true, though, that it was easier to have a close professional relationship with a man when there was no chance of it becoming any other kind of relationship.

"Five pickpockets arrested, so far," Bradley reported, "and three drunken arguments broken up, no arrests there."

His blue eyes sparkled. Was he actually enjoying himself?

"Pretty tame for Founders Day," he added.

"So far," I echoed, my tone acerbic.

He grinned and opened his mouth to respond.

An ear-splitting scream interrupted, temporarily silencing the noisy crowd.

Then the sea of people parted as a frantic woman surged toward us, dragging a two-seater baby stroller behind her.

"Officers, you've got to help me. My little girl is gone!"

My radio crackled with static. "Divers are on their way." Bradley's voice.

I turned away from the mother I'd been trying to both console and interview. "Can they even search in the dark?" I whispered into the radio.

"They say yes. They have lights, but it will be slow going."

I turned back, and said for the umpteenth time, "We're going to find her." But I wasn't as confident as I hoped I sounded.

This wasn't the same as the other kids, who had presented themselves to an officer when they'd realized they were separated from their parents.

This was a two-year-old. She'd pulled loose from her mother's hand and shoved through the legs in front of her, moving toward the riverwalk's railing.

The mother had called after her and had tried to follow, but people were slow to move aside to let her double-wide stroller through. Only when she'd screamed had they realized she wasn't just trying for a better view.

"My God," the woman sobbed now. "You can't know what it's like, to have to choose between your kids. I couldn't leave the baby..." She trailed off and cried harder.

"Of course you couldn't," I murmured. No, I couldn't know, because I'd never been a mother, but...

Why the hell did you let her out of the stroller?

My cell phone rang. I yanked it out of my pocket and glanced at the screen. It read *Dot Wilder-FDLE*.

Really bad timing, Dot. I opted to let the call go to voice-mail, even though it was from the director of the regional office of the Florida Department of Law Enforcement, the state equivalent of the FBI.

I spotted Jenny Coleman, pushing her way through the crowd, and breathed out a sigh. She was a social worker and the head of the Department of Children and Family Services for this area. She would take the mother off my hands, before I slipped and said some of my not-so-understanding thoughts out loud.

I introduced the two women and Mrs. Silva practically collapsed into Jenny's arms. "She insisted on walking. She hates the stroller," she sobbed out.

I rolled my eyes behind her back, and Jenny pursed her lips. "Come on," she said in a soothing voice. "Let's get you and the baby out of this chaos."

Good idea! The baby, seven-month-old Teddy, had been crying for the last ten minutes. But his mother had barely noticed.

I took a deep breath and decided I should cut her a break. Truly, I had no idea what she was going through, or why she'd made the choices she'd made.

And where the hell was her husband? It was a Saturday, so he shouldn't be at work. But maybe he was. Not everybody worked nine to five, Monday through Friday. All I'd gotten out of the mom was that he was an accountant.

I pulled out my phone and texted Jenny. *See if you can find out where the father is.*

The phone pinged in my hand. But it wasn't Jenny responding. It was a text from my assistant, Officer Gloria Barnes.

Chief, found something you need to see.

As I approached, the dim light from a street lamp revealed that Barnes was not her usual well-put-together self. Her uniform was rumpled after a day of herding pedestrians. And several tufts of dark hair had pulled loose from her bun and were hanging in frizzy clumps around her face.

And the expression on her face was the grimmest I'd ever seen. She pointed to a light blob, something resting on the railing of the riverwalk, about a hundred yards south of the spot where the little girl's mother had lost track of her.

Barnes pointed her flashlight at the blob. It was a stuffed bear, perched on the railing.

And balanced on his nose were the pink sunglasses the mother had said little Ashley was wearing.

CHAPTER TWO

I called my head crime scene technician. "Bert, I need you guys out here. We've got two sections of riverwalk railing to check for fingerprints."

He groaned. "On our way."

Standing next to me, Bradley said, "There are gonna be thousands of prints."

When I didn't answer, he ran his hand through his hair. "Should we call off the divers?"

"No," I said in a low voice. "She could still be in the water, or along the riverbank somewhere. Tell our people to keep searching."

"Yeah, will do, but..." He pointed to the bear. "This says to me she was kidnapped."

"Probably," I said, rubbing my aching chest with the heel of my hand. "Do we have contact info on the people around the mother when Ashley broke loose from her?"

He nodded.

"Send our detectives to their homes to re-interview them. See if they've remembered anything suspicious, anyone near the little girl or showing any particular interest in her."

He nodded again, blew out air.

I clapped a hand on his shoulder, gave it a squeeze. "Worst kind of case."

He grunted and turned away to organize his people.

———◆◇◆———

I stood under the tent-like canopy that constituted our temporary search headquarters on the riverwalk. Two long tables were beginning to fill with potential evidence—anything our people had found that might be related. It was mostly small toys and pieces of abandoned child-sized clothing. After a day of families jamming onto the riverwalk, there were lots of both.

Each item sat on top of an index card that gave the location where it was found, the officer's or volunteer's name who found it, and why they thought it was relevant.

I'd made myself examine each item as it had come in, even though the sight of those tiny shorts and tee shirts, baby dolls and pacifiers made my throat close.

Now I was staring out at the two divers' boats, my mind wandering. In the gathering darkness, the vessels were barely distinguishable from the charcoal-gray waters of the river. Except for the lights on their bows and back ends...*what is that called, the back end of a boat?* I knew the word but couldn't seem to pull it out of the recesses of my tired brain.

I shook my head, hoping that would help me focus.

I figured we were looking at three possible scenarios. One, an unstable woman had taken the child to raise as her own. That was the safest scenario for the child, but would make it harder for us to track her down.

Two, a pervert who likes them young had taken her. I shuddered.

Three, there would be a ransom demand.

As if he'd read my mind, Bradley said, "Should we be setting up to trace a ransom call?" His voice was a little tentative. He'd been a detective for years, but was still fairly new at being in charge.

As was I. I'd been the Chief of Police here in Starling for not quite a year, and we'd had no missing children cases in that time.

Indeed, *I* had never worked such a case at all. I'd been a homicide detective in Baltimore County for twenty years, before moving here and taking this sometimes quite thankless job.

So, new territory for both of us.

I grimaced. "They don't have a landline, only their cells. I explained to the mother that we would use Call Trace if she gets a ransom call. She freaked out all over again, but we finally got her calmed down. A uniform, Peters, is at the house with them."

"I'll send Wellbourne over to help them deal with a call, if one comes."

I nodded. Wellbourne was our only female detective. She was young, not all that experienced, but she had a knack for calming victims' frazzled nerves.

She wouldn't be happy about babysitting, but she'd do her job.

"What about the father, is he still MIA?" Bradley said, disgust in his voice. "I'm not a parent, but if I were and my child was missing, I'd be front and center."

"Jenny Coleman just texted me. He finally came home. Unfortunately, we missed seeing his body language when he was told Ashley's missing."

"You suspect him?" Bradley asked.

"At this point, I suspect everybody the least bit associated with that child."

"Can you take the interview with him?" Bradley said. "I want to check for similar cases in the past."

I nodded again. "And check the hospitals in the area for any woman who's recently lost a baby or young child."

Bradley walked away. Fifteen feet down the riverwalk he passed our newest unit in the Starling PD. Officer Robert Terry approached with his partner, a ninety-pound German Shepherd named Konig—although Officer Terry had anglicized it to King.

The humans exchanged a nod. The dog ignored Bradley, his focus straight ahead.

The corners of my mouth twitched upward, despite the solemnity of the current situation. *King knows he's on duty.*

"I figured all units included us," Terry said as he stopped in front of me. "But I don't know how much we can help. King is not trained in search and rescue."

I tried to hide my disappointment—Terry and King had only been with us for a few weeks. And they'd spent most of their time so far in training, getting to know each other. Terry was an experienced canine handler whom we'd lured away from a northern department with our tropical climate. And King was a trained police dog, purchased from a company in Germany for six-thousand dollars. I was praying I would be able to justify that expense with some results when called before the next City Council meeting.

I opened my mouth to respond.

"But I know of a local volunteer S&R group," Terry added. "I can call them for you."

Relief loosened the tension in my chest, a little. "Yes, please. We are going to scour the city until we find this child."

He took out his phone, poked the screen a couple of times, and held it to his ear. To me, he said, "King and I *can* help by checking dark alleys and warehouses and such, for firearms or explosives before people go in."

"That would be useful, especially now that it's full dark."

Terry nodded, then said, "Hey, Bill..." into his phone. He turned away from me.

I took out my own phone and looked at Jenny Coleman's text again. She'd reported that both parents were home now and waiting anxiously for news.

I was pleased by the tone of her text. Things had been a bit strained between us, ever since I'd almost gotten her killed in Mexico last fall.

Hopefully she had forgiven me by now, or at least, was putting it in the past.

My phone pinged. A text from Derek the Geek, our nickname for our sole digital forensic technician. And he was also our official liaison with the National Crime Information Center.

Everything entered on NCIC, the text read. *Amber Alert has gone out. FBI CARD team will be here soon.*

My stomach quivered. The Child Abduction Rapid Deployment team. I'd never imagined I'd be dealing with them.

My insides tensed at the thought of federal intrusion into *my* case, *my* city. Then my throat closed and my chest hollowed out—a foreshadowing of the guilt I would feel if this child died because I didn't have the experience to handle the investigation.

I didn't want the FBI involved, but I needed them. *How soon is soon?* I texted back.

Sometime tonight. They're bringing search and rescue personnel. And FDLE is sending 3 agents to help.

Hmm, that might've been what Dot Wilder was calling about earlier. I'd forgotten to check the message.

I quickly punched in a text to Dot. *Thx for the extra manpower.*

Should I call off Officer Terry's search and rescue group? No, the more, the better. And they were local, they would know the city.

I glanced down at the tables in front of me. *And we can definitely use the FBI's lab to help process all this junk.*

I blew out air and called over a uniform to take over manning the tables. If any of the junk turned out to be real evidence, we'd have to be able to establish chain of custody.

As I jogged to my car, I texted a friend in my home state of Maryland. Well, she wasn't only a friend. Kate Huntington was a psychologist, and she'd helped out with several of my tougher cases since I'd found myself, as Chief of Police, plunged into the deep end of the law enforcement pool.

I know it's kinda late, my text read, *but can you talk?*

I breathed out a sigh when my phone rang and her name appeared on the screen. That meant it was a good time to talk. If it wasn't, she would've texted back to that effect.

"Hey Kate," I said into the phone.

"Good to hear from you, Judith. How are things going down there?"

"Not so great, I'm afraid." I filled her in on the missing child, as I climbed into my car but didn't start the engine yet. Then I told her about the teddy bear and sunglasses. "I'm taking that to mean that the abductor isn't going to kill the girl."

"Probably," Kate said. "Unless it's a really sicko psychopath who's taunting you all."

My stomach clenched.

"But odds are good," she continued, "that you're right. He/she won't kill her."

Willing my body to relax—an order it ignored, I said, "I figure we've got one of three scenarios." I spelled them out for her.

"Any of those are possible," she replied.

"But what is the likelihood of each?"

A half-beat of silence. "I'd say unstable woman trying to replace a lost child would have a slight edge as number one, with kidnapped for ransom a distant third. If it's that, again the kidnapper would be taunting the parents with the bear."

My chest aching, I said, "So a pervert who's going to molest her, that's still a strong possibility."

"Yes, sadly. A fair number of child sexual abusers have love all twisted up with sex, usually because they themselves were abused—that's how they learned such aberrant behavior. And their own abuser may have told them something along the lines of, 'this is how adults love children.'"

Bile rose in the back of my throat. "Ick," I said out loud.

"Yeah." The sound of a heavy sigh. "They're convinced that they truly love children—as well as being attracted to them sexually—and that molesting the child isn't really doing any harm. I can see someone from that subset of abusers leaving the teddy bear to try to reassure the parents that the child will be loved."

"So lemme get this straight," I said. "They think it's perfectly okay, just another way to show *love*?" I spat out the last word. "But they must know it's wrong, they hide it."

"Because it's illegal. They know it'll get them in trouble...And on some level, they may know it's wrong." Another pause. "Unfortunately, the fact that they seem to love kids makes it easy for them to hide in plain sight. They become teachers, Scout leaders, youth ministers, et cetera."

I pushed words past clenched teeth. "And when they're caught, everyone who knows them says, 'Oh, he can't possibly be an abuser; he loves kids.'"

"Yep, exactly," Kate said, frustration in her voice.

I thanked her and we signed off. Then I took a deep breath and let it out slowly, trying to get the tension in my body to ease some.

Time to deal with the parents.

The Silvas lived in a development of newer homes—large and expensive-looking houses, but with postage-stamp lots and few trees. I stepped up on their front porch and reached out to ring the doorbell.

The door flew open. "Did you find her?" Mrs. Silva asked in a breathless voice. Her short blonde hair was sticking up in clumps. And her clothes—the same khaki capris and white sleeveless shirt she'd been wearing earlier—were disheveled. She tugged at the hem of the shirt, pulling in opposite directions until I feared the bottom button would pop. It held and she shifted to yanking on her hair instead.

"No, not yet. May I come in?"

A tall, thin, thirty-something man stepped up behind her. His face was handsome and tanned, with dark hair and gray-blue eyes. "Why are you here?" he demanded. "You should be out searching for our daughter."

"May I come in?" I repeated, trying to keep my voice neutral.

Mrs. Silva stepped back and collided with her husband. He flinched—had she stepped on his foot?—and moved aside.

I brushed past them and into a spacious foyer with a marble floor and crystal chandelier. Mrs. Silva smelled of sour milk and baby powder.

At least I assumed it was Mrs. Silva giving off those fragrances.

Mr. Silva smelled of some musky aftershave, and he was impeccably dressed in a deep purple polo shirt and chinos. I doubted he'd given the baby a bottle or changed a diaper any time recently. Maybe never.

I reminded myself not to jump to conclusions and turned slightly toward the couple.

They stood frozen for a beat. Then Mr. Silva made an after-you gesture in the direction of a double-sized open doorway, where Detective Wellbourne was standing.

I gave her a nod as I walked past her. She was a slender young woman, with a spray of freckles on her light brown cheeks and spirals of red-brown hair sticking out in all directions. Not everybody could pull off the look, but on her it was attractive.

Right now, her expression was grim, her brown eyes clouded with worry. I did not envy her this assignment.

I entered a large living room, with a black leather sofa and chairs and low chrome-and-glass tables. No flowers or throw pillows to soften the effect. It was a man's room.

Mrs. Silva rushed past me and began gathering papers that were spread out on a coffee table.

"Leave those be." Her husband's tone was sharp.

She turned to him, papers bunched in both hands, her eyes brimming. "Can't you be nice to me, even today?"

I froze in my progress toward an armchair.

Mr. Silva glanced at me, then hurried to his wife. "I'm sorry, darling. We're both on edge." He pried the papers from her fingers and dumped them on the table. Then he sat her down beside him on the sofa.

They both looked at me expectantly.

I sat on the edge of an armchair and pulled my notepad and pen from a pocket of my pantsuit jacket. I was debating where to start, how to ease into the bad news.

Or was it good news? The child was probably still alive.

Deciding to start off vague and see what I got, I cleared my throat. "Let me assure you that every member of my department is on this case, but we need more information. Can you think of anything, anything at all, that would explain your daughter's disappearance?"

Confused expressions. They both shook their heads. Silva's dark hair fell across his forehead. He quickly smoothed it back into place.

I tried vague again. "What's the first thing that popped into your head when you realized she was gone?"

Mrs. Silva's eyes filled again with tears. "That she'd fallen in the river."

I nodded and turned toward the husband. "And you, sir, when you heard what had happened?"

He gave his wife a hard look, which fortunately she did not see. She was busy swiping at her eyes with a tissue from a box on an end table.

He turned to me, and his handsome face became a neutral mask. "That Ashley had wandered off and gotten lost in the crowd."

The face might be neutral but his eyes were flashing with anger. I could pretty much read his mind. He thought his wife had not been paying attention.

"Does Ashley go to daycare or a preschool? Is she involved in any activities?"

"She's kinda young for that stuff," Mr. Silva said, as his wife shook her head.

"She's with me all the time," she said.

"Do you know of *anyone* who's taken a special interest in Ashley, especially lately?" Remembering Kate's words, I added, "They might've seemed like they really love kids."

Blank looks.

"Or maybe someone who seemed a little envious that you have such beautiful children?"

Mrs. Silva was shaking her head again. Mister was staring at me.

I noted, out of the corner of my eye, that Wellbourne was watching their faces as intently as I was. *Good girl!*

Should I even be thinking *girl* in reference to a grown woman? But then again, she was twenty years my junior, only twenty-seven. To me, she was a girl.

"Any strangers," I continued, "who've commented on Ashley out in public? Or on both children?"

Silva jumped up, his face now pale. "Oh my God, you think she's been kidnapped?"

Ignoring him, I made eye contact with the mom. "Does Ashley have a favorite teddy bear?"

More head shaking. "She has a stuffed duck that she drags everywhere with her. But it was still in the stroller when we got home."

My throat ached. The poor tike didn't even have her duckie.

I pulled out my phone and quickly found the photo of the bear on the railing. "Does this mean anything to you?" I held it up high first, near Mr. Silva's shocked face as he stood in front of me. Then I moved it down to Mrs. Silva's line of vision.

"Those are her sunglasses," she choked out, and buried her face in her hands, sobbing.

"How about the teddy bear? Have you seen it before?"

The woman shook her head without lifting it.

"Mr. Silva, please sit down."

He shook himself slightly and complied.

"Where were you this afternoon?" I asked him.

"Um, at my office," he said, in a distracted tone. He was glancing around the room as if searching for his missing daughter there.

It's finally hitting him.

"Can anyone verify that?" I asked, trying to keep my voice gentle.

His head jerked in my direction. "I don't know. I don't remember seeing anyone...Uh, I was catching up on some paperwork."

"Who would know whether or not people were working today?"

"Um, maybe, Mrs. Nelson. Maude Nelson, she's our office manager. She keeps track of the hourly people, but any accountants working..." He trailed off.

"Can I get this Mrs. Nelson's home number from you, please? And also those of the other accountants."

Silva hesitated, then nodded. "Let me get my phone."

He got up and headed out of the room. Wellbourne stepped aside to give him plenty of space. Then her gaze met mine.

I nodded slightly, and she trailed after him.

"Why are you asking about my husband working today?" Mrs. Silva said, her eyes still shiny and her face streaked with tears.

"Just ruling out all possibilities," I said.

Her pale face blanched even whiter, but she didn't say anything.

CHAPTER THREE

I sat in my car, the window down despite the muggy night air. I was half listening for sounds of arguing from the Silvas' house, as I made phone calls.

Interesting that Mr. Silva didn't question why I was asking about his whereabouts, but his wife had. And she didn't protest when she realized he was a suspect.

First, I called Wellbourne, who was still inside the house. She answered on the first ring. "Hello?"

Hmm, not Hi, Chief. Smart girl, too!

"Just answer yes or no," I said. "Have they been fighting tonight?"

"Yes."

"Do you think he gets physical with her?"

"Not sure."

"Okay, let me know right away if anything interesting happens, not just if they get a ransom call."

"Okay."

"And keep tabs on them and both of their cell phones at all times."

"Okay."

"Thanks, Wellbourne. You're doing great." The words sounded funny in my ears. Even after almost a year, I wasn't used to having to give positive support to my newer officers and detectives. The seasoned detectives under me at Baltimore County didn't need my *atta, boy* to know that they were doing their jobs.

"Thanks, Mom," Wellbourne said. "Sorry I can't come over tonight. See ya soon."

She disconnected and I chuckled.

Next, I called Bradley. After giving him a summary of the interview with the parents, I instructed him to try to get a warrant for the Silvas' phone records.

"Do you think a judge will go for that?" he asked.

Honestly, I wasn't sure. But I hesitated to express uncertainty to Bradley, not wanting to undermine his confidence by admitting that I too was feeling like a fish out of water with this case.

Fish made me think of ducks, and my chest ached.

"Maybe I should have Collins and Cruthers canvas the neighbors first?" Bradley was saying. "See if anyone reports hearing or seeing them fight. And I'll check for domestic violence calls to us."

"Okay, but go ahead and try for the warrant anyway, even if there are no reports of DV. Admit to the judge—verbally, not on paper—that it's a fishing expedition but it might give us a thread to pull on, and a child's life is in danger. If the judge balks, we'll go back and ask again after the canvassing."

"You're pretty sure the neighbors are going to have tales to tell, aren't you?"

"Yeah. You didn't see the way he looked at her."

"Oh, by the way," Bradley said. "Bert said they pulled two hundred and forty-three prints from the railing that were legible, although about half were partials."

I groaned.

"That was Bert's reaction. There were plenty more that were too smeared to be useful." He signed off.

Still sitting in my car, I managed to contact all four of Mr. Silva's fellow accountants at their firm. Most were not too happy that I was calling so late, but all reported they had not been in the office. Three of the four were at the Founders' Day celebration with their families. The fourth was single and had gone to the beach with friends for the day.

The office manager, Maude Nelson, didn't answer her phone. I left a message on her voicemail.

I drove back to the riverwalk and spotted Sam at our makeshift command center. He, or someone, had added another card table under the canopy, and he had maps spread out all over that one, weighted down by battery-operated camping lanterns.

They threw off a harsh light, but even so, he looked damn good in his khaki Clover County Sheriff's Department uniform.

I blew out a sigh. *If only we could go to my place, like a normal evening, and I could enjoy removing that uniform.*

As I approached, Sheriff Sam was giving instructions to two of his khaki-clad deputies. They walked away with their new assignments, and Sam turned to me with a small, sad smile on his rugged face.

"Thank you," I said, pumping as much heart-felt gratitude as I could into those two words.

"It's the least I could do." He ran a hand through his graying sandy hair, leaving tufts standing straight up.

I resisted the urge to reach up and smooth down that hair.

"This is a tough case for everyone," he added.

A flash to a sunny backyard and my mother calling names, "Judith, Paulie, Meredith." Only two of us kids responded.

I shook my head to clear it. "What have we got?"

"The divers have stopped for the night. They're coming back in the morning to search again, make sure they didn't miss anything. I divided the downtown area into grids, your people and mine are searching every alley and knocking on doors. And most of your auxiliary folks have shown up. They're searching as well."

I nodded. A lot of my sworn officers made fun of the auxiliary volunteers, calling them wannabe cops behind their backs. But at times like these, they were a big help.

Sam let out a frustrated sigh. "Unfortunately, a lot of the businesses are closed now, and many won't reopen until Monday."

"I'll get one of my detectives to compile a list of the business owners," I said, "and we'll contact those who are closed tonight and make arrangements to search their buildings tonight or tomorrow morning. If she's crawled in somewhere..." I trailed off as another searcher approached, one of my auxiliary cops.

While Sam talked to him, giving him a new assignment, I made the call to Bradley to assign someone the task of compiling that list. Then I stood there, staring into space and trying hard *not* to think about my cousin Meredith.

Sam had turned to me and said something, but I'd missed it.

"What?" I said.

"Did Dot Wilder catch up with you?"

"Uh, yeah."

"So you heard about John Black," Sam said.

It took half a beat for the change of subject to register. Black was my predecessor as chief of police of Starling, and he was currently on the run, with multiple outstanding warrants against him, for corruption and for jumping bail.

And the thought of him reminded me that I'd been hired for my reputation for integrity, despite my limited administrative and leadership experience. I'd soon discovered that being the head of a homicide unit in a large police force did not prepare me to run an *entire* albeit small department.

Unbeknownst to me, the Starling mayor and city council had pressured Black to retire and then had hired me to root out the corruption he'd left behind. With that as their main agenda, they hadn't seemed all that concerned about the multiple *faux pas* I'd made so far as CoP.

Until now... My stomach twisted. They would likely want my ass on a platter if this missing child turned up dead.

"Wait, what about Black?" I asked, realizing I'd let my mind wander, again.

"Dot said she could only spare a few agents because there was a sighting of Black, at a hotel in Palm Coast."

"Where's that?"

"On the east coast, near Flagler Beach."

"When was this?" I asked.

"Saturday morning. She sent agents down to check it out." Sam paused. "She said there was something else, but she wanted to talk to you about it first."

I took out my phone and opened voicemail. Dot's earlier message was only a cryptic request to call her back. And I realized she had called before she would've even known about the missing child, so her call had been about something else. No doubt the *something else* that she'd mentioned to Sam.

I put my phone away and stared into space. I was curious, but I really couldn't afford to get distracted right now. Or rather any more distracted than I already was, by the flashbacks to the worst day of my childhood.

And Dot hadn't called again, so the *something else* couldn't be that pressing.

"Penny for your thoughts," Sam said.

I grimaced. "They're not worth that much."

"Is it my imagination or is this case hitting you harder than usual?"

I shook my head. "As you said, it's a tough case for all of us."

"Have you ever worked a missing child case before?"

"Not unless they were dead." I winced when I heard the sharpness in my voice. "Sorry. No, I mostly worked homicide as a detective."

"I have," Sam said, "and this is stirring those ghosts for me." He looked at me expectantly, inviting me to open up about my own ghosts

I gave him a wry smile. "You missed you're calling. You should've been a shrink."

He chuckled softly.

I sighed, pushing aside thoughts of my cousin Meredith. "Yes, it's stirring ghosts, but not from old cases. And now is not the time or place to get into it."

"Whatever it is, it's been bothering you, off and on, for a while." He paused a half-beat. "Or is this something new?"

"No, same thing. I'll tell you soon."

He nodded, then swiveled his head back and forth. No one was nearby, so he gave me a quick peck on the cheek. "I've got things covered here. Why don't you go home and get some sleep? You're gonna need to be sharp tomorrow."

That was a tempting idea. But it would look like the captain had abandoned ship.

My phone pinged. I checked the screen. *CARD team ten minutes out,* Derek had texted.

"No can do," I said to Sam. "FBI is on its way. I've got to deal with them."

"Okay, go forth and liaise. I'll call if we find anything useful."

"Thanks." I gave him a small smile and turned away.

When did liaison *become a verb?*

The CARD team was made up of five agents, one female and four males. Very solemn faced and pasty skinned—even the female, who wore no makeup. They looked as tired as I felt. All wore suits, in various shades of navy.

The Special Agent in Charge introduced himself and his four Special Agents. Their names went right past my exhausted brain, except for the SAC—Dennis Trager.

What makes them so special *anyway?* I made a mental note to look up why they were called that, when I had a moment. Probably some time next year.

The SAC was a big guy, not quite fat but headed in that direction, with a little gray at the temples of an otherwise dark head of hair. He stuck out a big paw. "Call me Denny. Sorry it took us a bit to get down here. We were wrapping up a case in South Carolina. Our search and rescue people should be here soon."

I shook the proffered hand. "Judith."

Then the implications of what he'd said sank in. "Did you find the child up there?"

He pursed his lips. "Not in time."

My chest ached and my cheeks heated. Here, I'd been think-ing judgey thoughts. Who knew the last time these folks got any sleep?

"So, where can we set up?" the SAC asked.

"Follow me." I turned and headed for the largest of our conference rooms. The SAC, Denny fell into step beside me.

"How does all this work?" I asked, then hurried to add, "I've been a cop for a couple of decades, but it's been years since I had to deal with the FBI."

"Well," he said, "we're here to assist in any way we can, and we have a lot of resources to offer. But..." he paused, "if you want us to, we can take over the investigation."

I stiffened. He looked away, pretending not to notice. "It's up to you," he said to the hallway's wall.

A part of me was tempted to turn it all over to them. They had the expertise in this kind of case, expertise that my depart-ment, and I, sorely lacked. And I believed they were good at their jobs, despite the outcome of their most recent case.

But their obvious fatigue meant they were not at the top of their game. Plus, my people knew the city, and they didn't.

And I just plain don't want to give up the reins, I admitted to myself.

My chest tightened and my stomach churned anew. Was I letting territorialism cloud my judgement here? What if something horrible happened to this child? It wasn't only my job I was worried about... *I won't be able to live with myself.*

"I, uh, need to think about that some. In the meantime, feel free," I glanced over my shoulder at the others, "all of you, to offer any suggestions or course corrections."

The dead woman rose slowly from the floor. My whole body shivered.

She turned toward me. "Have you found your cousin yet, sweetheart?" Her tone was casual, as if she were asking did I have any homework.

I opened my mouth to answer her but nothing came out.

Then her face morphed from my mother's into that of a man—with salt and pepper hair and a rugged, tanned jaw line.

He grinned. "I've got her now. I've got little Ashley."

My head jerked up and a sharp pain in my neck made me gasp. It took a second to realize I was in my office. After bringing the FBI people up to speed, I'd left them to get set up and had come back here to think.

But I'd apparently fallen asleep instead, head on my crossed arms on my desk.

I scanned my office. Everything—my bookcase, the visitor's chairs, the desk—it all looked so normal.

I shuddered as the face from my dream flashed into my mind again.

It was that of a man I'd arrested five months ago—for child abuse, human trafficking, and several counts of assault.

CHAPTER FOUR

I tried to do some paperwork, while I waited for new developments in the case. But I couldn't focus.

Finally, I pulled my laptop out of my bottom desk drawer, booted it up, then opened my personal email account. I wrote an email to the private detective I'd hired, the husband of my friend Kate back in Maryland.

It was a very brief message. *Hey Skip, anything new? Judith*

I hit *send*, knowing full well that there wouldn't be anything new. If there had been, he would have immediately let me know.

And as he had gently reminded me a few weeks ago, my cousin Meredith had been missing for over forty years, so the trail was very, very cold.

I'd also involved the National Center for Missing and Exploited Children in my quest. They had DNA samples from me, my Aunt Jean—Meredith's mother—and my cousin Paul, plus some partially degraded hair from Meredith's own hairbrush.

The only news we'd received so far was from NCMEC. Their computers had done a thorough search nationwide of all unidentified female bodies over the last four decades and had found no matches.

That was good news, actually—the odds that Meredith was still alive had gone up.

But not all of the older cases had DNA samples available.

I sat back and sighed. "Might as well grab a shower," I muttered.

Twenty minutes later, I was somewhat refreshed after a quick shower in the minuscule bathroom off of my office. I'd donned the black pantsuit and white shirt that I'd left there this morning. Correction, yesterday morning, although it felt like a month ago now. My rumpled dress uniform hung in its place on the back of the bathroom door.

I walked through the bullpen and out into the hallway, pausing to take in the transformed area in front of me. The Starling PD was housed on the third floor of the municipal building, and previously there had been little to no security. The elevators had opened onto a spacious hallway—with floor-to-ceiling windows running across the front of the building.

And the watch commander's desk had sat at one end of the hallway, near the entrance to the bullpen, with nothing but that wooden desk separating the sergeant from the general public.

Concerned about the safety of my people, I'd convinced the mayor and city council to fork over the funds for better security. The mayor was an easy touch. He and I had been through a lot together in my short tenure as police chief, and his even shorter time in the mayor's chair.

The city council was another story.

But the project had managed to stay on budget so far, and was within weeks of being completed. That spacious hallway was now divided, with partitions of bulletproof glass, into a waiting area and a reception space. The latter contained our new departmental clerk's desk and a cubicle for the watch sergeant.

The waiting area, by the elevators, had been re-carpeted and would soon boast a dozen chairs, where folks could enjoy the cityscape beyond the windows as they waited. Currently, a few metal folding chairs were scattered about.

Barnes had suggested holding off on having the new furniture delivered until the construction was completed. The layer of sawdust on the folding chairs attested to the wisdom of that suggestion.

The part still under construction was another partition—this one a reinforced, solid wall with a metal door—separating the waiting area and elevators from the conference rooms, interrogation area, locker room and holding cells. The doors in both partitions were locked at all times, and our officers and staff now had key cards. It was a pain having to unlock doors every time one moved around the department, but a necessary evil for security's sake.

The clerk's desk was empty—she wasn't in yet. But the watch commander's cubicle was occupied by the Chief of Patrol, Sergeant Armstrong. He greeted me through the open doorway.

Glancing past the all-glass wall of the reception area to the windows beyond, I noted that the dark sky had a pale gray edge near the tops of the buildings across the street. And a few of the windows in those buildings were now brightly lit. A new day was beginning.

"Anything happening?" I asked Armstrong.

He shook his shaved head. "No. The divers are out on the river again, waiting for enough daylight to get started."

Bradley was coming toward us from the other end of the hall. He wore a fresh light blue shirt but the dark gray suit he'd changed into yesterday evening was now rumpled. He'd probably slept on the small couch in his office.

If he'd slept at all.

Armstrong hit a buzzer on his desk to unlock the door, so Bradley wouldn't have to fumble for his key card.

After an exchange of half-hearted "good mornings," Bradley said, "I've got some things to report."

I made an after-you gesture back toward the entrance to the bullpen.

"No domestic violence calls to the Silvas' house," he said, as we crossed the bullpen. "But there was something else that was very interesting. Two months ago, they filed a theft report, of some jewelry, and..." he paused for effect.

A spark of annoyance in my chest.

"They accused their nanny," he finished, "but there was no proof."

The annoyance evaporated as my chin dropped. "Oh, *really*. Then why did they say no when I asked if anyone had a reason to take Ashley or might want to hurt them through her?"

"An excellent question."

In my glass-walled office, I started my coffee maker before taking a seat behind my desk.

Bradley sat in one of my visitors' chairs, the sole comfortable one. The other two were not so comfy, and were reserved for people I didn't particularly want to linger.

When he stretched his long legs out, his feet almost touched the front of my desk.

The office was cramped, to say the least. In general, the department needed more space, but that was next year's battle with the city council.

"We only got to some of the neighbors last night." Bradley skimmed light brown hair out of his eyes, which were a cloudy blue-gray this morning. "Collins is picking that up today, as well as tracking down other people whose fingerprints were on that railing. The FBI and FDLE agents are helping with that. And one of the FBI crew is checking on the current whereabouts of people on the sex offenders' registry who are supposed to be living in northern Florida or Georgia. And I touched base with Bert and Ernie."

Hmm, not even a flicker of amusement on Bradley's handsome but somber face.

Our crime scene techs even looked a little like their Muppet counterparts. But they were excellent and dedicated personnel, so we were careful not to laugh in front of them. In private though, their names usually elicited a smile or a soft chuckle.

"The feds took most of the stuff from the riverwalk to their lab in Jacksonville," Bradley was saying. "Our guys are focusing on the fingerprints. And another way that the FBI is useful—they have access to a lot of databases that we don't."

"Such as?"

"Such as anyone who's ever had to have a background check, for a job for example. Bert's checking the fingerprints against them, and he's gotten some additional hits...Anything on Silva's alibi?"

"It can't be verified," I said. "The HR lady finally called me back last night, but she was evasive about who might be working. The only definitive thing she said was that *she* wasn't there. She was at the Founders' Day celebration, as were all four of his fellow accountants I talked to, but one. He was on Jacksonville Beach working on his tan."

Bradley frowned. "Oh, forgot to mention. Nothing came of my search for similar MOs in child abductions. Only thing that came close was thirteen years ago in South Florida. A two-year-old girl was taken from her yard, and her teddy bear was left sitting on top of the fence near the gate. It was too high for the child to have put it there, so the Miami PD assumed the kidnapper had left it on purpose, as some kind of message."

"You're thinking that's not similar enough to be relevant?" I asked.

"And it was so long ago, plus they never found the girl or her abductor."

"Did they have any forensic evidence we might find useful?"

He shook his head. "She disappeared without a trace. Only prints on the gate were accounted for as those of family members, a neighbor, and the mailman."

A flash to a sunny backyard. I closed my eyes and swallowed hard. *Not now!*

The flashback had most likely been triggered by the words "without a trace," a phrase used often when Meredith's disappearance was discussed. Discussions that had only happened recently, though. For years, no one in my family mentioned it.

"Chief, you okay?" Bradley asked, as his cell phone rang. He held it to his ear. "Bradley."

"It's Wellbourne." He laid the phone on my desk. "You're on speaker. I'm with the chief."

"Uh, I could use some help here," Wellbourne's high-pitched voice rose above the sounds of yelling in the background. "Mr. Silva is losing it. Something about their neighbors."

The yelling got closer. "How dare you cops–" Silva's voice, cut off by Mrs. Silva's, sounding frantic, but her words were garbled.

"Mr. Silva," Wellbourne yelled. "If you don't calm down, I *will* arrest you."

I jumped up. "Come on, Bradley. It's time for another chat with the Silvas."

Wellbourne was standing on the Silvas' front porch. Her spiral curls were almost all sticking straight out. She had a habit of yanking on them when she was stressed.

"He tossed me out," she said as we approached.

Ignoring the doorbell button, I rapped knuckles against the door, hard. "Mr. Silva, it's Chief Anderson. Let us in. Now!"

The door flew open and we stepped into their expansive foyer. But we got no farther than that.

Silva stood between us and the doorway into the living room. Wellbourne hadn't been exaggerating. He was damned close to out of control, going on and on about how we were ruining his reputation by talking to his neighbors, and asking them intrusive questions. That's the word he used, *intrusive*.

Who uses that word in normal conversation?

And despite the volatile energy behind his rant, it seemed a bit off.

Like maybe he rehearsed it in his mind ahead of time?

Trying to calm him down, I said, "Sir, we need to ask the neighbors certain things, like whether they have noticed anyone hanging around your house, maybe watching the kids when they were outside."

And our people had asked about that, along with their other *intrusive* questions about the Silvas' relationship.

Bradley's cell phone chirped, indicating he had an incoming text. He pulled out the phone and glanced at it.

Eyebrows high on his forehead, he turned the phone so I could see the screen.

The text was from Collins. *Next door neighbors confirmed they had a nanny, but haven't seen her for about two months.*

"Mr. Silva," Bradley said, "when were you going to tell us about the nanny?"

The question effectively halted the man in mid-rant. He blinked twice. "What?"

Bradley turned slightly toward the wife, directing the same question to her. "When were you going to tell us about the nanny you had up until a few weeks ago?"

"Cara?" Annie Silva said. "She was our *au pair*. We, uh..." She glanced at her husband. "Gabe let her go. We thought she might have been stealing from us."

I scowled at the couple. "And you didn't think that might be relevant?"

Mr. Silva deflated. "No, we just didn't think...of mentioning her, that is. We were kind of rattled last night."

I should've conceded that point. Of course, they were rattled. But it still felt like an awfully big omission.

"Tell us about the theft," I said, my voice no-nonsense.

"I had this diamond bracelet, a family heirloom," Annie said. "It had been my mother's and I'd planned to give it to Ashley..." Her voice faltered, then she swallowed hard. "When she was o-older."

"She foolishly showed it to Cara," Silva said, his tone scornful.

"A few days later," Annie turned her shoulder, as if excluding her husband from the conversation, "it was gone. I looked everywhere for it."

"It had to be Cara," Silva said. "No one else was in the house during that time."

"Not even a cleaning lady?" Bradley asked.

Annie's cheeks pinked and she opened her mouth.

But Silva cut her off. "No," he said definitively.

I frowned at him. "We'll need Cara's contact info, and that of the cleaning person."

"It's a service, not always the same people come," Annie said.

Silva said nothing, glaring at us.

"I don't have a forwarding address for Cara," Annie continued. "She stayed with us. But I have an emergency contact, a friend of hers here in Starling." She walked into the living room and over to a small antique rolltop desk, the only somewhat feminine thing in the room.

We trailed after her, Wellbourne bringing up the rear behind the husband.

The top was open and Annie extracted an actual address book from a cubby, then thumbed through to a certain page.

She gave me a weak smile, as she handed the opened book to Bradley. "I'm old-fashioned about some things."

Bradley jotted the contact info in his pad and handed the address book back. "We need to see her room."

Annie blinked. "Her room?"

"Why?" Silva demanded.

"Standard procedure," I said.

"Why are you wasting time with all this?" Silva's voice was rising again.

Ahh, and here comes the line I've been expecting.

"You should be out there," he poked a finger toward the front door, "searching for our daughter."

"We are searching, sir," I said, from between gritted teeth. "But we are also investigating any leads that may tell us where she is. Now we *need* to see the *au pair's* room."

But after all that, the room revealed nothing useful. Indeed, it had been swept clean of even fingerprints, thanks to the Silvas' aggressively efficient cleaning service.

Bradley got the number of that service and put in a call from the car, asking them to check their schedule of visits to the Silva house for the last couple of months.

Then he asked to speak to whoever cleaned the nanny's room. It was unlikely that person would remember anything they'd thrown out during that job, which was likely a hundred or so jobs ago by now. But we had to pursue every lead.

While he was on the phone, I contemplated whether we should be relieving Wellbourne. She'd been with the Silvas now since last evening, and had probably gotten no sleep. But when I'd taken her aside for a quick check-in, she'd said she was fine.

And we didn't really have anyone to replace her, not a detective at least that we could spare. I could ask the FBI folks to take over liaising with the parents.

I smiled grimly. *There's that word again.*

They would be happy to jump into that role, but not unless I asked. Unlike the portrayals in a lot of books and TV shows, the FBI did not storm in and take control away from local law enforcement, only if the local department asked them to take over.

I'd keep that option on the back burner. As long as Wellbourne was still standing upright, I preferred to have her keeping an eye on the parents.

"They'll have the cleaner contact us," Bradley said as he disconnected. He started his engine. "And they didn't clean the week the bracelet went missing, so Silva was right about that."

A soft rap on the glass of Bradley's window. He jumped a little, but I'd seen Mrs. Silva coming from the house.

He lowered the window. She glanced nervously over her shoulder. "Chief, Lieutenant, I wasn't quite honest with you." Her voice was rushed. "I've actually been in touch with Cara, since she left us. She's living with that friend. And she's met us in the park a few times. I didn't want there to be a sudden break in contact. Ashley asks for her a lot."

She paused, sucked in air, glanced over her shoulder again. "But Cara would never take her from me. She wouldn't do that to me or Ashley."

"We still need to talk to her," Bradley said.

She pinched her lips together. "But you're wasting time. Like my husband said, you should be–"

I held up a hand from the passenger's seat. "We need to ask her if she's seen anyone taking an interest in the children, in the park and such."

Annie rocked back on her heels a bit. "Oh... Of course. That makes sense. Thank you for all you're doing."

"It's our job, ma'am," I said, "and thank you for telling us this. It's helpful."

—◆—

We stood in a hallway that smelled of cat urine and cooked cabbage. Bradley knocked a second time.

The door opened a crack, and a Latina woman looked out at us. "*Si?*"

"Cara Hidalgo?" I asked.

She shook her head and pushed the door almost all the way closed. "Cara," we heard her yelling on the other side of it.

A moment later, the door opened again. An extremely fair skinned, blue-eyed blonde asked, "Can I help you?" Her accent was British with a hint of something else.

"Are you Cara Hidalgo?" Bradley asked, a slight note of surprise creeping into his voice. He opened his badge wallet and held it up for her to see.

Her fair skin paled even further. "Uh, yeah. Caroline."

"Don't worry," I quickly said, as I adjusted my own assumptions about what Cara *Hidalgo* should look like. "You're not in trouble. But can we come in? What we need to discuss, well, I don't really want your neighbors hearing us."

If the crying baby and raised voices we could hear from nearby apartments were any indication, the walls were thin in this building.

"Sure," she said with little hesitation. She stepped back and opened the door wider.

The main room of the apartment was spacious, with big windows making it feel light and airy. An open kitchen area was off to one side, and three doors sat open at various points around the living area. They revealed a powder room, a bedroom with a neatly made daybed against one wall, bookcases on either side, and another bedroom that was quite chaotic. The Latina roommate was laying on the double bed in the middle of the chaos, flipping through a magazine. She wore loose-fitting red lounging pajamas.

Cara, in denim shorts and a royal blue tee shirt, ushered us to a sitting area—older furniture but in good shape, a sofa and two armchairs circling an oval coffee table.

"Have you heard about Ashley?" I asked, as we all sat down. The lack of preamble was intentional. I wanted to see how she responded to an abrupt introduction of the topic.

She nodded, while biting her lower lip.

"How did you hear?" Bradley asked.

It was too early for the Sunday paper, although it would be hitting the streets soon, and my nemesis at the Starling Sun, Stuart Frost would no doubt have the missing child on the front page. The accompanying story would most likely be couched to make the Starling PD sound incompetent.

Still the exposure would be helpful if someone came forward who'd seen the child. But sadly the deluge of calls to the PD from the citizenry would be mostly cranks and the curious.

"Annie called me last night," Cara said, "she was hysterical." The girl's own voice caught some.

I sat forward in the overstuffed armchair. "Had anyone shown any particular interest in Ashley or the baby in recent months? When they were playing outside at home or at the park, or elsewhere?"

Cara quickly shook her head. "That's the first thing I wondered and I've been wracking my brain. But I can't think of anyone odd who's paid undue attention to them."

"How about someone who wasn't necessarily all that odd?" Bradley said.

I gave him an approving glance. He'd been paying attention when my friend Kate Huntington from Maryland had been helping us with a case last spring. She commented that child abductors/abusers usually presented as normal, law-abiding people. Rarely, did they appear to be the monsters that they were.

Cara was shaking her head again, then she froze. "Wait. There was a girl there sometimes. She'd sit on a bench near the playground and watch the kids. But she didn't have any little ones with her."

My stomach clenched, even as excitement bubbled in my chest. Finally, something resembling a lead.

CHAPTER FIVE

"What did this woman in the park look like?" Bradley asked the nanny, his notepad and pen poised.

I leaned even farther forward in my chair.

"Mid-twenties maybe," Cara said. "A little plump. Blonde hair, short and kinda spikey, like some girls wear it. Dark clothes. I remember they were too tight on her, not very flattering. I guess she had kind of a Goth look to her."

"Eye color?" Bradley asked.

"I never saw her eyes. She wore sunglasses." She picked up her phone from the coffee table and scrolled for something. "Here's the park." She showed Bradley the screen. I caught a flash of a Google map.

He jotted the address down, then handed her one of his cards. "If you see the young woman around, don't approach her but call me right away."

Cara nodded.

"Out of curiosity," I asked, "how'd a young British woman like yourself end up with the name Hidalgo?" It wasn't only idle curiosity, however. Anything out of sync could be significant.

She gave me a small smile. "I'm from France." She pronounced *France* with a French accent. "My great grandfather was from Spain. He married a French woman. My *grand-pere*, one of their many children, also married a French woman. Their youngest was my *papa*. And he married a British woman."

The small smile again. "Thus, I am bilingual in English and French, with a Spanish surname."

"And why did you come to the US?" I asked.

"I met a chap, at *université*. We fell madly in love." A feeble grin this time. "Well, I was in love. He was just mad... I followed him over here. He was doing graduate work at the University of North Florida, but I didn't want to go to school anymore. So I got the job with the Silvas through this agency that hires young women in Europe to come to the US as nannies. And then a few months later, the mad boyfriend and I broke up."

Cara grimaced. "I'm trying to find another job, before my visa runs out."

"But why do you want to stay," I asked, "since you and this guy broke up?"

"I like it here."

I nodded and rose from my chair. "May I use your powder room before we go?"

"Of course." She gestured toward that open door.

Bradley glanced my way, then quickly said, "Be sure to call me if you see that woman hanging around again."

His diversion tactic worked. Cara turned toward him, giving me a chance to veer over to the door of the room with the daybed—the one I assumed was hers—and peek inside.

But there were no signs of a pint-sized inhabitant.

───◆───

I had Bradley drop me at the riverwalk, while he went to that park to see if Goth Girl was hanging out there today.

Sam was there again, or maybe it was there *still*. His uniform didn't look all that fresh. Had he been here all night?

A few new items were scattered on the tables under the canopy, but most had been shipped off to the FBI's lab.

"Hey," he said as I approached.

"Hey yourself," I said. "You look as tired as I feel."

He shrugged and quickly glanced around. No one was nearby, so he put an arm around my shoulders and gave me a quick peck on the temple. Then he let go.

I appreciated the human contact, even when accompanied by the fragrance of manly sweat.

"This is hard," he breathed out on a sigh.

"Yeah, it is. You said you had worked child abduction cases before..." I trailed off, hoping he would offer some pearls of wisdom.

"A couple of times, in Albany, when I was in the sex crimes unit." He grimaced. "I hope this one ends better."

He fell silent.

Duh, if he had any suggestions, he would've made them by now.

So I didn't ask questions. I wasn't real sure I wanted to know the details of cases that didn't end well. And he didn't seem to want to talk about them.

"The divers are packing up," he finally said. "And I think we can call off the search along the riverbanks. We've been the whole length of it within the city limits twice. And JSO is checking its banks down where it joins the St. John's."

I shook my head slightly as Sam led me toward a nearby bench. I was still getting used to the fact that the Jax law enforcement agency was called the Jacksonville Sheriff's Office, and the head honcho held the title of sheriff, while everyone else on that force were called police officers. It was due to the merger of Duval County and the city of Jacksonville several decades ago. The Duval Sheriff's Department and been blended with the Jax police. Even their shoulder patches had both *Office of the Sheriff* at the top and *Police Department* at the bottom.

Sam fell onto the bench with a groan. "Feels good to sit down."

I sat down beside him and he surreptitiously took my hand in his, hidden between our thighs.

"How are you holding up?" he asked.

I opened my mouth to say "fine," but suddenly my eyes were stinging and my vision was blurry.

He squeezed my hand. "Now would be a good time to tell me what this is stirring up." He paused, glanced sideways at me. "Or not, if you're not ready."

My throat tightened. I loved that this man was so patient. I really should've told him months ago.

I took a deep breath. "My cousin was abducted when I was six."

He pulled a little to the side to look directly at me. "Your cousin? Paul?"

I shook my head. "No, his older sister. She was ten, and he had just turned eight."

"Oh my god, no wonder this is hitting you hard."

"It actually got stirred up last March, when we had that Jane Doe case and it became apparent that she'd been kidnapped as a child."

Sam said nothing, waiting for me to continue.

"I'll give you the details at some point, when we have more time. Short version, the three of us were playing hide-and-seek, and she was it. She seemed to vanish into thin air. We've never seen or heard anything about her since." I paused. "Remember I told you that my friend Kate's husband is a private eye?"

"Yes."

"He's searching for Meredith for me." My stomach churned, and I wasn't sure why. Was it guilt that I wasn't doing more myself? Or maybe dread that Skip would find something—would discover that my cousin had suffered some horrible fate. My stomach twisted even more.

I should've looked for her sooner, much sooner.

"I uh, can't really do anything myself," I justified to Sam. "Not until this..." I waved a hand in the air to indicate the tables of evidence and the divers carrying gear up from the river, "...is resolved."

After a couple of beats of silence, Sam said, "Hey, I'll get things packed up here and get these additional items to the FBI folks. Then I'll bring you lunch later."

"Sounds good." I squeezed his hand and let go, rising to my feet. My stomach growled. Apparently, it had untwisted enough to realize it was empty. "Make it an early lunch," I added, "I never had any breakfast."

He gave me a small smile, and I turned and started walking to my office a few blocks away.

I hadn't taken into consideration how stinking hot it was when I'd had Bradley drop me off. Sweat was dripping down my cheeks by the time I got back to 3MB, and my shirt was quite damp, even though I'd removed my jacket along the way.

Barnes was at her desk. "Hey, Chief." She handed me a tissue to wipe my face, then continued, "There's a Beatrice Gardner here, asking to talk to a detective."

I raised my eyebrows in the air.

"Collins left his card in her door early this morning, while she was at church."

"And where is he?" I asked.

"I texted him, and he texted back that he was in the middle of an interview with a neighbor of the Silvas. *And* that Mrs. Gardner's fingerprints were among the ones Bert and Ernie got off that railing."

I opened my mouth, but she went on before I could ask, "I checked with Bert. They found the prints match because she used to work for the school system, as a cafeteria supervisor. So there'd been a background check done when she was hired."

I hid a smile. Barnes was like a walking, talking AI computer. Her ability to read my mind and anticipate my questions was improving daily.

"She's in the smaller conference room," my assistant said.

I gave her a small nod, shrugged back into my jacket, and turned in the direction of the hallway.

"We might want to take her a refill," she added. "I gave her some coffee, from your personal stash, but that was awhile ago."

I pursed my lips but nodded again. I kept walking, and Barnes scurried into my office to get the coffee.

"You saw something last evening, Mrs. Gardner?" I asked the plump, middle-aged woman across the conference table from me. She wore stretch denim capris and a pale pink short-sleeved sweater that did nothing for her pasty complexion.

"Please, call me Bea, or as the kids in the neighborhood do, Aunt Bee. You know, like on the Andy Griffith Show." She chuckled, then waved a hand in the air. "But of course, that was before your time."

According to the scant info we had on the woman, it was before hers as well. She'd been thirty-two when she'd applied to work for the Starling school system, and the background check had been done. That was twenty-five years ago, so she was now fifty-seven—although her silver-gray hair made her seem somewhat older.

I knew what she was talking about, though. Many Americans of our era had been exposed to Andy Griffith and his Aunt Bee via re-runs on TV.

But why was she pretending to be older than she was? And was she always this gregarious, or was she nervous?

"I'm sorry I missed your officer this morning." Another wave of her hand. "I was at church."

"Well, thank you for coming in, *Bea*." No way was I calling her *Aunt Bee*.

I opted not to mention the fingerprints—the way we had tracked her down—and cut to the chase instead. If this woman was wasting our time, just hoping for her fifteen minutes of fame, I was not going to be a happy camper.

"What did you want to tell us?" I prompted.

The woman's face sobered. "I think I saw the girl, the one who's missing. Right before that woman screamed, I saw a small child standing by the railing. I was worryin' that she seemed to be by herself."

My heart rate ratcheted up several notches.

"But then I saw someone take her hand," she continued. "And she didn't seem scared. She looked up at the person, and if anything, seemed to relax."

Fighting to keep the excitement out of my voice, I asked, "Can you describe the person?"

She shook her head. "Not really. I couldn't see them very well, in the crowd, only an arm and part of a hand. I'm not even sure if it was a woman or a man, but I think maybe it was a man." She closed her eyes, as if to focus better on the memory.

And I realized I was holding my breath.

"They wore a gray long-sleeved shirt," she said. "A knitted fabric, I think, like a tee shirt."

She opened her eyes when Barnes entered the room, juggling two steaming cardboard cups. She sat one down in front of each of us and removed the empty cup from in front of our guest.

I took a sip, waiting for Mrs. Gardner to continue. It tasted a tad bitter. Probably the last of the pot I'd made earlier. Good thing Barnes hadn't made it. Her coffee was undrinkable.

"What happened next?" I finally prompted.

Barnes walked to the conference room door, then hesitated, looking back over her shoulder. I nodded slightly, and she leaned her butt against the closed door's frame and took out her note pad.

"A boat sounded its horn, and I glanced that way," Mrs. Gardner was saying. "When I looked back, the child and whoever was with her were gone."

Hmm, I didn't recall hearing a boat horn at that time. But it wouldn't have necessarily registered, since the boat parade was starting. Actually, the parade was over almost as soon as it had begun, once we realized a child might have fallen in the water.

"That's when the woman screamed," Mrs. Gardner continued, "and some people were running away. I guess they thought there was some danger or something. I was looking around, trying to figure out what was going on."

I mentally groaned, wishing we had contact info for those people who'd immediately ran away. "And what did you do?" I asked.

She hung her head a little, and her fair cheeks pinked. "I left. Everybody seemed to be running around, getting all worked up. I hate a fuss like that...And I'd already seen my favorite boat."

"How far away were you from the girl?" I asked.

She scrunched up her face. "I'm horrible at estimating distances. Maybe ten or fifteen feet."

I nodded. Close enough to see Ashley, amongst people's legs, but maybe not see the person next to the girl.

"Did you see anyone carrying a teddy bear?"

"What, a child?"

"No, an adult."

She shook her head slowly. "No, and I think I would've noticed that."

I asked a couple more questions, but that seemed to be all the information the woman could give us. I thanked her again for coming in.

She hefted a large purse from the floor and followed Barnes out of the room.

I stayed in the conference room for a few minutes, thinking. But my tired brain came up with nothing new.

Other than the observation that—if Bea Gardner hadn't fabricated the whole story—Ashley *was* indeed abducted. It was very unlikely she'd fallen into the river.

Halfway across the bullpen, Bradley fell into step with me and followed me into my office. "Nobody at that park that even vaguely resembles the Goth girl that Cara described."

I grunted as he flopped into my visitor's chair. I started another pot of coffee and held up one of my empty china mugs. "Want some?"

He shook his head. "I've had four cups already this morning, and they're burning a hole in my stomach as we speak."

"Have you had any food?"

He shook his head again.

I pulled open my bottom desk drawer and grabbed a granola bar from my own stash. I tossed it across the desk. "Eat!"

He picked it up but didn't open it. "Caroline Hidalgo checks out. She's here on a work visa through the European Society for Cultural Exchange."

He peeled back the paper from the end of the bar. "And the divers have gone over the floor of the river from the spot where Ashley and her mom were standing to where it joins the St. Johns River."

I opted not to tell him I already knew that from Sam.

He took a bite of the granola bar and grimaced. "It's stale."

"Eat it anyway. Man does not live by caffeine alone."

"Says the woman who sucks it down like it's nectar from the gods."

"It *is* nectar from the gods," I said. "But we need calories as well. Here I'll set a good example." I pulled out another bar and unwrapped it.

"If she went in the river," Bradley grimaced again, this time not because of the granola bar, "she's well up the St. Johns by now, maybe even in the Jacksonville harbor."

Up, not down? Then I remembered, the St. Johns was one of the few rivers in the world that flowed from south to north.

"That's a lot of riverbed to search," Bradley was saying, "and no guarantee the divers won't miss her."

"Sam's arranged for the JSO to search the riverbanks in Duval County. But I'm thinking that if she'd fallen in, someone would have seen it. How many people who were nearby have we interviewed now?"

"Between our four detectives, two of the FBI agents, the three agents the FDLE sent over, and our uniforms, almost two hundred already. And more interviews are happening as we speak."

"Good. I don't care if we have to talk to every person in this city, twice," I said, my tone emphatic, "or more. We are going to find this child."

I paused, making a mental note to thank Dot Wilder again for the assistance.

"And with all those interviews," I said, "no one has mentioned seeing her fall off the boardwalk, or hearing a splash or anything?"

Bradley shook his head.

"Okay, for now, we operate under the assumption that she was taken." I filled him in on the interview with Mrs. Gardner, concluding with, "Assuming the woman isn't making the whole thing up to get attention, it's further evidence that Ashley was kidnapped."

He nodded. "The question is, by whom?"

I had opened my mouth when his phone rang.

He sat up straighter and fished it out of his jacket pocket. "Unknown caller," he said, but he answered it anyway. One does not ignore calls on a police-issue cell phone.

His eyes went wide. "I'm putting you on speaker. Repeat what you just said."

He set the phone down between us on my desk.

"I was wondering," Cara Hidalgo's British-accented voice came from it, "if the woman in the park was Ashley's birth mother."

CHAPTER SIX

I was still reeling from the news that Ashley was adopted as Bradley continued his briefing. We'd told Cara Hidalgo we'd get back to her.

"We've got some goodish news in the pervert department," Bradley was saying. "With the FBI's help, Cruthers has been tracking down everybody on the sex offenders' registry who lives in or near Starling." He pulled out his pad to consult it. "Thirteen in Starling, all men, and twice that in Jax, three of whom are women."

"That few?"

"Yeah. Surprisingly, the Florida registry only has about 86,000 names on it, and we're one of the more diligent states about keeping those records. But only about four hundred of them still live in the state…" He paused. "According to the registry that is. Sex offenders don't always notify properly when they move, especially if they're no longer on probation."

He paused again, glanced at his pad. "Most of the ones in Starling and Jax are from cases of sexual assault of adults, a few are statutory rape. But eight are child abuse cases. Three have solid alibis, two have somewhat iffy alibis and the other three—two live in Jax and one here in Starling. Cruthers is bringing him in and the Jax Sheriff's Office is tracking down the other two."

"What constitutes a solid alibi?" I asked.

"One guy was having an emergency appendectomy yesterday afternoon."

I let out a short bark of laughter. "That's pretty solid, all right."

"Collins is checking out the ones with iffy alibis. You wanna participate in the interrogation of the guy Cruthers is bringing in?"

"Maybe. Lemme think for a minute." We'd gone from barely a lead to three strong ones. Goth girl, especially if she was Ashley's birth mother, this guy Cruthers was bringing in, and the Silvas were looking more suspicious now, having withheld the info that Ashley was adopted.

"How about I observe Cruthers's interrogation, and back him up if he needs it. Should we double team him?"

"I'd leave that up to Cruthers. Sometimes that shuts these guys down. They don't think of themselves as criminals, they're just misunderstood." Bradley pursed his lips as if he'd tasted something sour. "One sympathetic-seeming cop can often get more out of them."

I nodded, acknowledging his superior experience in that area, since I'd never worked sex crimes—other than those that ended in the victim's death.

"You go confront the Silvas about their faulty memories," I said.

Bradley pushed himself to a stand. "I'll swing by the park again, on my way back, and see if Goth Girl has shown up."

I stood as well. "Maybe you can get more out of Silva. I don't think he likes women."

Bradley turned in the doorway. "I didn't get the sense that he's gay."

I shook my head. "Me neither, but I suspect he prefers the women around him to be barefoot and pregnant."

Bradley gave me a long look up and down, a small smirk on his face. "I have trouble visualizing you in either condition."

I snorted and waved him on his way.

As he left, I called after him, "Find out if the baby boy is adopted as well."

———⊙———

Cruthers had agreed with Bradley's assessment. He went into the interview room alone, while I entered the observation area.

I could watch the interview on the video screen as it was recorded, but I opted to turn out the light and open the blinds over the old-fashioned one-way mirror still imbedded in the wall. I could see more details through the large window.

The guy sitting at the stark metal table was not the obvious sleazeball that my imagination had drummed up. Instead, he was the clean-cut kid next door whom you'd hire to mow your lawn.

And wouldn't think twice about letting your kids be around him.

Mid-twenties, with brown eyes, longish brown hair, and smooth boyish cheeks, he wore a faded red tee shirt and jeans with ripped knees.

Cruthers informed him that the interview would be recorded. "Am I under arrest?" he asked, anxiety in his voice.

Was that significant? Or would any sex offender be nervous when he's pulled in for questioning, even if he hasn't done anything wrong? Recently.

"No," Cruthers said. "We only want to know what you've been up to lately." His tone was casual, his body language relaxed, as if this were truly a routine check.

The guy, Peter Richards, did not seem reassured. "Look, if this is about that little girl who went missing, I had nothing to do with that. I intentionally stayed away from the riverwalk Saturday, so I wouldn't be around kids."

"Ah," Cruthers said, "but your fingerprints were found on the railing about a hundred feet from where she was standing with her mom."

Bradley hadn't mentioned that part. Maybe Cruthers was making it up. Contrary to common belief, police *are* allowed to lie to suspects, to see if they can trip them up.

But Richards didn't missed a beat. "So, I go to the river-walk sometimes. Most people in this town do." He tossed his head, flipping too-long bangs out of his face. "Look, I've been working on this, um...you know, goin' to therapy and everything. I don't want to be like that again."

Cruthers nodded and scribbled something on his pad in front of him. It was probably a doodle since this guy hadn't said anything relevant yet.

"Besides," Richards added, "I don't go for girls, only boys."

"So you're a homo?" Cruthers said.

I winced, glad that Bradley wasn't here. But he would know Cruthers didn't mean it. He was using the language this kid could hopefully relate to.

"No," Richards said emphatically, glaring at Cruthers.
Or maybe not.

"And I'm not homophobic either," he added in a huffy voice, crossing his arms over his chest.

Cruthers said nothing.

"And I've *never* kidnapped a child. I *seduce* them."

More silence, although Cruthers maintained a pleasant expression on his face.

I swallowed a chuckle, admiring the seasoned detective's astuteness. He'd realized the guy was basically interrogating himself.

"My therapist says I'm only replaying what my father did to me, to take my power back."
Psychobabble BS, I thought.

"Do you realize you're using present tense," Cruthers said. "I thought you weren't doing that anymore."

"No, no," Richards's tone was panicky. He'd leaned forward, his butt partway off his chair. "I meant I *was* doing that. She said that was what I was doing, in the past."

Cruthers waved him back into his chair.

Richards complied, but even from fifteen feet away, I could make out beads of sweat on his forehead.

"Seduced them how?" Cruthers asked, after a long pause.

Richards had been staring down at his hands, folded on the table in front of him. Now his head jerked up. He swallowed hard, his Adam's apple bobbing. "Candy, sodas. Then I'd buy them video games, get them talking about their favorites. Eventually I'd tell them I had a new game that was really cool and I wanted to show it to them."

"And you'd take them to your place and molest them," Cruthers said, his voice a little choked, as if he were struggling a bit to keep his tone neutral.

"No," Richards said, "I mean...uh, yeah. I'd invite them to my place, and lead up to things slowly. I'd start touching them, but innocently. Hand on the shoulder, ruffle their hair." He mimicked that motion. "Stuff like that. Then I'd roughhouse with them and–"

Cruthers held up his hand in a stop gesture. "I get the picture."

"And another thing, I didn't go for little kids. My boys were all ten or older."

"His *boys?*" I muttered. Bile rose in the back of my throat.

I'd heard enough, and apparently so had Cruthers. He ended the interview and handed the kid off to a uniform to be escorted from the building.

I met Cruthers out in the hallway.

"We'll have to cut him loose," he said, "but can we put him under surveillance?"

I thought for a moment, decided that was a good idea. "Yes. He made a good point, that he's only ever gone after older boys. But he may hang out with other child abusers."

It was a long shot, but I was willing to put some manpower on it, especially with the FBI and FDLE agents helping out. "It'll have to be uniforms, though," I said. "Sergeant Armstrong is officially off duty today, but he came in to volunteer anyway. We can put him and Peters on it, in plain clothes."

Cruthers nodded as my police-issue cell phone rang in my pocket. I fished it out and, without looking at caller ID, barked, "Chief Anderson."

"Well, good afternoon to you, too, Lieutenant...uh, Chief." Skip Canfield's mock cheerful voice in my ear.

"Sorry," I said crisply, although I wasn't all that remorseful. Canfield had the worst timing sometimes. "It's a bad day. And Judith will suffice."

"I left a message on your personal phone, but I thought you'd want to hear this. I can wait though, until..." he paused. "I know you've got a tough case going on—a child abduction, Kate said." His tone had shifted from mockery to sympathy. I wasn't sure I liked that better.

But I took a deep breath. "Yeah, tough case," I acknowledged. "Uh, lemme get to someplace private." I waved Cruthers off.

"I'll tell Armstrong," he whispered, and I nodded.

"By the way," Skip said conversationally, as I crossed the bullpen, "why do you go by Judith, not Judy?"

"Long story." I ducked around Barnes's desk, where she was hunched over her keyboard, doing background checks on various suspects. "Short version. A bully in second grade kept calling me Punch and Judy and punching my arm. So one time, I punched him back, bloodied his nose."

The low rumble of a chuckle came through the line. "And you've been Judith ever since."

"Yup." I closed my office door. "Okay, what's going on?"

"The National Center for Missing and Exploited Children got a hit," Skip said, his voice sobering. "A partial DNA match to Meredith's."

CHAPTER SEVEN

"It's mitochondrial DNA," Skip added.

"So related through the mother's line," I said, my voice sounding breathless in my own ears.

"She may very well be Meredith's daughter. This is a woman in her early thirties. She's in Ohio. I need your permission to spend the money to go out there and interview her."

Heart pounding, I dropped into my desk chair. "Did you try calling her?"

"No. I have a feeling I'll get farther in person. Over the phone, she may think I'm some kind of scammer."

I made myself stop and think. I could readily afford the airfare for Canfield to go out there, and he was an experienced PI. I should trust his instincts.

"I'll try not to spend too much of your money, Judith," he added.

"No worries. Yes, go to Ohio."

"I'll keep you posted." Skip disconnected.

I sat back in my desk chair, willing my skittering heart to settle down. "Hang in there, Meredith. We've got a lead," I said under my breath. "We're gonna find you."

———◆———

Mid-morning, I sat at my desk contemplating what I should do next. Where could I be most helpful?

Bradley had reported that confronting the Silvas about their failure to mention the adoption had been a waste of time.

Damn! I'd been hoping the husband would slip and say something incriminating. Based on his withholding of the adoption info and on Mrs. Gardner's report that someone had taken Ashley's hand—someone the child was comfortable with—I was leaning hard toward suspecting him.

But all he'd done was repeat that of course they'd forgotten to mention some things, they were rattled. Then he'd blustered on about how the police were wasting time interrogating them—the victims—when we should be out there searching for Ashley. Bradley said he'd given a convincing performance.

"But I'm not sure I *am* convinced it was totally sincere," he'd added. "Silva could just be a good actor. Oh, and the baby is his. It was one of those cases of adopting, and then the wife gets pregnant soon after."

Was Silva planning on leaving his wife and taking a runner with the kids? So he hired someone to take Ashley first, since it would be difficult for him to hustle both children out from under her nose at the same time?

Or maybe the goal was to drive Annie crazy, so he could get her committed? I made a mental note to have Bradley dig deeper into their finances. They lived well. Was that all from his income, or did she have money of her own?

Maybe he wanted to make her look like an unfit mother, so he could get the kids.

We needed to talk to that lawyer! The one who'd arranged the adoption.

Cara Hidalgo had remembered his name, having met him once. She'd been hired two weeks before the baby was due, and had already been living with the Silvas when Ashley was born. The lawyer had brought the baby to their home when she was a few days old.

Cara had also said that there'd been no contact between the birth mother and the Silvas, that the mother had wanted it that way. The lawyer had handled everything.

Unfortunately, the only phone number we could find for the lawyer was his office, which was closed on a Sunday. And Barnes's attempts to find his home address had ended at a Mailboxes and More storefront. She was trying to locate the owner of the private mailbox service franchise. But I held out little hope that said owner would fork over a mailbox owner's name without a subpoena.

I jumped some when Wellbourne and Collins suddenly appeared in my doorway.

"Sorry for startling you, Chief," Wellbourne said, "but we think we have an idea."

"A crazy idea," Collins added.

"Who's with the Silvas?" I asked.

"The head FBI guy," she replied, looking a bit sheepish. "He said he wanted to get a feel for the family." She frowned. "I guess I should've called you first."

I thought about chastising her for not doing just that, but decided to save that discussion for another time. The dark circles under her eyes said she hadn't gotten much, if any, sleep. And I suspected she was more than a little intimidated by Special Agent in Charge Trager.

I waved my fingers at them in a come-in gesture. "So what's your idea?"

Wellbourne deferred to Collins regarding the comfy chair, perching her butt on the edge of one of the others. Barnes followed them in, taking up her usual spot leaning against the doorjamb.

They were right. It was a pretty crazy idea—a minor sting operation for the park, to try to catch the Goth Girl. Wellbourne would pose as another nanny in the park, and Collins would be nearby.

But, as they talked, the idea began to grow on me. After all, neither the sex offender lead nor the Silvas withholding info had taken us anywhere solid, at least not yet.

Collins held up a finger. "I've got Cara Hidalgo on hold. Can I put her on speaker? She's willing to go with me, to identify the young woman."

I nodded, thinking, *if Goth Girl even shows up.* But if she didn't, that might tell us something as well—that she might indeed be Ashley's birth mother and/or her kidnapper.

Either way, the two detectives could observe and question other nannies and parents about the stranger who frequently sat on that bench mid-day watching the kids.

I'd almost talked myself into it, but the haste with which we were throwing together the operation was making my stomach queasy. Undercover ops were usually weeks in the planning, or at least days.

"The problem is we need a kid," Barnes was saying. The detectives had apparently filled her in on their idea before entering my office. "And," she added with a chuckle, "we don't have any undercover preschoolers on duty today."

I gave her a sharp look.

"Sorry, trying to lighten the mood." But she only seemed slightly chagrined.

I considered chastising her some more, but I really couldn't fault her. The intensity of the situation was already getting to us, and it was only halfway through day one.

Dear Lord, let there not be a day two. The longer this child remained among the missing, the greater the chances that she'd never be found.

I flashed to a sunny backyard and three kids innocently playing hide-and-seek. Tragically, one of them—Meredith—was sought but never found.

I shook my head to clear it.

"We've got that covered," Collins was saying, a small grin on his boyishly handsome face. "My five-year-old would love to play cops. He's bored silly after being off from school all summer."

My stomach churned. *No!*

"Don't worry, Chief," Collins quickly added, "I'll stay near him the whole time."

I leaned forward. "Absolutely not. We're not putting a child at risk." Although, all the children at that park would be somewhat at risk, if this young woman freaked out on us.

"You..." I pointed to Wellbourne, "will pretend you're supervising a divorced father's visit." I turned to Collins. "You'll hang out near some kid and try to act like he's yours."

Barnes snorted softly. "He may get arrested as a predator."

I glared at her again, and this time her expression sobered.

"I'm going with you," I told the detectives. "Cara and I will be in my car nearby." I paused. "I'm concerned, though, that some vigilant mom or nanny might get suspicious that we're up to no good."

The sound of Cara clearing her throat came from the phone. "Um, that's not unusual. Some mums drive the nanny and kids to the park, then sit in their cars and call their friends, or text or whatever."

"That's nuts," Barnes said. "Why have kids only to have someone else play with them?"

As a non-kid person, I kinda got it, but I let that whole issue go. "Wellbourne, you need to go see Derek and get yourself wired."

She jumped up and hustled toward the door, apparently not wanting to give me time to change my mind.

Barnes shifted to let her by.

"*You* hold down the fort here," I said to her.

Her face fell.

"One," I said, "you're in uniform–"

She opened her mouth and I held up a hand. "And two, we don't want a whole crowd of strangers showing up. That will make the regulars suspicious."

She made a face, but then nodded and headed for her desk.

———◆◆———

The park was smaller than I'd imagined, tucked away in a residential neighborhood. The playground consisted of monkey bars, swings and a sliding board.

Collins stood near the monkey bars, his eyes on the little boy currently attempting to crawl along the top of them.

Wellbourne strolled around the play area's perimeter, taking it all in. "Is that her?" she said in a low voice, tilting her head slightly toward a young woman on a bench on the opposite side from my car.

Of course, we've ended up on the wrong side.

I nodded to Cara, in the passenger seat beside me. I'd instructed her not to speak unless I said it was okay, so as not to distract the detectives.

"Yes," she said.

The woman was somewhere between mid-twenties to early thirties, pale faced, and a little pudgy around the middle. She wore all black, her blonde hair sticking out in clumps from under a knit cap.

Why a knit cap in August? I wondered.

I was contemplating whether moving my car closer would draw attention to us, when Wellbourne plopped down on the bench next to the woman. "Pretty day," she said, "not too hot yet."

The woman turned slightly toward her. "Yeah." But her eyes darted back over her shoulder.

I followed her line of vision. She was staring at a little girl, about three, with blonde hair. But she was taller and thinner than Ashley.

Cara held a pad and pen on her lap. She jotted something on it and held it up for me to read.

She looked at Ashley that way sometimes.

I nodded. There was definitely something going on with this woman.

In the meantime, Wellbourne had gone through her spiel about supervising her young charge's visit with his father, the non-custodial parent in a contentious divorce. "It's a real drag," she concluded, while snagging a red-brown spiral curl and tugging on it. "I'd much rather be playing with little Joey myself. It makes the time go faster. Which kid is yours?"

"Um, none." The woman's voice was low, barely audible. "I'm on my lunch break, from work."

"You work near here?" Wellbourne asked.

And she's working on a Sunday? I didn't see any evidence of food on or near the bench either.

The woman gestured toward a taller office building, peeking above the trees in the distance. "Over there."

Long way to walk for a break, I thought, just as Wellbourne said, "That's a bit of a trek."

The woman shrugged and started to turn away.

"What do you do?" Wellbourne asked, "at work, I mean."

"Computer programming." The woman's lip curled up. From this distance, I couldn't decide what that meant.

And why wasn't Wellbourne asking why she's working on a Sunday?

No! I resisted the urge to smack the side of my head, to get my tired brain in gear—Cara would think I was losing it. Wellbourne was on the right track. Asking about working on a Sunday would *not* be relevant, and it might get the woman's back up.

"You must like kids," Wellbourne was saying, "since you come here for your lunch break. Why don't you become a nanny?"

The lip curled again, this time a tad more pronounced. "No offense but I suspect programming pays better."

Wellbourne smiled. "None taken, 'cause you're totally right."

The woman didn't return the smile, but her shoulders slumped, indicating she was relaxing some.

"Hey," Wellbourne said, "did you hear about the little girl that got lost during the boat parade yesterday?"

The woman lifted her head some, but her shoulders stayed relaxed.

Wellbourne nodded. "I think she used to play here. I'm pretty sure I've seen her before."

Some tension now in her body, but the woman seemed more engaged in the conversation. "Now that you mention it–"

"Stop that, Jimmy." A woman's sharp voice. "You're gonna get hurt."

I glanced over. The woman was gesturing to the boy on top of the monkey bars. "Jimmy, get down," she ordered. "Now!"

Collins stepped forward, arms raised to lift the boy down. "Here. I'll help you."

"Jimmy?" our woman on the bench said, "Isn't that your charge? I thought you said his name was Joey."

"Uh, yes. Well his dad calls him that, named after himself, Joseph, Jr." Wellbourne was talking fast. "Kinda narcissistic, if you ask me. His mom calls him Jimmy, his middle name, after her dad, I think she said."

Lame, but nice try, Wellbourne.

Our Goth Girl wasn't buying it one bit. Her shoulders were hunched upward and she was edging away from Wellbourne on the bench. "Why's that woman telling him to get down? It looks like she's his mother."

Wellbourne jumped up, perhaps realizing belatedly that she should be reacting to her charge being in danger.

I glanced quickly at Collins. He stood frozen beside the monkey bars, looking past the mom and boy—now safely on the ground—at Wellbourne and our suspect.

It was a good thing Wellbourne was on her feet, because the young woman slid off the far end of the bench. "Gotta go," she muttered and power-walked away.

"Hey, hang on," Wellbourne called after her, jogging a few steps. "You wanna do coffee some time?"

In the passenger seat, Cara rolled her eyes. I swallowed a snicker.

The woman shook her head without looking back and broke into a half run. Wellbourne sprinted after her, calling out, "Police! Stop."

"Damn it to hell," I muttered and threw open my car door. "Stay here."

Crap! I should've put my sneakers on when we got in the car. My low-heeled pumps, fine for the office, were not good running shoes.

I took off anyway, now glad we were on the opposite side of the park. The woman was running right toward me.

Then she saw me and veered off. I shifted direction as well and was easily going to cut her off.

I lifted my left foot. My shoe stayed on the sidewalk. Thrown off balance, I stumbled a couple of steps.

When I looked up, I expected to see the woman pulling away from me and Wellbourne. But Collins was intercepting her from the other direction. He grabbed her arm and brought her abruptly to a stop. "Police," he said, pulling his ID out with his other hand.

And he isn't even breathing all that hard.

He began tugging the woman in black toward me.

I retrieved my shoe and discovered a huge hunk of chewing gum on its sole.

Damn!

CHAPTER EIGHT

Back at 3MB, I left it to Wellbourne and Collins to interview our Goth Girl and headed for my office. I needed to be able to hide behind my desk and slip my not-running shoes off for a while. I was pretty sure I had a blister on one heel.

I'd carried my sneakers in with me, planning to put them on once my feet had a few moments of freedom.

I found a bag of deli sandwiches on my desk, and a note from Sam telling me he and some of his deputies were helping out with the canvassing.

I texted him a thank you and unwrapped a sandwich. *Ah, egg salad.* Sam's go-to sandwich choice when he knew it was both my breakfast and lunch.

I picked up a gooey half of the sandwich and moved it toward my mouth.

My desk phone rang. I glanced down at caller ID—*Watch Desk.*

I juggled the messy sandwich into one hand and hit the button for speaker. "What's up, Sarge?"

"Sergeant Armstrong just called in," Sergeant Johnson's voice. "Somethin's going down with that guy Cruthers interviewed earlier. But I can't reach Lieutenant Bradley."

"I'll go. Is he still at the per...suspect's apartment building?"

"No, he gave me a new location. I'll text it to your phone."

"Thanks."

I jumped up from my chair and called out, "Barnes, we're going out to back up Armstrong and Peters."

I took three steps and realized I was barefoot. Turning back, I grabbed my sneakers. I jogged through the bullpen, my naked feet garnering funny looks from some uniforms who were at the desks typing out their reports from this morning's canvassing.

At the elevators, I took the time to actually put the sneakers on. Barnes was trying, and failing, to hide a smile.

"Oh, shut up," I said, but then snickered in spite of myself.

Nothing like a couple of shots of adrenaline to lift my mood some. My stomach gurgled and I thought longingly of the sandwich abandoned on my desk, wishing I could've gotten a couple of bites in me before I had to run off.

On the way to the new location—a warehouse in an older industrial park on the Bennett side of town—I filled Barnes in on the details of Cruther's interview with Peter Richards.

She grinned. "That's really his name, Peter Dick? What was his mother thinking?"

Internally I chuckled too, but I didn't want to encourage her. Instead I said, in an acerbic tone, "I doubt she was thinking her little babe would grow up to be a child molester."

She arranged her expression into something closer to somber, but one side of her mouth still tilted upward in a slight smirk.

I concluded my summary of the interview with, "Richards is a slimeball, but he made a good point, that little girls are not his thing. But–"

"Maybe he knows other child abusers," Barnes finished my sentence.

"Yup, thus the surveillance."

The Bennett area was made up of mostly working class to poor neighborhoods. The warehouse, indeed the entire industrial park, looked abandoned.

We left my car behind a building two over from the designated warehouse, and slipped between dumpsters and piles of wooden pallets—gray from years of sitting out in the weather—to where Armstrong had reported he was parked. He and Peters were in his private vehicle, tucked away in an obscure spot but with a view of the side of the warehouse.

I knocked gently on the back passenger window.

The locks clicked open, and Barnes and I piled into the backseat.

"We followed Richards here. He went to that side door." Armstrong pointed through the windshield. "He knocked and someone let him in."

"Five others have gone in during the last twenty minutes." Peters's brown eyes sparkled with excitement, belying her bland tone of voice. She wore jeans and a medium brown short-sleeved sweater a shade lighter than her skin. "Four men and one woman. All White, except one of the men was Black. No cars that we've seen."

"Richards got here via the bus," Armstrong added, "then walked the rest of the way. Maybe the others did too. I got pics of most of them and sent them to Derek."

I nodded. If anyone could get an ID from a photo taken from a distance, Derek the Geek could.

As if on cue, Armstrong's phone pinged. "Oh ho," he said after checking it. "Geek Boy came through. On two of them, at least. Some of our friends from the sex offenders' list." He turned his phone so I could see their mug shots from the backseat.

I tilted my head toward Barnes, and he shifted the phone for her to see them.

"Why," I asked, "would half a dozen perverts be meeting in an abandoned warehouse?"

"Maybe an SAA meeting?" Barnes said.

"A what?" Peters asked.

"Sexual Addicts Anonymous," Armstrong answered before Barnes could. "Maybe, but why here?"

"Wouldn't they get in trouble for being around each other?" Peters asked. "Those still on probation, that is."

"I think twelve-step meetings are an exception," I said. Still, they could be worried about that, thus the choice of an abandoned warehouse for a meeting place.

But somehow I doubted it. These people were up to something.

I paused a moment to appreciate how well the rookies were participating in the brainstorming. Barnes was used to it—she sat in on most brainstorming sessions between me and the detectives—but Peters had been strictly patrol up to this point.

However, she wasn't quite a rookie anymore. She was coming up on her two-year anniversary with the force, which would mean the end of her probationary period.

The side door of the warehouse opened. It hung there for moment, most of its blue paint peeled off, the wood underneath gray. Then a figure stepped out. It was a woman.

Armstrong held up his phone and snapped a shot. "Good, I didn't get her on the way in." He poked at his phone, no doubt sending the pic to Derek.

The woman looked all around, then took off at a slow trot.

"Barnes," I said, "sneak around back and see if anyone is going out that way. But stay out of sight, since you're in uniform. We don't want to spook them."

She nodded and slipped out of her door.

Two more men exited over the next ten minutes. Then one more came out.

"That's our guy," Armstrong said, as the man jerked his head back and forth, checking to make sure no one was watching.

"You two stick with him," I said, as I started to open my door. "Barnes and I will check out the warehouse after the other one leaves."

"There are two more people in there," Peters said. "Someone was already there, opening the door for the others, before we got here."

"Good point," I said. "And there could have been others who arrived before our guy."

Armstrong was looking back over his shoulder, his eyebrows raised halfway up to where his hairline should be.

It took me a beat to figure out the question that he dared not ask out loud of the police chief—in front of rookies, no less.

"Don't worry," I said. "I'll call for backup if we need it, but I'm not planning on arresting anybody. Not until we know what's been going on here."

He nodded, apparently satisfied, and I slipped out of the car.

I hid behind a nearby dumpster. It didn't even smell. Which meant it had been a very long time since anyone put anything in it.

I texted Derek to research the owners of the property, both the industrial park and the warehouse. Then I sent a text to Barnes's phone, filling her in. I hoped she'd remembered to put it on vibrate only.

My phone pinged a few seconds later and I felt my cheeks warm. I'd forgotten to put my own on vibrate. I did that first before checking the text.

Got it. Nothing happening back here.

A scraping sound, from a distance.

I peeked out around the dumpster.

The door was hanging open again and a man stepped out. I snapped a shot of him, in case he was another one that Armstrong had missed on their way in.

The door didn't close this time behind him. The man jogged away.

A beat later, another man came out, a big black duffle bag in one hand. It bulged and he carried it like it was heavy.

Is that big enough to hold a little girl?

I didn't think so, and I suspected Ashley was heavy enough he'd have to carry it with both hands if she were in there. The guy wasn't very big—short and wiry.

I clicked a couple of shots of him as he turned and locked the door behind him.

But he kept his head down and wore a straw cowboy-style hat. I doubted my photos had captured much but I sent them off to Derek.

I texted Barnes. *Last guy out, maybe. Might be more inside. Check the windows, but be careful.*

I slipped from the dumpster to a pile of empty crates, then to the corner of a building and on to more dumpsters and piles of various abandoned containers and supplies, until I reached the building next door to our target.

I ran the fifteen feet between the buildings and flattened against the wall. I was halfway down it, peeking through filthy windows when my phone vibrated.

Found an unlocked window, Barnes had texted.

I meant look IN the windows, I replied.

I was. But found one unlocked.

Sit tight.

I finished peeking through the windows on my side. Some opened onto a large room, empty with a thick coating of dust on the floor, that had been stirred in places. A couple of the windows accessed smaller rooms, maybe nine feet by nine feet. One of those rooms held an old-fashioned wooden and metal student's desk, the kind with the desk attached to the arm of the chair, hinged so that it could be pushed up to get in and out of the seat. The second of the smaller rooms was empty, but again the dust on the floor was disturbed, and two deep tracks led from the center of the room to the doorway, which was open. Through it I could see what looked like the larger room.

I headed to the back of the building.

Barnes stood next to a high, square frosted window. She'd found a crate and dragged it over, as evidenced by tracks dug into the sandy dirt.

"We need a warrant," I said in a low voice.

"To just look around?" She asked. "What if Ashley's in there?"

I debated. We had very little probable cause to enter the building. So some folks had come and gone there. Richards had completed his parole, so the fact that he was hanging with other questionable people was not a crime.

But the child could be in there. And a half dozen people might have just abused her, or one, while the others watched. I shuddered and my stomach heaved.

My phone vibrated in my pocket. I pulled it out. A text from Derek read, *Two brothers own both park and warehouse, Harry and Frank Tobin. Both have sheets long as your arm.*

He'd sent copies of mug shots and arrest reports. I scrolled down.

Forget my arm, his sheet was as long as my leg. And on it, among the breaking-and-entering, robbery, and assault-and-battery charges, were two arrests for distribution of pornography via the internet. Neither stuck, charges were dropped.

Maybe due to insufficient evidence? Or had this creep been one of the criminals who'd paid off John Black to look the other way? I'd also found out last fall that the former assistant state attorney for this area was probably part of the old chief's corruption circle. Dot Wilder was still gathering evidence against him.

I scrolled to the mug shots and mentally compared straw-hat dude to them. One of them could very well be the same guy.

"Did you look in all the other windows?" I asked.

Her cheeks pinked. "Um, no, not those last two." She gestured toward two filthy windows between her and the end of the warehouse wall.

"You take that one. I'll get the other."

Mine revealed nothing but the large dusty room. A quick movement in my peripheral vision had me jerking around.

It was Barnes, ducking down below her window. "Someone's in there," she hissed in my direction.

I pulled my Glock as I walked over there, being careful not to bump into any of the debris that would make noise.

I quickly glanced in the window, showing only a sliver of my face along the window frame, then pulled my head back. My brain processed what I'd seen. The back of a man walking out the door, dragging what looked like a garden hose behind him. And in the center of the floor was another student desk, dripping wet.

"Why was he washing the desk?" Barnes whispered.

"Good question," I whispered back, although I had an inkling now of what was going on here.

"Let's get back to the side door." I pointed to the far end of the warehouse. "Stay below the windows."

We crouched over and awkwardly moved down the length of the building. I pointed silently to another pile of wooden pallets about fifteen feet from the corner of the building.

Barnes nodded.

I ran for the shade behind the pallets. She followed, again staying low.

We made ourselves as comfortable as one can get while crouched down in a dusty warehouse yard in the Florida heat. And we waited.

Ten minutes later, the door screeched open and a man stepped out. He too carried a duffle bag that seemed heavy.

He walked past our hiding place and we held our breaths.

Another couple of minutes ticked by, then we heard the roar of a car engine from a couple of buildings over.

Barnes audibly blew out air and rose to her feet. She took a step around the pile of pallets.

I stood and reached for her arm to drag her back down.

The engine roared louder and she turned to me, her eyes wide. Beyond her I spotted a sporty-looking blue car headed our way.

We both dove head first back behind the pallets.

CHAPTER NINE

The car roared past, stirring up gravel and sand that rattled against the wooden pallets.

Neither of us moved until the sound of the engine was long gone.

I stood, brushing off the front of my clothes. "After this case is over, you get to take this pantsuit to the dry cleaners."

"No problem," Barnes said meekly as she batted dust off her uniform, with only partial success.

She looked up. "Now do we go in?"

I shook my head, pulled out my phone and showed her the mug shots Derek had sent. "They both have rap sheets for a lot of things, including distributing porn. Do you recognize them?"

She nodded. "The guy who just left and the other guy with the duffle bag."

"Yup. I'm pretty sure Ashley isn't here, but we're going to get a search warrant right away to make sure. I think I know what's going on here, and I don't want these assholes to get off because of a search some judge decides later was illegal."

Barnes looked baffled. "What's going on, Chief?"

"Think about it. Six people come in, most of them known sex offenders. Several rooms with desks in them and scuff marks in the dust on the floor, indicating recent use. And the owners of the building leave, carrying heavy bags of–"

"Laptops! He's showing them porn."

I nodded.

"Ewww." Barnes's expression shifted to a deep frown. "I think I've figured out why the desk needed a bath."

I dropped Barnes off at her car in the municipal parking lot. She was to go home and get a fresh uniform, then go to my apartment and check on my cat. And bring me two sets of clean clothes as well. The way things were going I figured it would be wise to keep a spare pantsuit and shirt handy.

Then she would write up the search warrant request for that warehouse. It was a good opportunity for her to learn how to do that.

Yes, I wanted to put a stop to whatever the Tobin brothers were up to there, but it wasn't our current priority.

Ashley was.

As I entered the bullpen, Officer Terry and King were leaving. "What happened to you?" Terry blurted out.

"A dive into the dirt to avoid being seen by the bad guy," I replied.

His eyebrows went up. I gave him the short version of what had gone down at that warehouse, de-emphasizing the slimier sexual aspects. "We're going to try for a search warrant," I concluded.

"I want in on that," Terry said. "That's exactly the kind of operation where King can be helpful. He goes in first to make sure there are no guns or explosives."

I nodded. "I'll keep you posted."

Unfortunately, the rest of Sunday afternoon was pretty much a bust.

At six, Bradley came to my office to fill me in. Barnes followed, taking up her post against the doorjamb.

Bradley reported that the young woman from the park, whose name was Lola Dexter, had admitted she'd given up a baby for adoption, and now regretted it. But she'd done so fairly recently—a couple of months ago, and it was a boy. She went to the park on her breaks and daydreamed about what he would be like when he was the ages of the preschoolers playing there.

"Why does she torture herself like that?" I asked.

"Maybe the torture is the point," Barnes observed. "Punishment to appease her guilt."

I nodded.

"She said," Bradley continued, "that she was still struggling with postpartum depression, but she knew it would pass."

"Hmm, what does that suggest to you?" I asked.

"That she's given birth before," Bradley said with a sigh. "I'll dig deeper on her."

"She still could've taken Ashley," Barnes said. "Maybe she was still hanging out in the park to throw off suspicion."

"Somehow I don't see Lola being that clever," Bradley said.

"Me neither," I said.

"And who's watching the toddler while all this is going on?" he asked.

"Good question," Barnes and I said in unison.

"Wellbourne located her employer in that office building," Bradley added, "but no one was there late on a Sunday afternoon."

"We'll have to check that out tomorrow," I said.

"We've got no grounds to hold her," he said, "so I cut her loose. But I assigned a couple of seasoned uniforms, in plainclothes, to keep an eye on her."

He shrugged. "She went home. One of the uniforms, on the pretense of looking for someone else's apartment, knocked on her door. He said the place was tiny, although there was a separate bedroom that he couldn't see into. But there were no signs or sounds indicating a toddler was in residence, and Lola willingly opened the door and didn't seem nervous."

I made a mental to-do list for the next morning—talk to the lawyer who'd arranged Ashley's adoption, check with Bradley re: his deeper dive into Lola Dexter's background, and maybe confront the Silvas again about their failure to mention the adoption. And it was time for a press conference, with the poor parents begging the kidnapper to send their child home safe.

My chest ached and my stomach clenched.

I studied Bradley, slouched in the comfy visitor's chair, and Barnes sagging against the doorframe. They looked as exhausted as I felt.

I hated to break off the investigation, even for a little while, but we were all running on fumes at this point. "Go home, get some rest," I instructed. "Come back when you feel you're fit for duty again."

On my way out, I checked in with Sergeant Johnson at the watch commander's desk. He informed me that the FBI agents had left to get hotel rooms.

"Everyone else, our detectives and the FDLE agents, are still interviewing folks," he said.

"Tell them to stop at dusk and go get some sleep," I said. With Florida's stand-your-ground law, there was a distinct risk that some crazy homeowner would open fire on a stranger on their porch at night, without even asking who it was.

Halfway home, my phone pinged and a text message appeared on my dashboard screen. It was from Sam. Just the sight of his name had my shoulders and chest relaxing some.

Are you still at the office?

I instructed Bluetooth to respond, *No, on my way home. Pizza in 20 minutes?*

Make it 30?

Sure.

I smiled at the dashboard, then I fantasized about the hot shower I was going to take during that thirty minutes. I'd washed off the worst of the dirt from that industrial park's dusty lot in my minuscule bathroom at work. But I needed a longer shower at home to wash away the gruesome thoughts clogging my brain.

Guilt tightened my chest. What was happening to little Ashley right now? Was she safe, or scared to death? Was she in pain?

I shook my head vehemently as I pulled to the curb in front of my building. My landlord, bless his heart, had given me a designated space near the door, so I could come and go quickly, when I got a call about a major crime. Technically, the little sign saying *Reserved for Chief of Police* wasn't legal, but I wasn't about to look this gift horse in the mouth. It shaved off valuable seconds during which I would otherwise be running around the block to wherever I'd managed to find a spot.

By the time Sam rang my doorbell, I was showered and dressed in a sleeveless white silk shell and black cotton shorts.

"Too hot for your lounging PJs?" he asked as he let himself in with his key and walked to the breakfast bar. He deposited the pizza box there and turned to me with a smile.

The lounging getup was a champagne-colored long sleeved and loosely fitting outfit he'd given me last Christmas. It actually made me feel elegant, and it was one of the few things in my closet that wasn't black or white. I like to keep my wardrobe decisions simple.

But he was right. *Too damn hot!* "Yeah, the less clothes the better," I said out loud.

He wiggled his eyebrows in an exaggerated leer. "Sounds good to me."

I laughed. "Down, boy."

We settled at my breakfast bar with glasses of wine and devoured the pizza.

Sam glanced at his watch. "Wow, I think you set a new record there, half a pizza in eight minutes."

"I'm pretty sure it's the first food I've had all day. I have a vague memory of unwrapping the sandwich you left me, before getting called away."

"Without a single bite?"

I pulled a long face and nodded.

He reached out, gently tugged me off my stool and wrapped his arms around me. "Poor baby."

That immediately reminded me of Ashley, and my body stiffened.

He held me slightly away from him so he could look into my face. "What's the matter?"

I grimaced. "This case. I can't stop thinking about it."

He sighed and pulled me against him again, gently nudging my head toward his shoulder. I settled my cheek against his khaki uniform shirt and breathed in his scent. Male sweat mixed with a remaining hint of his woodsy aftershave.

A very slight hint. Based on the length of the stubble on his jaw, it had been a long time since his last shave.

I sighed and willed my body to relax. Only some parts of it obeyed.

"Still dredging up the past?" he whispered in my ear.

I nodded my head, still against his shoulder.

He nudged me slightly away, tilting his head toward my old leather sofa. Sliding off his stool, he picked up our wine glasses and hooked the neck of the bottle.

I gave him a small smile and touched the brown splotch of dampness on his khaki shoulder. "My hair got you wet."

He put the wine and glasses down on my coffee table and shed the shirt. "It's filthy anyway, after two days."

The white tee shirt under it was sweat-stained as well.

Sam grinned at me. "But don't be gettin' any ideas, little lady," he drawled in a fake Texas accent. "I can't stay the night," he added in his normal voice. "Staff meeting at the jail bright and early tomorrow. And I need a fresh uniform."

I settled on the sofa. "I can't say I'm in the mood for anything but cuddling tonight anyway."

He sat down beside me and put an arm around my shoulders. My white cat, Pipsqueak jumped into my lap, kneaded my shorts leg a bit, then curled up and closed her eyes.

"You do have a simple life, don't you, little one?" I said to her.

An ear twitched but she otherwise ignored me. I was only a comfy cushion to nap on, apparently.

Sam gently scratched her ear with his free hand. She twitched again and shook her head, without opening her eyes. But she was purring. That soft steady hum was one of my favorite sounds.

"You feel up to talking about your cousin?" Sam asked.

I blew out air. "There's not a lot to tell. Paul and Meredith, eight and ten respectively, were at my house. Their mom, Aunt Jean, had a doctor's appointment. We were playing hide-and-seek. I hid under a bush, but minutes went by and nothing happened. Um, other than the ringing of the phone inside the house and the screen door slamming as my mother went in to answer it. Then my mother started calling our names. Paul and I came out of hiding, but Meredith...she...was just gone."

My voice caught as my throat closed up.

Sam squeezed my shoulders but said nothing.

"It destroyed my family," I continued after a moment. "Aunt Jean was devastated, of course. But her brother, my father..."

I paused, sucked in air. "He went from being a social drinker to a full-blown alcoholic. And when he was drunk, he beat my mother."

Sam already knew that last part, that my father was a drunk and a wife beater, despite his PhD and prestigious job as a university professor.

"Aunt Jean told me a few months ago that he used Meredith's disappearance as an excuse for the beatings, that he was angry with my mother for not watching us better. But Jean said their father—my grandfather—was like that too. I never met him. He died before I was born." Another pause, another deep breath. "Aunt Jean thinks that Dad couldn't resist following that role model any longer."

"Humph," Sam said, "your friend Kate would say he was decompensating, because of the trauma of losing his niece."

"If that means he was overwhelmed by the feelings and lost control of himself, yes, that's probably what happened."

I shifted, cuddling closer against his sweat-stained tee shirt. "And I could've forgiven him for that. But he never seemed to try all that hard to rein himself again. And then he left her for a younger woman."

Sam knew the rest of the story. "And she spiraled downward," he said in a low voice, "and eventually killed herself."

I nodded and cleared my throat.

"Do you think the phone call was from the kidnapper," he asked, "to draw your mother away?"

"Hmm, I never thought of that." I sat up some, but not enough to pull away from the comforting arm around me. "But this was before the days when cell phones were in everybody's pocket. We're talking early 1980s. And no caller ID."

"He could have had an accomplice," Sam said.

"Hunh, maybe. But who would help a pervert steal a child?"

"Another pervert."

I cringed at the thought of that, little Meredith with two monsters.

"Or a wife or girlfriend," he continued. "Women in love can do crazy stuff."

"I'll have to tell Skip about those possibilities. He's checking for anybody who lived near us back then who seems suspicious, maybe has a record, et cetera."

My personal phone, which I'd dumped on the coffee table earlier, pinged. I leaned forward to check the screen. "Speak of the devil. It's a text from Skip."

I read the text out loud. *Spoke to the young woman. She's meeting me at a coffee shop on her way to work. I didn't tell her much yet, only that I might have info about her mother. She seemed kind of ambivalent. Hopefully, she shows. Will keep you posted.*

Normally, I would be ecstatic at this news—soon we might know more about what happened to Meredith. But for some reason, Skip's text left a brick of dread in my stomach.

What if we find out she's dead? That thought sprang into my mind unbidden. And I flashed to a childhood fantasy, one that I'd harbored for several years after my cousin disappeared.

I'd imagined her with a new family, sitting at a dinner table, happily telling her new parents about her day at school. The fantasy had always left me with a lump in my throat—sadness that she had so easily forgotten us, her original family. But I'd also felt relieved and happy that she was okay.

I was thirteen when I realized that fantasy was the least likely outcome of Meredith's abduction. Indeed, it was extremely unlikely. Babies and toddlers might be abducted by some troubled soul looking for a child to raise, but not a ten-year-old girl.

"Penny for your thoughts," Sam said.

I turned toward him. "Not sure they're worth that much."

"Try me." He gave me a soft smile, and his eyes...

I both loved and hated it when he looked at me that way. The blue of his eyes deepened and they sent the message, *I love you*, as loud and clear as if he'd spoken the words out loud.

I squirmed a little on the leather of the old sofa. I'd never been good with feelings, nor with relationships. But this one was different. For one, it was the longest romance I'd ever had. Six months was my old record, and Sam and I were now coming up on a year.

You've kept Meredith a secret long enough, I thought and made myself sit back in the circle of his arm again.

I told him about my fears, and that childish fantasy.

The dead woman rose slowly from the floor. My chest tightened.

Here we go again, I thought, somehow aware that I was dreaming.

The woman turned and smiled at me. "You still haven't found your cousin, sweetheart?" Again, the casual tone.

"I'm trying, Mom," my own teenage voice, a little whiny.

She turned toward the kitchen counter. "Do you want a sandwich?"

She looked back over her shoulder. And I froze.

The face had morphed again into a man's. This time, he wore a straw hat.

The warehouse owner!

"We've got them all," he said in a deep guttural voice. "And you'll never find them."

I jolted upright, gasping for air.

And slowly oriented to my own mundane bedroom. The ambient light from the cityscape beyond my window, which filtered around the edges of my curtains, revealed the flat duvet on what was usually Sam's side of the bed. And Pipsqueak sleeping in a curled-up ball at the foot.

She opened one eye, and her ear twitched. As if to say, is it morning already?

Then she meowed and glanced toward the open bedroom door and the kitchen beyond, where her empty bowl waited for her breakfast to magically appear.

"That's all you care about, isn't it?" I said out loud. For such a diminutive creature, she had a very hearty appetite.

She meowed again, looked back toward me, and her tiny pink tongue slid out and licked her lips.

With a sigh, I threw back the covers. Might as well get going.

CHAPTER TEN

It's Day Two, it's Day Two. The mantra kept repeating in my brain as I drove to 3MB. My empty stomach roiled.

Too much time was slipping away, and with each passing hour, the odds of us finding little Ashley diminished. And especially the odds of finding her alive and well.

I shook my head to clear it. That tactic didn't work.

It's Day Two, it's Day Two.

The pre-dawn sky was charcoal, with only a slight lightening at the horizon. I chewed on my lower lip.

I so wanted to call my people and get things rolling, but I didn't want to wake them.

I settled on Bradley. He didn't require a lot of sleep—a good thing for a police detective. Odds were good he'd be up by now.

I instructed my Bluetooth to text him. *You awake?*

Yes, in the office, came back within seconds. *Digging deeper into Lola Dexter.*

Anything else happening?

Afraid not.

On my way in. See you soon.

Okay, that had stopped the mantra, but only for a few minutes.

It's Day Two, it's Day Two.

At 3MB, Barnes was already at her desk, staring at her computer terminal. I cleared my throat and she glanced up. "I'm helping with more of the background checks."

I nodded.

"And I got my hands on that lawyer's home number. It's unlisted but..." She wiggled her eyebrows, "...I have my ways."

I nodded again but said nothing. I was better off not knowing too much about Barnes's "ways."

"You've got a seven-thirty appointment," she said, "at his office. He said he'd talk to you before his morning clients begin arriving at eight."

Excellent! The day was off to a good start.

"Good work," I said to Barnes.

She grinned and turned her gaze back to her monitor.

The lawyer's office address turned out to be a one-story brick building on one of the busiest streets in Starling. And the morning rush hour had already begun.

An impatient driver behind me honked his horn as I slowed, looking for a parking lot attached to the building. There didn't seem to be one.

I turned down a side street and ended up parking at the curb in front of someone's house. Just in case there were resident-only restrictions here, I took out the small sign Barnes had made for me, with *Chief of Police* stenciled on it along with the SPD logo. I slipped it on top of the dashboard, where it could be seen through the windshield.

As I exited my car, a jackhammer started up. In the lot on the opposite corner, a steel skeleton of a new structure rose above piles of dirt and gravel.

I wasn't sure how I felt about that. New development in the city meant new jobs, a stronger economy—but also more people and more crime. I sighed and headed for the office building's front door. It was unlocked.

A long, straight corridor dissected the building, with two suites on each side. Three were lawyers' offices, and one was an accounting firm. Even inside, you could hear the muffled sounds of road noise and the jackhammer.

I stopped at the first polished wooden door on the right, which sported a brass sign reading *Herbert Campbell, Esquire*. I grabbed the knob, but it was locked.

My knock elicited a clicking sound and the thick door swung open. A well-put-together woman in a tailored royal-blue suit greeted me. "You must be Chief Anderson."

A few threads of silver in her short dark hair and faint crow's feet around her brown eyes pegged her as early to mid-forties.

I opened my mouth but she didn't give me a chance to speak.

"Right this way." She ushered me through a well-appointed but empty waiting room. Lots of chrome and glass and tan leather loveseats. "Herb has a very tight schedule this morning. Mondays are always like that. But he knows how important this is."

We'd reached a closed door. She opened it, stepped aside and gestured for me to go in. The door clicked closed behind me.

Herbert Campbell stood behind a broad mahogany desk. He was a big man, a bit jowly, with pasty skin. I doubted he got outside much. His medium brown hair was graying at the temples, and his silver-gray suit looked expensive. The office was plush, befitting an established attorney—with wall-to-wall oak bookcases, a file cabinet with a wood veneer so it fit right in, and more tan leather chairs.

"Mr. Campbell," I began, as I crossed the room.

"Call me Herb," he said with a smile that didn't reach his eyes. The latter were a muddy brown, clouded with some emotion I couldn't decipher—perhaps just worry that we were throwing his morning schedule off.

He gestured for me to sit.

I perched on the edge of a chair. It looked like the kind that enjoyed swallowing people whole. "Herb, I know you're a busy man, so I'll cut to the chase. We really need the name of Ashley Silva's birth mother."

He grimaced as he sat down. "I wish I could give it to you, but..." He shook his head. "I can call her, though, and ask if it's okay to breach attorney/client confidentiality."

My turn to grimace. "I'd rather you didn't. If she's taken Ashley, a warning that we're coming would give her time to hide her."

Or worse, I thought, but I doubted she'd harm the child.

I huffed out a short sigh. "Let me ask you this, how ambivalent was she about giving the baby up?"

Herb sat back in his oversized desk chair. "Probably the least ambivalent I've ever seen. Um, let me speak hypothetically."

Sure, I thought, *if that will ease your conscience about confidentiality.*

"Some women who get caught up in violent relationships," he laced his fingers together over his substantial stomach, "and then find themselves pregnant...well, they may want nothing to do with the child."

He shook his head slightly. "It's a reminder of that horrible mistake they made. And if it were a boy, those women who are savvy about such things may worry that a genetic predisposition toward psychopathic tendencies might override upbringing, and the boy could follow in his father's footsteps."

I swallowed a smile. He sure was using a lot of words to try to avoid saying too much. "But it turned out to be a girl," I said. "Would that make this hypothetical woman waver?"

He squirmed some in his chair. "Perhaps. Some women in those circumstances might still become a little reluctant when it comes time to actually let the baby go. But that's pretty normal. It's not an easy decision to make."

I nodded and waited for him to continue. When he didn't, I asked, "Can you talk to me some about the Silvas? Did they approach you about an adoption?"

A fair amount of the tension left his body. "Yes, but that's not unusual. I have a reputation for discreetly arranging private adoptions, and Annie's father is a friend of mine."

He paused, took a deep breath. "But even so…Well again speaking hypothetically, I would have pointed out that I would be representing the mother, despite the fact that they would end up covering my fees."

"Is that usually how it works?"

"It is for me," he bluntly said. His eyes had turned shiny. *What's that about?*

"I feel that the young women involved do not have the advantages within the system as the well-to-do potential adoptive parents do. I need to look out for their interests."

I had a feeling there was something more to that story, but I wasn't sure it was relevant to finding Ashley.

"So you can speak more freely about the Silvas?" I asked hopefully.

"Yes, up to a point."

"Were they both equally interested in getting a child?" I hoped that wasn't too leading a question.

"At first. Mr. Silva particularly wanted a son, and wanted to know why they couldn't adopt a child that had already been born. I pointed out that most mothers who wanted to give up their babies turned them over to the Department of Children and Families for placement, and there was a long waiting list for healthy infants." He paused, rubbed a large hand across his face. "If they wanted to skip the line, so to speak, they needed to arrange with a pregnant woman ahead of time to take her baby, and pay her expenses during the pregnancy, plus my fees."

"Did Mr. Silva try to back out of the deal at any time?"

"No, not really. But he seemed disappointed when a sonogram was inconclusive regarding gender. The little one wasn't turned the right way to tell anything."

"Do you think he would've tried to back out if it had shown that the baby was a girl?"

He shrugged. "I reminded him that they had signed a contract. They'd still be obligated to pay all the mother's expenses, even if they didn't take the child."

So in other words, yes, you were concerned.

"Did you have any other concerns about the Silvas?" I asked. "Anything at all that seemed the least bit off?"

He started to shake his head, then stopped. "Well, he is from Brazil. Did you know that?"

"Yes."

"He came as a student and never left, other than to go home to visit. He got a green card after he married an American, and I think he's a citizen now, but I'm not sure about that."

I nodded. "He's got dual citizenship." Our background checks on the parents had given us that.

Campbell hesitated, his expression conveying an internal conflict. "I, uh, don't want to cast aspersions on the young man, just because of his nation of birth. But the Brazilian government is not very good at obeying international laws when it comes to returning children who are taken to Brazil by a Brazilian parent, even if the other parent is from another country. There was a rather notorious case, in 2004. A Brazilian woman took her toddler son to see her parents. Once in Brazil, she divorced her American husband and refused to give him any access to his son. She remarried down there, got pregnant and then died during childbirth. The Brazilian government still made it difficult for the biological father to get his son back, because the mother had designated her new husband as his guardian. It took two more years–"

A light rap on the door and it cracked open.

"I said no interruptions," the lawyer called out, his voice annoyed.

His admin assistant stuck her head in. "I think you'll want to take the call on line three."

His face softened, but then he scowled. "Who is it?"

"Emma."

He smiled. "Ah, this is why I love you."

She smiled back. "Watch it or I'll have to report you for harassment." But she winked.

It had the feel of an often-repeated exchange, so I wasn't the least bit surprised when Herb Campbell gestured in her direction. "My wife, Jannie."

She smiled again and left the room.

He picked up his phone's receiver and punched a flashing button on the large console. "Emma, my dear, how are you?"

He listened, his face sobering. "You know I can't confirm that," he glanced my way, "but I have the Chief of Police in my office. May I give her your contact info?"

I was scowling now. I'd specifically said I didn't want the birth mother warned, and that was obviously who he was talking to.

"Good. She'll be in touch." He hung up the phone and called out, "Jannie–"

But his wife was already coming through the door, closing it behind her. She had a slip of paper in her hand. She handed it to me. "Emma's address and phone number."

I swallowed my anger—too late now—and gave them both a genuine smile. "Thank you for your help."

Jannie left the room again, and Herb Campbell came around the desk to escort me out.

In the doorway, I spotted a face I recognized in his waiting area—Mrs. Gardner.

Boy, this really is a small city.

We only had a little over eleven thousand residents. Some would call it a large town.

Mrs. Gardner glanced my way, then did a double-take. "Well, *hello*. Fancy meeting you here."

Campbell muttered something behind me. I only caught part of it. "...fooled the rest...this time."

I turned back toward him. "What did you say?"

He waved a hand in the air. "Thinking about another case."

Mrs. Gardner rose from her chair. "Herbert, I'm here to add another heir to my will. I have a new grandchild." She beamed as the scattering of people around the waiting room smiled and murmured congratulations.

She headed our way.

"Of course, Bee." To me, he added in a whisper, "I keep telling her that the clause 'all issue of said offspring' covers all her grandkids, but she likes to name them." He gave the woman an indulgent smile. But again it didn't reach his eyes, which were once more clouded.

The outer door opened, offering a possible explanation for his anxiety. I really had thrown his morning schedule off.

I quickly thanked him again and shook his hand. And when I turned I was face to face with Starling's mayor, Mark Hayes.

"Ah, Mr. Mayor," Campbell said. "Jannie has those papers for you to sign."

Hayes nodded my way, *his* eyes definitely worried. "Wife's probate," he muttered, and turned to enter a glass cubicle where Jannie had settled at a small conference table.

Campbell ushered Mrs. Gardner into his office and closed the door. Leaving me standing there, wondering why Mayor Hayes, who was normally Mr. Nice Guy, was acting so strangely.

My phone rang in the car, as I was driving back to 3MB. *Dot Wilder-FDLE* the dashboard screen read.

Damn. I'd never called her back.

I hit the button to accept the call. "Hey, Dot."

"How's it going, Judith? Any leads on your little girl?"

"Some, but nothing that's panned out yet. And thanks again for sending some agents to help out."

"Wish we could do more, but the manhunt for Chief Black has heated up. You got a few minutes? I don't want to take you away from your missing child."

"I'm in the car so I've got a couple of minutes" I said. "What's happening with Black?"

"Someone who once lived in Starling, and is now a cop in Palm Coast, he recognized the former chief leaving a hotel, with a woman. The hotel clerk told our agents that they'd only stayed one night. Checked in under false names apparently, but my agents showed him photos of Black and his wife and he said they looked like the couple."

"The cop didn't follow them?" I asked.

"He was off duty, had his family with him. He got the plate number of their car, though. Turns out to be a rental, also rented with the same fake ID, which the rental company photocopied. *But* the car was already turned back in, after only one day."

"Why would they rent a car for only a day?"

"Good question, but there's another wrinkle. The agents got there before the room was cleaned. It had been wiped of prints, which is odd in and of itself. Only one partial on a small lamp on a side table."

"Lemme guess, it matches Black's."

"Yes, left thumb. But the agents also found something else."

"What?" I said, trying to rein in my impatience.

"A toy mouse, cloth, well used, with the smell of catnip still on it. Um, the only person I know who's at all related to this case, and has a cat, is you."

My stomach twisted. *Pipsqueak's mouse?*

"I'm sending you a photo of the cat toy," Dot was saying. My phone pinged.

"Hang on." I pulled into the entrance of a fast-food place and parked. I grabbed my phone and checked the pic.

The well-chewed brown and green felt toy barely resembled a mouse, but I recognized it. My chest tightened. "That looks like one I threw out last week. But why the hell would anybody fish it out of my garbage?"

"More important question, how did John Black get his hands on it?"

"Could be a coincidence. Maybe left by another guest, earlier, before Black got there..." I trailed off, fully aware that I was grasping for straws.

"Unlikely," Dot said. "No pets allowed in that hotel."

I stared at the photo. The toy was so shredded, maybe it wasn't even the one I'd thrown away.

"*And*," Dot added, "it was in the middle of one of the pillows on the bed."

Left there on purpose. I swallowed hard.

"We're getting the lab to test it for cat saliva. Can we get a sample from your kitten?"

"Of course," I managed to get out in a relatively normal-sounding voice.

"I know you've got your hands full. I'll send an agent over to get it."

"Thanks."

Uh, there's more." Dot's voice was hesitant.

My heart rate kicked up a notch.

"This morning, the agents tracked Black and his wife to another hotel, just over the state line in Kingsland, Georgia. He was gone by the time they got there, but he left another present."

I tried to speak, but my throat had closed.

"A wine bottle," Dot said, "with yours and Sheriff Pierson's fingerprints on it."

CHAPTER ELEVEN

I left a spare key to my apartment, which I kept in my wallet, with the watch commander, for the FDLE agent to use to get Pipsqueak's saliva sample. I hoped the cat wouldn't draw too much blood in protest to having a swab jammed into her mouth.

I'd wanted to ignore the whole mess. I had a little girl to find.

But I'd texted Sam about the developments with Black and whatever game he was playing with his little presents. Sam didn't deserve to be blindsided, finding out about it from someone else.

I ended with, *Can't talk about it now though. Too much going on here.* I hit send, then worried. Was that too abrupt?

His reply was *Holy shit! I'll take care of it.*

What the hell does that mean? I shook my head, resolutely shoving the cat toy and wine bottle and all associated questions out of my mind. I could *not* afford these distractions.

We gathered in my office for a regroup session. *We* included Bradley, Collins and Wellbourne—Cruthers was still out in the field with the FBI and FDLE agents, knocking on doors. And Barnes was in her usual place, leaning her butt against my doorjamb, notepad in hand.

Collins leaned forward from his perch on the edge of one of the uncomfortable chairs. Wellbourne fidgeted in the other one. Bradley of course, as Chief of Detectives, got the comfy chair.

Maybe we should put those other contraptions out in the waiting area, I thought, *and get new chairs for my office.*

Bradley clearing his throat brought my focus back. "I've got some news from Foster over at JSO."

"Good news or bad?" I asked.

He pursed his lips. "Not sure. He found the two guys from the sex offenders' registry who live in Jax. Both have decent alibis. He's verifying them for us."

I nodded. Detective Foster in Jacksonville was a good cop. He'd do a thorough job.

"The two who live here," Collins said, "who had iffy alibis. They checked out."

I nodded again, silently agreeing with Bradley. The local child abusers, those we knew about at least, didn't have Ashley. That was good. But it brought us no closer to finding her, which was bad. And Bradley had put out feelers with nearby hospitals, birthing centers, and even pediatricians, to identify any grieving mothers who'd lost a young child recently. So far *nada*.

"Lola Dexter did give birth," Bradley was saying, "six months ago. That was a boy. *But* she gave another child up earlier, almost two years ago." He paused, his eyebrows arched. "A girl."

"She would be about Ashley's age now," Wellbourne pointed out.

"So maybe," Barnes said, "she was watching Ashley because she reminded her of her little girl."

"And maybe she saw her chance," Wellbourne said, "and grabbed her at the Founders Day parade."

"Maybe," I said, "but the teddy bear on the railing says it was a premeditated kidnapping."

Wellbourne shrugged. "Or maybe she had the toy with her, a reminder of the kids she gave up."

I gave her an intense look.

"I guess that's a bit of a stretch," Wellbourne admitted in a weak voice.

I tried to work up the energy to say something supportive, but couldn't think of anything.

"Yeah," Collins was saying, "I don't think she would be carrying around stuffed animals in her pockets."

Wellbourne shot him a don't-rub-it-in look.

"Hey," Bradley said, "we're brainstorming. No idea is too far out there to at least mention."

Thank you, Bradley. That was exactly the right thing to say.

To bring us back to Dexter, I said, "If Lola's so remorseful about giving up her kids, why did she do it twice?"

"Maybe she wasn't all that remorseful," Barnes said, "with the little girl initially. Maybe after giving up another baby, the boy, that's when it really hit her."

"Could be," I said. "She checked out otherwise, correct? She really is a programmer for a company in that building near the park?"

"Sort of," Bradley answered my question, then added, "but I just had another thought. Maybe she's a prostitute."

"She could be turning tricks on the side," Wellbourne pointed out, "even if she has a day job."

"The long answer to your question, Chief," Bradley said, "is yes and no. She works for a company called Starling Digital Solutions, third floor of that building, but she's not a programmer. She's a data entry clerk."

"Which doesn't pay nearly as well," I said. "So yes, she might have a side gig going. We'll keep her under surveillance for now."

Bradley made a note on his pad, then looked up. "I also talked to Emma Blackstone, Ashley's birth mother. As the lawyer said, it was a closed adoption. She hadn't known who got her baby before, but when she saw the news she started putting the pieces together. So she called the attorney for confirmation."

He tilted his head in my direction. "Which turned out to be while you were there asking about her. She said she had no regrets about giving the baby up before, because she knew the child was better off than she would've been with her. But now she's furious. She's looking into how she can get custody back, once Ashley is found."

Wellbourne snorted. "Good luck with that."

My tired brain experienced a moment of confusion. Did she mean we weren't likely to find the child?

"I know someone who tried to get a child back after six months," Wellbourne continued. "She was told, 'Once the ink dries, the adoption is final.'" She made a karate-chop motion with her hand.

"The background check on Emma Blackstone came up clean," Barnes said. "As did the deeper dive into the Silvas' backgrounds. But I found out something interesting. She's the one with the family money, not him. He's from an upper-class family in Brazil, but they've fallen on hard times, after his father made some bad investments."

Bradley's expression perked up. "That's very interesting, especially since he has some charges on his credit cards from rather high-end stores."

"I take it that means," I said, "that you did get the warrants for his financials and phone records."

"Yes." He shoved hair back off his forehead. "Still waiting for his cell company to cough up his records."

"High-end stores, as in?" I asked.

"Couple of jewelry stores—one charge six months ago, the other last month. A very expensive meal at a fancy restaurant three weeks ago, and several thousand dollars charged at a travel agency two months ago, I'm assuming for plane tickets."

I sat up straighter in my chair. "Find out what that one is about." I told them about my conversation with the lawyer regarding Mr. Silva, and his concerns regarding Brazil's loosey-goosey adherence to international child custody laws.

"It's probably too late," I concluded, "if he did send the girl out of the country, but we need to check flight records since Saturday evening. See if a child matching Ashley's description flew out of any of the airports near here."

Collins whistled. "That's gonna be a huge task. We've got Jax airport and Orlando, and Gainesville Regional, for that matter."

"Maybe the FBI folks can help with that," I said.

Bradley nodded and stood up. "I'll talk to them, then go check out that travel agency." He headed for the door, which his sister had helpfully opened.

I turned to Wellbourne. "Did you get any rest recently?"

"Some sleep last night."

"Good. Go relieve the uniform who's at their house and escort the Silvas here. We're doing an eleven-thirty news conference."

She frowned but nodded.

"I guess I'm back to knocking on doors again," Collins said, his expression somber. "My pic of that little girl is already getting ratty around the edges, I've shown it to so many folks."

"For now," I replied with a sigh, "yes, more doors."

Everyone trooped out of my office and I sat back in my chair, thinking about all those doors my people had knocked on.

I flashed to running into Mrs. Gardner at the lawyer's office this morning. *Damn, it's not that big of a town!* We should have found *something* by now, some sign of what had happened to Ashley.

A few minutes after eleven, Wellbourne escorted Annie Silva into my office, then discreetly withdrew.

Annie was a hot mess.

Not physically—she looked fine. Her makeup had obviously been carefully applied, although it was currently at risk from the tears pooling in her eyes.

"Where's your husband?" I asked.

She opened her mouth, sucked in air, then blew it out. "He's not coming. We had a big argument. He said going on TV would look bad for his firm. And it might encourage other kidnappers to go after accountants' families, if they thought they were worth big bucks."

She paused, sniffed loudly, still fighting the tears. "Plus, he said these pleas from parents never work. Kidnappers don't just say, 'Oops, sorry, here's your kid back.'"

"No," I said, "but sometimes these news conferences lead to a citizen seeing something and reporting it. Speaking of ransoms, you haven't been contacted by anyone?"

We'd had at least one officer at their house the whole time, but I asked anyway. If a kidnapper called when that officer wasn't nearby, they might have instructed the parent they reached not to tell the police.

I watched Annie carefully as she shook her head. She maintained eye contact and showed no signs of dissembling or nervousness.

"Nor has your husband?"

She shook her head again.

"Okay, then do *not* mention ransom or paying money for Ashley's return. If you do, our hotline will be flooded with calls from people pretending to be the kidnapper and demanding a ransom."

She nodded this time, but her face went even paler. "If they'd wanted a ransom, they would've been in touch by now, right?"

"Correct." I tried for a reassuring look. I wasn't at all sure I'd succeeded. "But we've got several leads we're working on. Let me ask you something else. Do you know anyone who has recently lost a child, maybe a stillbirth? Or someone, besides Ashley's birth mother, who put a child up for adoption in the last three years?"

Annie thought for a moment. "No, I can't think of anyone."

"Okay. Tell me what you plan to say."

"I was going to offer a reward for information," she said. "Fifty-thousand. Should it be more?"

I shook my head. "That's a good sum. Enough to be enticing. More than that would mostly encourage tons of fake calls."

Although we'd certainly get plenty of false leads anyway. Again, the auxiliary folks were going to be very useful.

"But make it clear," I added, "that it's for information leading to us actually *finding* her."

A few minutes later, we were in the elevator, headed for the mayor's conference room on the fifth floor where the press would be gathered.

"If reporters start asking you questions before we begin," I said, "tell them to wait for the formal statement, or better still ignore them."

"But I don't want to piss them off," Annie said. "Then maybe they won't cover the story."

"Oh, don't worry. They'll cover it. And they're used to being rebuffed. They don't take it personally."

The reporters were standing outside the conference room. I shooed them off to the sides, making a path for Annie. A few of them called out questions, but she shook her head, which she kept down, as if she were unsure how to keep putting one foot in front of the other on the lush carpeting.

I wondered if she realized how strong she really was. Her husband acted like she was weak, too emotional. But what men often didn't get was that emotions didn't make one weak. Indeed, after spending most of my life in the male-dominated law enforcement world, I hadn't realized that myself. Not until recently, thanks mostly to Kate's influence.

Showing up when it counted, despite how you were feeling—that was strength. And Annie Silva had it all over her husband on that score today.

Carol, the mayor's admin assistant was guarding the door. "Mayor Hayes will be here in a moment," she whispered as we moved past her. She deftly stepped behind us, blocking the door to keep the reporters out for now.

"I need to talk to the mayor briefly, before the press conference starts," I whispered to her.

She made a face. "I'll try." She took out her phone and sent a text. A ping signaled a responding text. Carol lifted her head. "He wants to know what about."

"Just tell him not to mention ransoms. Otherwise, we'll get flooded with fake ransom calls. Mrs. Silva's going to offer a reward for information leading to finding the child. That will bring out more than enough crazies and fakes."

She tapped quickly on her phone, then nodded. "Done."

A minute later, Mayor Hayes came through the door. Back straight and with a confident expression on his face, he was much more put together than he'd been earlier this morning in Campbell's office. His well-tailored gray suit accented his salt and pepper hair—which contained a lot more silver than a year ago, when I'd first met him.

And somewhere along the way during that year, he'd slowly morphed from a kind but intense man—sincerely dedicated to helping Starling be the best city it could be—to a smooth politician. He probably was still sincere under the veneer, and probably still kind as well, but he was learning to play the game.

Carol had started to block the reporters again, but he said, "Let them come on in."

He gave me a grim smile. "Morning, Chief."

"Morning, Mr. Mayor," I replied, while wondering if he would even acknowledge our brief encounter earlier this morning, and his lack of courtesy then.

He didn't.

Instead, he turned to the podium. "Please, folks, take your seats."

The news conference went well, or as well as could be expected. The mayor spoke very briefly, promising that the city was using all possible resources to find the missing child. Annie shed a few tears as she begged her daughter's kidnapper to bring her home and offered the $50,000 reward for information leading to her safe return.

When Annie had finished her formal statement, of course the press began bombarding her with questions.

I raised a hand in the air. "That's all for now, folks. We'll keep you updated as we go along."

"I have a question for you, Chief," Stuart Frost, the reporter for the Starling Sun and the local TV station, called out over the heads of the other reporters—most of whom had come from nearby Jacksonville and Gainesville.

Those others paused in their exodus toward the door, turning curious faces my way.

"If the police are, quote, 'putting all their resources into this search,'" Frost said, a slight sneer in his voice, "then where are the officers that you normally have standing behind you during a press conference?"

I mentally counted to five, very quickly, and managed to restrain my urge to call him an idiot. "Mr. Frost," I said slowly, emphasizing each word, "they are out *searching* for Ashley."

He called out something else, which I didn't catch, thanks to the chuckles of nearby reporters. Carol and Barnes ganged up on him and practically shoved him out the door.

Grrr, why does the Starling Sun insist on hiring the most obnoxious reporters they can find?

I looked around for the mayor, but he had managed to escape while my attention had been on Frost.

I'd planned to ask him about his visit to the lawyer's office earlier, but apparently, I would have to wait to satisfy my curiosity about that.

Bradley was waiting to pounce as I entered the bullpen. "I got the phone records, and I may know what those credit card charges are about," he said in a low voice.

I nodded and kept walking toward my office.

He waited until my door was closed behind us before continuing, "The travel agency was pretty much a bust. Silva did charge plane tickets, to Costa Rica, but he came back two days later and cashed them in."

"Names on the tickets?" I asked as I sat down behind my desk.

"His and his wife's. And when I say cashed them in, he insisted they give him a refund, in *cash*. Since his firm uses that agency regularly for business travel, they decided to be accommodating."

"Hmm, good way to get his hands on some money without his wife knowing about it."

Bradley nodded. "And Silva has made regular calls, at least several a week—sometimes several a day—to a young woman who works for his firm, a Cynthia Hampstead. But she doesn't work directly for him, so I'm thinking these calls are more about a personal matter. The calls have tapered off some recently, down to about two or three a week now."

"An affair?"

"Could be," Bradley said. "Definitely merits having a little talk with her. Maybe the tickets were for the two of them, and she turned him down. Would explain the fewer calls lately. She's cooled off, but he's still trying."

I thought for a moment. "Let me and Barnes take Ms. Hampstead. And we'll have another little chat with Lola Dexter, to ask her why she keeps having kids and then giving them up. That way, you can stay on top of things with the canvassing."

We'd tracked down as many owners of fingerprints on the riverwalk's railing as we could. Bert and Ernie and the FBI folks were continuing to review the remaining partial prints, trying again to find matches.

Now, we had turned the focus of our door-to-door canvassing to neighborhoods near any places that Annie and the kids frequented—the playground and park, but also their favorite ice cream shop, the library, etc. The questions included several about anyone who seemed to pay particular attention to young children in the area, especially anyone who professed to "love" children.

I shuddered, and my chest ached. I would never look at a playground or schoolyard the same way. The innocent world of childhood had been invaded by perversion and paranoia, where we had to suspect the very people who seemed the most dedicated to the kids.

Shaking my head to clear it, I stood, and we exited my office. I gestured for Barnes to join me, and we traipsed back across the bullpen.

CHAPTER TWELVE

"Ms. Cynthia Hampstead?" I asked the thirty-something, fair-skinned woman who answered the apartment's door.

"Yes?" She clutched the neck of a pink silk robe closed.

Why's she answering the door at one o'clock on a Monday in a robe? Is she sick?

I resisted the urge to step back. Last thing I needed was to catch a cold right now—or worse yet, Covid.

I held up my badge. "Chief of Police Judith Anderson. This is Officer Barnes. We have a few questions regarding the missing child, Ashley Silva."

"Yes, that's horrible. I, uh, heard about it on the news, but, um..." she glanced over her shoulder, "now's not a good time."

Aha, thus the robe is explained. Would we find Silva in her bedroom?

"I'd love to be more accommodating, Ms. Hampstead," I said, my tone slightly acerbic, "but I'm afraid time is of the essence."

"Yes, of course. Um, there's a coffee shop on the corner. Can I meet you there in ten minutes?"

I leaned forward and lowered my voice. "I take it you have company?"

"Um, no, but..." another glance over her shoulder, "but my dog is sick, and strangers would upset him."

"Uh huh." I didn't even try to hide my disbelief.

Her cheeks pinked, matching her robe.

"Ten minutes," I said. Barnes and I pivoted and walked toward the elevators.

"Her dog is sick?" Barnes whispered.

"Yeah, right. You stay here and watch her apartment door from around that corner." I pointed down the hallway. "See who comes out."

Ms. Hampstead arrived at the coffee shop in nine minutes. I'd just gotten through the short line and had settled at a table with a much-needed cup of caffeine.

Hampstead wore jeans now, and a green sweater that went well with her auburn hair and blue-green eyes.

She didn't bother to get a drink but came straight to my table and sat down. "Look, I was thinking about what you said, about time, so I'll save you some. Yes, Gabe Silva and I... We, um, had a short fling, but it's been over ages ago."

"Then why did he call you three times in the last week?" I asked.

"That was work related."

I raised my eyebrows at her.

She frowned and blew out air. "One was work related. The other two were him trying to get me to...go out with him again."

"You hesitated," I said. "You don't actually go out, do you?"

"No, because his wife might find out. They're really...booty calls, which I *don't* go along with." She said the last part emphatically, but she also dropped her gaze to her hands folded on the table in front of her.

"And how long ago did you stop going along with these booty calls?"

"Two months ago." She glanced off to the side.

"You've caved a few times since then, though," I said.

She nodded, looked back in my general direction. Her eyes were shiny with tears.

"Is this a 'me too' type situation?" I asked.

She nodded again, bit her lower lip, but she was now making eye contact.

"Ms. Hampstead–" I began.

"Please, call me Cindy."

"Cindy, why don't you start at the beginning."

She stared down at her hands on the table again. "At first, I thought he was really interested in me. And I didn't know he was married. He doesn't wear a ring, and he has no pictures of his family in his office. I was hired to be his admin assistant, but he kept telling me I was too smart, that I belonged higher up the ladder."

She paused, sucked in a deep breath. "I thought I'd hit the jackpot. He dangled a promotion in front of me and wined and dined me almost every evening. I was so happy—better job, new boyfriend. He even bought me some jewelry, not that I'm all that into such things."

She shook her head. "I got the promotion, but then the attention dwindled away. No more nice restaurants or gifts. He'd just show up at my apartment, with carry-out food most of the time. By that point, he'd admitted he was married, but told me he was filing for divorce soon. But there were some things he needed to take care of first, so he could get the kids."

She stopped.

After a moment, I prompted, "Did you ask what things?"

"Yes, but he was pretty vague about it. Something about proving she couldn't care for them like he could. I thought he meant because he had money. His family is rich."

Or so he says, I thought but kept that to myself.

She shook her head slightly. "After a while, he didn't bother with the carry-out. The final straw was the Sunday afternoon when he showed up, pulling off his shirt as he was coming in the door, demanding that I hop right in bed because he only had a half hour to spare."

She sucked in more air. "I told him to get out. Surprisingly, he did, but he sneered at me as he was leaving. 'Don't think that I don't own you,' he said and slammed the door."

"And he's been pushing for booty calls ever since," I said.

"Yes, and threatening my job if I don't comply. But I've got a new boyfriend now..."

I gave her a small smile. "Your sick dog."

She responded with a lopsided grin. "Yeah. And he's the real thing. He's so good to me, and it's made me realize what a scumbag Gabe Silva is."

"Has he said anything more about his kids recently?" I asked.

"No, not recently, but shortly before that day I threw him out, he'd said something about having come up with a solution to the *girl* problem. I'd asked what he meant but he said not to worry about it."

"Do you still work directly for him?" I asked.

"No, which is the only reason I can stand being there. I'm assistant to one of the senior partners now. Not an admin, but an actual accounting assistant. I do bookkeeping and such. And as it turns out, I love it. I'm going to school to become a CPA, and the firm is paying my tuition. My boss, Eloise, is a good person, and she said she wants young women to succeed."

"Is there anything else you can think of that might help us find Ashley?" I asked.

"No, I never even met the little girl. There was an office family picnic during the time that Gabe and I were theoretically dating. He brought his baby son, but said his wife had to stay home because their daughter was sick."

"Nothing else you can think of?" I asked again.

She shook her head.

I drained my coffee cup and stood. "Thanks for your time, Ms. Hampstead. And may I offer some unsolicited advice?"

Her hesitation was minimal before she nodded.

"Go to your current boss, whom you believe is a good person, and tell her what's been going on with Silva's booty calls."

"I've thought of doing that. But I'm not sure I want the hassle, and the embarrassment if it comes out that I actually dated him before."

"I get that, but if he's doing this to you, he may be doing it to other women in the firm."

"I'll give it some thought."

I texted Barnes as I left the coffee shop.

She joined me a couple of minutes later. "Nobody came out."

"I'm not surprised. Okay, on to our second stop, Lola Dexter's."

I filled Barnes in on young Ms. Hampstead's up and down love life as we headed for my car.

Lola Dexter lived on the third floor of an older apartment building in the Bennett area of town. It was the poorest quadrant, containing some dicey neighborhoods. But Lola's place was in a more stable working-class section.

Barnes and I checked in with the uniforms—currently in plain clothes—who'd been watching her. They said she'd been in her apartment all day.

We discovered the elevator was out of commission, but two flights of steps wasn't all that onerous.

Several knocks on her door elicited no response. After the fourth round of knuckles against wood, I yelled, "Police, Ms Dexter. Open up."

A full minute ticked by. It's amazing how long a minute is when you're braced for a hostile confrontation, adrenaline pumping through your system.

"Shall I find the manager?" Barnes asked.

I nodded, and she took off for the stairs. At least *she* would get to use up some of that adrenaline.

Seven minutes later, she returned with a scruffy-looking and rotund middle-aged man in tow. He was huffing from the stairs.

"This is the owner of the building, Mr. Powers," Barnes said.

"Open the door, please," I asked.

He huffed and puffed another second or two, then asked, "Do you have a warrant?" His gravelly voice said he was or had been a heavy smoker.

"No, but we have reason to be concerned that Ms. Dexter may be...in trouble." The word that came to mind was *suicidal*, but I opted not to say that out loud.

"We can't insist," I added, "but you, as the owner, have the right to enter the property to check on her."

The owner shrugged and extracted a ring of keys from his pocket. He unlocked the door.

"Step back, please," I said, as I pulled my Glock from my small-of-the-back holster. Barnes took out her weapon as well.

Mr. Powers's eyes went wide, and he backpedaled to the top of the stairs.

Barnes turned the knob and flung the door open. She went left, while I went right. It took only a minute or two to clear the small one-bedroom apartment.

It was empty, and the window over the fire escape was an inch open.

Powers stomped over and slammed it shut. "I keep telling these people, keep the damn windows closed when the AC is on."

"Lock it, please," I said.

He did so, and I hid a smirk. Now she'd have to come around to the front of the building to get back in.

There was no sign of a child's presence in the apartment. I wasn't sure if I should be disappointed or relieved.

We thanked the owner and went down to the street. I sent one of the uniforms around to the back of the building, in case Lola decided to take off when she found the window shut. The senior cop would remain out front, and he promised to be diligently observant.

Those were his words, and I suspected that he'd expected a dressing down for letting Lola slip away from them.

But I could spare neither the time nor the energy for that.

Once in my car, I called the watch desk. Johnson answered.

"Sarge, send a couple of uniforms to Ms. Dexter's place of employment, and if she's not there, to the park where we first apprehended her. They're not to do anything if they find her, just report on where she is."

"Got it, Chief," Johnson said.

"Maybe she realized we had people on her," Barnes said, "and she didn't want them following her to work."

I shrugged. "Maybe."

But that was about to backfire. Instead of being followed discreetly by cops in plainclothes, some in uniform were about to show up at her workplace.

———◦———

Back at 3MB, I found a pizza on my desk, and a note from Sam on top of the still warm box.

I'm making an educated guess, based on your past pattern, that you aren't eating much.

The note went on to tell me that he and some of his deputies were helping out with the canvassing. I smiled, my chest filling with a pleasant warmth.

I'd just taken a bite of pizza when Bradley knocked on the frame of my open door. I wiggled my fingers to indicate he should enter the office.

"Want a piece?" I gestured toward the pizza.

He shook his head. "I had a protein bar, not all that hungry really. My mind keeps going over various scenarios of what might be happening to that little girl, wherever she is. Most of those scenarios are... Anyway, it's kind of an appetite killer."

I dropped my piece of pizza back into the box. "Did you talk to Silva again?"

He closed my door and settled in my visitor's chair. "He's not home. Wife's pretty upset. I got an earful."

"He didn't go to work, did he?"

"No, but not for the reasons one might assume. He told her that he couldn't go in because the 'media scavengers,'" Bradley made air quotes, "who were now hanging around their house, thanks to *'her* press conference,'" more air quotes, "might follow him to the office and cause a scene."

"But he didn't stay home?"

What was with this guy?

"Nope. Wife said he left for a walk about an hour ago. He does that a lot, apparently. And he left his phone at home, either accidentally or on purpose, she wasn't sure which."

I rolled my eyes. "What parent does that when one of his children is missing?"

"One who doesn't seem to be all that invested in that child. I called Cara Hidalgo and she agreed with what the lawyer told you. Mr. S, as she calls him, seemed to lose interest in Ashley, once the baby boy was born."

"His own flesh and blood," I said.

Bradley nodded. "And a male."

He paused, an odd expression on his face, a mix of excited and grim. "Um, I've got some more of that good, slash, bad news. The FBI team thinks they have something—some related cases, going back over a decade."

CHAPTER THIRTEEN

I sat up straighter in my desk chair. "Oh?"

Bradley nodded, his expression now mostly grim. "One of the FBI agents expanded the search for similar cases, varying the elements some. He found four other cases in the region, including the one I found in Miami. In each one, the child was female, blonde, and between eighteen months and two years old. And in each case, the abductor left something related to the child in an obvious place."

Despite being in the comfortable visitor's chair, he now sat forward, perched on its edge. "The first one was that one in Miami in 2009. The child's stuffed toy was on top of the fence, too high for the child to have put it up there herself. Three years and two months later, in 2012, a little girl went missing from a ladies' room in Atlanta. The mom had her in the stall with her, but the little girl turned the knob and ran out. By the time the mother got herself decent and went out, the girl was gone." He paused for a quick breath. "The child had a tiny pink purse. It was found dangling from the outside handle of the ladies' room door."

I realized my mouth was hanging open. I closed it. My heart was starting to pound in my chest, and a lump of dread was growing in my stomach. No wonder he had mixed emotions about this news.

"Then roughly three years, six months later," Bradley continued, "in early spring of 2016, another toddler was taken in New Orleans. Her mother had put her down for a nap and opened the window to let in some fresh air. When she went in to check on her an hour later, the window was pushed farther open, the screen was out on the grass below, and the child was gone. The police thought maybe she had climbed out on her own and wandered off. They put out an Amber Alert and conducted a search. Later in the day, a relative who had come to stay with the distraught parents went out to check the mailbox, in case there was a ransom note."

He paused again, sucked in air. "She noticed something on the ground behind the mailbox post. It was a stuffed rabbit, and its arms were wrapped around a small baby doll, that had been in the child's bed with her."

"But the rabbit wasn't her toy?" I asked.

Bradley shook his head, then glanced at his notepad in his hand. "In January of 2019, another child disappeared in Birmingham, Alabama. That mom had a four-year-old and the two-year-old. The older kid, a boy, was hyperactive. They were in the grocery store. He suddenly took off and Mom chased him down the aisle. She caught him, gave him a short lecture, and turned back to her cart. The little girl was gone from the seat in the cart."

He looked up at me, his eyes red-rimmed. "The girl had a bead necklace she loved, wore it all the time. It was found around the neck of a stuffed dog that was sitting on top of the stacked row of carts outside the store."

He sighed. "In that case, someone remembered seeing a car racing out of the parking lot, and a child's crying was coming from inside it. But they didn't get the license or note the details of the car. Only that it was a dark sedan. At the time, they assumed the child belonged to the driver of the car so they didn't think anything of it, not until they were questioned by the police later."

His face drooped. "These cases have got to be related."

I nodded. My body had gone numb as my brain continued to process what he'd told me. "If it were only a couple of cases, I might say it's coincidental, but four, five including Ashley. And the timing, each three to three and a half years apart..." I trailed off, thinking.

I picked up my desk phone and punched a button to put it on speaker. Then I dialed Kate Huntington's number. Normally, I would text first, to make sure it wasn't a bad time, but in this case, I needed her now.

"Judith," her voice sounded a bit breathless, "what's up?"

"A development in the case, and I need your help. You're on speaker."

"Sure. Tell me what I can do."

It took me a full three minutes to repeat what Bradley had told me, including about a child crying from a car in Birmingham. "I'd like your take on what this might mean," I concluded.

The sound of a long sigh being blown out. "It's not good."

I sat, elbows on my desk, my forehead resting in my hands.

"She was right," Bradley said, his tone grim. "Not good."

Kate had just informed us that the kidnapper taking a child every three years or so was a strong indication that he or she was a sexual abuser—someone who was fixated on girls of that tender age. And when they reached five or six, i.e. stopped being pudgy, cute preschoolers, the abuser lost interest.

"And what about leaving something of the child's behind?" I'd asked.

"That could be meant to reassure that the child isn't lost or dead, that someone is going to take care of her," Kate had paused, "but I'm more inclined now to take that as a taunt."

Now Bradley let out a noise suspiciously like a moan. "I've had Derek looking into where the teddy bear might've been bought. But we're going to need to see if there's any connection between it and the other two stuffed animals, in New Orleans and Alabama."

He pushed himself to a stand and shuffled toward my office door.

"Let's keep this possible connection to the other cases to ourselves for a while," I said.

He turned in my doorway, one eyebrow halfway up his forehead.

"The media would have a field day with it, and it would freak the parents out. Plus, I'd rather that the kidnapper not know we're on to the pattern."

He nodded and left.

A couple minutes later, I was mentally editing *the parents* part of my statement to *the mother. Mr.* Silva didn't seem to be the least bit freaked out by any of this.

His wife had just called again, beyond frantic. He'd now been gone for over three hours. "He's never gone for more than two," Annie said, her voice panicky.

Even a two-hour walk seemed excessive to me. Heck, one could hike across the entire city in two to three hours.

A quick internal debate. Normally finding errant husbands wasn't our job. But what if Silva was missing because he'd gone to wherever he'd stashed Ashley? "Okay, I'll be there as soon as I can, and we'll look for him."

"Thank you so much, Chief."

I grabbed my Glock and my pantsuit jacket and left my office. Barnes was not at her desk. I called her as I headed for the watch commander's office. "Where are you?"

"The lab. I was checking with Bert to see if they had anything new."

"Do they?"

"Not much. They went over the bear again. It's made in China," Barnes made a scoffing noise, "of course. They've confirmed it's new, or at least has never been in contact much with people. No trace DNA anywhere on it. Fur doesn't hold fingerprints, but Ernie found a small partial on the bottom of its plastic nose. Not enough to run through the system but it can help verify once we have a suspect. Sunglasses were wiped clean."

"Have Bert check the partial against the perverts," I said.

"Which ones?"

"The ones that were in that warehouse. Actually, tell Bert to check it against all the people on the sex offenders' registry who live in Florida or Georgia. No, make that the entire southeast."

"Got it, Chief."

At the Silvas' house, I was surprised when Cara Hidalgo answered the door.

"Oh, Chief," she said, "thank God you're here."

I processed the significance of her presence as I introduced Barnes and we stepped inside. So Annie was ready to buck her husband, at least on the nanny subject.

She was in the living room. The baby was lying on a quilt on the floor. Cara dropped cross-legged next to him.

I looked at the young woman, then at Annie, and raised my eyebrows.

"My phone is ringing practically nonstop. Most are reporters—not sure how they got the number—but I dare not ignore it. It could be the kidnapper."

I nodded. The part left unsaid was that she couldn't deal with an energetic baby and the phone at the same time.

As if to prove that point, the rug rat flipped himself over and started moving toward the edge of the blanket. He was belly crawling, resembling an infant soldier in a combat zone.

Cara leaned forward and scooped him up, set him down on her lap, cooing to him the whole time.

I nodded again, this time in her direction. She was good at what she did.

Annie's phone rang. She picked it up, listened for a second, then disconnected. "Reporter. I don't even bother with 'no comment' anymore."

Time to get down to business. "Where does your husband usually go on his walks?"

"To Holly Park. There's a stand of trees, with a bench. He likes to go there and read, says he can't hear himself think here at home with the kids making noise."

I was familiar with that small thicket of trees. It was where the previous mayor had been shot last winter. He'd survived, *that* time.

"Holly Park's not the safest place in town," I said.

"I told him that, but he says it's safe enough during the day, and he likes the fact that not many people go there."

"Okay," I said, "we'll begin our search for him at the park."

"Um, you don't think..." Annie's voice sounded a little choked. Her eyes pooled with unshed tears. "Could the same person have kidnapped him?"

"It's a possibility, I guess. But I can't imagine why." I intentionally paused. "Can you?"

She shook her head, her expression miserable.

Personally, I didn't think Silva was in any danger. He was just being a jerk.

And apparently that reality was slowly sinking in for her as well.

I gestured for Barnes to head for the door. "We'll keep you posted," I told the poor woman and gave a nod to Cara as we left.

Holly Park wasn't very big. It only took Barnes and I about twenty minutes to search it thoroughly, including the small building that housed restrooms and a tiny museum of Native American artifacts from the area.

We had climbed back into my car, and I was about to call the watch commander to put out a BOLO on Silva, when Barnes said, "Chief."

She pointed to a red compact car that had just pulled into the parking lot. It had stopped in the middle of the asphalt instead of pulling into a space.

And Gabe Silva was stepping out of the passenger's side of the vehicle.

I jumped out of my car and called out, "Mr. Silva."

His head jerked my way, then he scrambled back into the car and it peeled out of the parking lot.

What the hell?

I dove back into my own car and gave chase.

CHAPTER FOURTEEN

I hit the button on my dash for my siren, and one-handed, pulled the light bubble out from under my seat. I tossed it to Barnes, who turned it on and lowered her window to put it on the roof. The strong magnet in its base would keep it there.

Silva and whoever was driving the red car had a head start, but I had training in chasing bad guys down semi-busy city streets. We soon caught up, and Barnes scribbled down the license plate number. She called it in.

The car tried to go around another car. It almost hit a panel truck in the oncoming lane, veering back in at the last minute. Then the traffic light at the end of the block turned yellow. The car sped up, roaring through the intersection as the light went to red.

Even with lights and siren, I had to slow down to make sure there were no oncoming drivers who weren't paying attention. I looked up once we'd cleared the intersection, only to see the red car making a sharp right onto a side street.

By the time I got to that corner, it was gone. My heart fell into my stomach. *Damn!*

I cruised along the side street, Barnes and I scrutinizing each crossroad. Barnes's phone pinged.

"We can stop chasing them," she said.

I glanced over. She had a smirk on her face.

"The car is registered to a Penelope Atkins. And her address is two blocks away." She pointed straight ahead. "That way."

A couple of minutes later I pulled up in front of a two-story townhouse. My red and blue lights still flashing, I parked across the end of the short driveway that took up half of the house's front yard.

The red car, parked in that driveway, wasn't going anywhere anytime soon.

A curtain in the house front flicked sideways for a second.

I glanced at Barnes. She was grinning.

Curtains flicked in the houses on either side of our target.

My turn to grin. I decided to leave the lights on, flashing patterns of red and blue against the brick facades of the houses.

A young woman, somewhere between mid-twenties to early thirties, opened the door as I was reaching for the doorbell button.

"Come on in, Chief," she said with a sigh.

I held up my badge anyway, even though she seemed to recognize me, maybe from the news conference on TV.

"This is Officer Barnes." I jabbed my chin in my assistant's direction.

The woman backed up, waited for us to enter, then closed the door. "Follow me." She walked down a short high-ceilinged hallway, open at the second level on one side.

I eyed the railing above my head to the right, a little concerned about who might be lurking up there. The edge of a table and the side of a refrigerator identified the room as the kitchen.

The woman came to a split set of stairs, half going up, half going down. She went up.

I paused at the split, peering sideways through the banister into a lower-level rec room, complete with a pool table. The house was actually three stories, built into a small hillside. I could see a small portion of a sliding glass door beyond the pool table. And sand sloping away beyond the door. A soft lapping sound told me there was a body of water behind the house. Apparently the row of attached houses was built along the banks of one of the many inlets off of the Sofki River.

"Clear down there," I whispered to Barnes, tilting my head toward the stairs.

She nodded and went down to the rec room, her hand on her gun butt.

I went up, reaching behind me to the butt of my own Glock in its small-of-the-back holster.

Silva, in a long-sleeved, medium blue tee shirt and blue jeans, sat in the living room/dining room combo. One foot rested on top of his other knee, an arm stretched across the back of the sofa. His other hand was in his lap, empty.

I glanced into the kitchen. A double-sized open doorway gave me a fairly clear view of cabinets and appliances. There was a narrow door, closed, that led to a small section carved out of the corner of the room. Probably a pantry, and not really big enough for someone to hide in.

Barnes appeared at my shoulder, gave another small nod.

I relaxed some.

Across the room was a set of stairs leading upward.

"Do you mind if Officer Barnes takes a look around the bedrooms up there?" I nodded toward the stairs. "She won't disturb anything."

"What," the young woman said, "you think we're hiding Ashley up there?" Her voice dripped with sarcasm.

"The thought had crossed my mind."

"Let her search, Pen," Silva said.

She nodded, and Barnes headed for the stairs.

"So, Chief," Silva continued, "now you're following me around, looking for *new* places to harass me?"

"No, not at all," I said. "We had a couple more questions for you, but when we called your house, your wife was frantic that you'd been gone so long." I didn't mention that the fired nanny had come over to help with the parental duties he seemed to have little interest in. Nor that she was pinch-hitting as moral support for his wife as well.

"Annie said you often walked at that park," I added.

Silva shrugged. "So, now you know my dirty little secret."

Penelope Atkins bristled.

"I wasn't surprised. We've already talked to your previous 'girlfriend.'" I made air quotes, since Cindy Hampstead hadn't been a willing girlfriend toward the end. "Or should I say, your previous rape victim."

He stiffened. "That bitch is a pathological liar. That's why I broke things off with her."

"Uh, huh," I said, while thinking, *Pot. Kettle. Black.* regarding the liar part. I was inclined to believe Cindy's version of what happened rather than his.

A slight clacking sound as the accouterments of law enforcement rattled against each other on Barnes's duty belt. She came into view, descending the stairs. A shake of her head.

"You said you had questions," Silva said. "Get on with it."

"What were you wearing Saturday?" I asked.

He looked up at the ceiling, making a show of trying to remember.

"It was only two days ago," I pointed out.

"A dress shirt and slacks, in case one of the stodgy older partners was there. They get cranky if one is underdressed, in their opinion." There was a slight sneer in his voice. "No tie though. I draw the line at being strangled on a Saturday."

"Short or long-sleeved shirt?"

"Long. The AC tends to be a bit aggressive, I guess to keep the old guys from roasting in their three-piece suits." The sneer was now more pronounced.

"So you don't like working there?"

He shrugged. "It's fine. But I'm biding my time, until I can open my own agency."

"Oh yeah, when's that going to happen?" I asked.

Another shrug, but he'd stiffened again.

"What color was the shirt?"

"Light blue with a darker pinstripe."

"That's not what you were wearing when you showed up at the police station," I pointed out.

"No, I'd gone home and changed by then."

"Despite your wife's frantic calls?"

"I had my phone on mute, so I wouldn't be disturbed. I was working on a tricky issue with a client's business finances."

"What type of tricky issue?"

He sneered at me. "That's confidential."

Hmm, he'd said originally that he was "catching up on paperwork," not dealing with a "tricky issue." But I wasn't sure that what he'd been working on was all that relevant.

I gave an exaggerated shrug, mimicking his.

He scowled at me.

I managed not to smile. It was fun, getting under this guy's skin. But back to business. "So how about," I raised my eyebrows at him, "you accompany us back to your house and reassure your wife, then show us that shirt?"

"Uh," Ms. Atkins spoke up, "it's here. In the laundry basket."

I shot her a startled look. "You do his laundry for him?"

She crossed her arms. "Sometimes."

"Well, get it, please." I turned back to Silva. "You were wearing a dark purple polo shirt when we saw you later, at your house, if I'm recalling correctly."

"It was dark red."

I nodded, even though I trusted my memory more than his.

Ms. Atkins returned with the shirt and handed it to me.

"This is light gray," I said. Although the pinstripe was indeed a medium blue.

"What?" Silva dropped his foot to the floor and sat forward. "No, it's not."

Atkins cleared her throat. "He's color blind."

"Well, damn, that was my favorite shirt... Um...Annie gave it to me, said it matched my eyes."

I was pretty sure he'd been about to say *Cindy*, his ex-girl-friend's name.

His current girlfriend was apparently thinking the same thing—she had stiffened. "It does match them," she said, her tone acerbic. "Your eyes are gray."

"Well, damn again. Annie said they were blue."

I struggled to hide my disgust. *What does Atkins see in this guy?* He seemed to think women were as interchangeable as his socks. Did she know he'd still been calling the old girlfriend for booty calls?

"Bluish gray," Atkins was saying, her voice somewhere be-tween annoyed and soothing. I wasn't real sure how she pulled off that tone.

But I was impressed. And I noted that the shirt probably did look good on him.

My mouth twisted as I fought back a smirk. Wouldn't it be ironic if he ended up with no woman at all, only the shirt that matched his eyes?

"I need to take this for now," I said and handed the shirt off to Barnes. She dangled it from two fingers like it had cooties.

I suppressed another smirk.

"Was it freshly laundered when you put it on Saturday morning?" I asked.

"Yes," Silva said, "but I got kinda sweaty coming over here, in the heat."

"And he'd lost a button," Atkins added. "I kept it here to fix it."

I resisted asking how he'd lost a button. I had a mental image of these two tearing each other's clothes off. It was not a pretty picture.

"You're from Brazil, Mr. Silva?" I asked.

"Yes, originally. I came here as a student at UF and decided to stay."

"Your English is excellent," I said. I hadn't picked up on an accent at all before. But now, after my discussion with the adoption lawyer, I was noticing a few places here and there where he pronounced or phrased things a tad differently than a native speaker would.

"I've been here sixteen years," he was saying, "and the University of Florida has a very good language program for international students."

"Do you have family still, back in Brazil?" I asked.

"Yes, my parents and grandmother."

"Siblings?"

"I'm an only child. Where are you going with all this?"

I shrugged. "Have you been back to Brazil to visit recently?"

"Not for several years."

I debated if I should go any further with the Brazil angle just yet. I wasn't sure I wanted to let on about Herb Campbell's suspicions, that Silva might have secreted the child away to his homeland.

And his body language hadn't changed while discussing Brazil. He was obviously irritated, but there was no new tensing or fervent looks when I'd brought the topic up.

"I think I'm done answering these stupid questions." Silva's tone was now disgusted. "Go find my daughter."

"Hmm," I said, "I think we need you to come to the station, then."

He glared at me. After a thirty-second staring contest between us, he said, "I definitely want my lawyer present." He'd tried to maintain the disdain in his voice, but it no longer rang true. His gaze darted to Penelope Atkins and back to me.

"No problem," I said, trying hard not to sound cheerful about it. "Officer Barnes, would you wait here? I'll call the watch desk and have them send a patrol car for you and Mr.

Silva." I turned back to Silva on the sofa. "In the meantime, you and Ms. Atkins need to wait in separate rooms. Why don't you go upstairs, Mr. Silva? You can call your lawyer while you're waiting."

Atkins ran to him. He embraced her. "Don't worry, I'll be fine." He headed for the stairs.

You narcissistic prick, maybe she's *not so fine.*

I whispered to Barnes, "Get her statement, but take her downstairs where he can't hear you. I want to know what time she says he got here Saturday. If she's not cooperative, feel free to cite her for reckless driving."

She nodded.

"I've got another quick stop to make on my way back to 3MB." I took the shirt back from her. "I'll put this in an evidence bag."

She wrinkled her nose.

This time, I did smile.

I pulled my car up in front of the address the watch sarge had gotten for me, from Collins's report that he'd left a card stuck in her door on Sunday morning.

Another car sat at the curb. I ran the plate. Yup, the car was registered to Beatrice Gardner. She was home.

The house was white clapboard with black shutters. The design was known in Florida as Cracker-style, with dormers poking through a silver metal roof.

I strode up the front walk and rang the bell. I waited a bit and rang again.

A curtain in the window nearest the door twitched. That twitchy disease seemed to be going around today.

Another minute ticked by. Finally the door opened. Bea Gardner, looking somewhat bedraggled, said, "Well, Chief, this is a surprise. I, uh, can't talk long." She glanced over her shoulder. "I have my grandkids here. Their mom just had a baby."

I faintly heard children's voices and possibly a giggle.

"Sorry to bother you, ma'am," I said, "but I wanted to double check something."

She nodded.

"You said the person who took Ashley's hand was wearing a long-sleeved shirt, correct?"

"Yes, gray, and I think it was tee shirt fabric."

"Not a dress shirt then?"

She pursed her lips and wrinkled her brow. "Maybe...I don't know for sure."

I was tempted to show her the dress shirt I now had in an evidence bag locked in my car. But that could contaminate her perceptions and give a defense lawyer ammunition, should all this come to a trial and we needed her to testify.

"And going by the length of the arm," I said, "would the person have been the height of a man or woman?"

"Um, I think a man."

"Mom-mom," came a young child's plaintiff voice from behind her.

Mrs. Gardner whirled around. "I told you to stay in the bedroom." Her tone was a little harsh.

I caught a glimpse of a little girl over the woman's shoulder. She was maybe five years old.

"I know but...Allie too, she won't listen to me," the child whined. "She climbed up on the bed and is jumping on it." She put her little hands on her hips. "With her *shoes on!*"

"Okay, okay. I'll be right there." Mrs. Gardner made a shooing gesture, and the child headed down a hallway.

The grandmom turned back to me. "As you can see, I have my hands full." She gave me a sickly half smile. "Maybe I can come to the station later, if you have more questions?"

"That's okay, no need. Thanks for your time." I started to turn away, then asked, "She called you Mom-mom, not Grandmom?"

"Oh," Mrs. Gardner let out a weak chuckle, "that's what they call me—Mom-mom. The oldest called me that, when she first began to talk, and it stuck."

I smiled. "Sorry. Just curious. Occupational habit, I guess. Thanks again."

"No problem, Chief. Happy to help all I can."

"She's adorable, by the way."

"Who?"

"Your granddaughter." I made a vague gesture in the direction of the hallway down which the girl had disappeared.

"Oh, yes, thank you." She gave me a bright smile and slid the door closed.

I walked away, shaking my head slightly, once again grateful that I'd never had to deal with rug rats up close and personal.

I had barely settled into my driver's seat and started the engine when my phone rang. The Bluetooth screen read, *Wilder FDLE.*

I sighed and opted not to put the car in gear. Something told me I would need to give this call my undivided attention. I hit the button to accept the call. "Please tell me there has *not* been another John Black and wife sighting."

A short chuckle. "No, not another sighting, but I do have some news." Her voice had sobered, and I braced myself.

"The cat toy, it does belong to your cat. Our rapid DNA test came back a match."

Damn that rapid DNA gizmo that the FDLE lab had bought a few months ago. Under normal circumstances—with DNA results taking weeks, at least—I would be well past this missing child case before having to deal with more of the former chief's craziness.

"Dot, why is Black doing this?" I blurted out. "Why is he risking being caught in order to harass me?"

"I don't know," her tone was mournful. "But I'm afraid the bad news doesn't end there." A beat of silence. "The governor has gotten wind of all this, and he's pressuring your mayor to suspend you until an investigation is completed."

"What?" I shouted. I was very glad I wasn't trying to drive right now. "Does he really believe I'm part of Black's corrupt circle? I helped bring the man down!" I paused, sucked in air. "He can't make Hayes do that, can he?"

"Well," Dot said, "the governor is the head of the executive branch of the state, which means he can suspend any executive branch elected official suspected of corruption, and order an investigation. You're somewhat insulated from that, since you're hired by the city, not elected. But he could threaten to suspend Mayor Hayes if he doesn't do his bidding. And..." Another short pause. "He hinted that he might go after Sheriff Pierson as well as you, maybe as leverage to push you to resign."

"Shit." My heart had already sunk into my stomach. Now the latter was churning. "But what if he doesn't have just cause for the suspension?"

"That should come out in the investigation, but that takes time."

"Time that I don't have. Dot, a little girl could die because of this. I can't be pulled off this case right now." I choked on the last few words.

"I know. I'll do what I can, but I don't have a lot of influence with the governor's office."

"Have you talked to Mayor Hayes about it?" I asked.

"Yes, that's how I know what's going on. He called right after the governor. The latter asked what I thought of you and Sam. I said you were both highly ethical and competent law enforcement officers. He thanked me and hung up. Then I heard from Hayes."

"And?"

"And he didn't seem to know what he could or should do. Obviously, he doesn't want to suspend you, especially right now. He said he was going to call a special meeting of the city council."

"Oh lord, that's his answer to everything. He forgets sometimes that he's not the council chair anymore. He has the authority himself."

"Actually, in this case, having the council's backing might help."

I shook my head, no longer willing to even try to understand the political machinations involved here.

Movement at a window of Mrs. Gardner's house caught my eye. The curtain was twitching. She was probably wondering why I was still sitting here.

"Okay," I managed to push past the lump that had formed in my throat. "Thanks for the heads up."

I disconnected and sat back in the driver's seat, blowing out air. What was I going to do? If I was suspended now, taken off Ashley's case, she might... I couldn't abandon her.

Like I abandoned Meredith. I placed my hands at the top of the steering wheel and dropped my forehead against them, fighting back tears.

That was crazy thinking. I was only six years old at the time. What was I supposed to have done?

But then I hadn't done anything later either—after I was grown. Even after I was a lieutenant in the Baltimore County Police Department.

I lifted my head and shook it, glanced at the house. The curtain twitched again. Maybe it was the elder grandchild. She seemed the take-charge type.

She also reminded me of Meredith. Everything seemed to be reminding me of my cousin these days. Some of my earliest memories were of her telling Paul and me that we had to do what she said because she was the oldest.

Swiping at my wet cheeks with the back of one hand, I jammed the car in gear and pulled away from the curb.

CHAPTER FIFTEEN

I must have succeeded at covering my emotional turmoil, because Barnes didn't seem to notice. She had flagged me down as soon as I'd entered the bullpen and informed me that Silva was stewing in one of the interview rooms and his lawyer was on the way. But he would be about a half hour. He was in court.

"The girlfriend says Silva arrived on Saturday afternoon at two," she reported. "At five-thirty, they called out for pizza. He texted his wife that the project he was working on was taking longer than expected and he'd be working into the evening. Then he turned off his phone. He left the girlfriend's around eight-thirty."

I nodded, but Barnes wasn't done. "And I looked up color-blindness for the color blue. It's called tritanomaly, and it can be caused by different things, including diabetes that isn't well controlled."

"Is Silva diabetic?" I asked.

"Don't know," Barnes said. "I can see if I can find out."

I shrugged. "Or I can ask him. Has anybody else got anything new?"

"Not much. Peters and Sergeant Armstrong are still surveilling the pervert. Danny...I mean, the lieutenant tried for a search warrant for his place." Sometimes Barnes forgot that at work she should address her brother by his last name and/or his rank.

"No luck though," she said. "Judge felt there wasn't enough probable cause."

I grimaced. It had been a long shot. "What about the warehouse?"

"The lieutenant's working on getting a warrant for there."

"Okay. What's happening with Lola Dexter? Did the team on her catch up with her?"

Barnes nodded. "She'd only gone to work. Said she didn't want them following her–"

"She'd made them as cops?" I interrupted.

"Yes. Said she didn't want her boss thinking she was in trouble with the law."

"So she makes them go to her office and ask for her instead."

Barnes snorted softly. "As Franklin, the senior officer of the team said, 'Fool girl,'" she lowered her voice to a gruff imitation, "'if she'd acted normal, we would've followed at a discreet distance and all would be good.'"

I faked a chuckle. It was getting to be a strain pretending that all was good in *my* world. "You wanna observe while I go at Silva again?"

She nodded, although without her usual enthusiasm. "I hope he can give us a thread to pull on." Her voice sounded depressed.

I put a hand on her shoulder for a brief moment. "Let me know when his lawyer gets here."

"Oh," Barnes said, "I put your pizza in the break room fridge. It wouldn't fit in your mini-fridge."

Break room was a misnomer. It was a converted supply closet.

"Thanks," I said, but I had no appetite at the moment.

I entered my office, closed my door and fell into my desk chair. Suddenly I was exhausted.

But I had to call Sam. I couldn't let him be blind-sided by all this.

He answered in the middle of the second ring. "Hey there, how ya doing?"

"I've been better," I said. I managed to get through the whole blinkin' story without choking on my words.

"Boy, his timing couldn't be any worse," Sam said.

"Yeah. I wish I knew why the hell Black is doing this? Why is he risking getting caught? We'd assumed he was long gone, in the Bahamas, or some such place, by now."

"That's where I'd be, in his shoes. But I've been giving that question some thought. You remember that gang that tried to take over last winter?"

"How could I forget. We assumed they were bribing Black to look the other way, but we had no proof of that."

"Well," Sam said, "they were masters at pretending to be people they weren't."

That was certainly true. They'd even had one member posing as Sam for a while.

"I'm wondering if they've found somebody who looks enough like Black," Sam continued, "and with the right get-up, and–"

"A middle-aged woman who resembles his wife," I finished his thought.

"Yup. they could be pretending to be Black and his wife and leaving those little presents for the FDLE to find. And if they got caught, they'd just play innocent. After all, they *aren't* really fugitives on the run, only a man and a woman seeing the sights of Florida."

"And *I'm* wondering," I said, "if the cop who originally spotted him maybe was paid to do so. Damn, I wish I could spare a detective to check that out."

"Don't worry. I've got someone working on it."

"Wha..."

"And I installed cameras around your building's dumpster. I'm headed there now to see if anyone has been looking for new souvenirs."

"Wow, why'd you do that?" I blurted out.

"Because we're in this together." His tone sounded a bit exasperated. "You and me, for better or worse."

Panicky butterflies fluttered in my chest even as the area around my heart grew warm. That sounded suspiciously like some kind of wedding vow.

"Judith, rein in your imagination."

Damn, this man knows me too well.

"I only meant," he said, "that they're trying to implicate both of us in their corruption, so it's as much my problem as yours. And you have your hands full with a missing girl."

I blew out air and my stomach relaxed some. The butterflies simmered down, and the warmth spread.

"Try not to worry about all this," Sam continued, his voice low and soothing. "I'll take care of it. You focus on little Ashley."

"Okay, thanks. Um, have I told you lately that..." I paused to swallow the lump that was back in my throat.

"That you love me?" he chuckled, "Yeah, a few days ago. And that's twice in one week, a new record for you."

"Okay, make fun of me if you must, but know that I've only ever said that word to family before."

"I know, and I'm honored. Even though you still trip over it every time you try to say it."

"Oh shut up. I've gotta get back to work."

"Love you too."

I chuckled despite myself. "You had to get in the last word, didn't you?"

"And what a great little word it is." He was laughing as he disconnected.

———◇———

I felt much calmer as I walked to the interview rooms. I even smiled a little as I thought of Sam. He'd become such a steadying force in my life—which both comforted and scared the crap out of me. What if something happened?

Don't borrow trouble. My mother's voice in my head.

You should talk. My own voice, but as an angry teenager. And my mind flashed to the dead woman on the kitchen floor.

I shook my head to clear it. Now was not the time to be sorting out my "relationship issues," as Kate called them.

Just be grateful for Sam, I told myself. He'd helped me get my focus back.

And I would need it in order to get anything out of Silva.

Unfortunately, Mr. Silva didn't give us much. Only one tiny thread to pull on, and it was pretty thin.

Apparently his lawyer had advised him to answer only yes or no, because that's all we got. Except to the question, "Are you a diabetic?"

"How'd you know that?" Silva had spat out before the lawyer could stop him.

I hid a smile. Had I hit a nerve?

Then something dawned on me. This guy was from Brazil.

"How is it, Mr. Silva," I asked, "that a Brazilian has gray-blue eyes?"

He bristled, but looked first to his lawyer, who nodded.

"My family goes all the way back to the original Portuguese settlers." His tone was pompous.

Hmm, I wonder how the family feels about an adopted granddaughter, then.

"So, no inbreeding with the indigenous people?" I put a slight sneer in my voice.

He stiffened even more. "That's not exactly how I'd put it. We are proud of Brazil's rich and diverse heritage."

Okay, enough of getting him rattled.

"Uh huh," I said, as I leaned back in my chair across the metal table from him. I folded my hands together on my stomach. "Convince me, Mr. Silva, that you didn't take your daughter."

The lawyer leaned forward. He was thirtyish, tall and thin, and wore a light blue suit that matched his eyes but made his fair skin seem even more washed out.

Those pale blue eyes were now boring into mine. He probably thought he was being intimidating, but I'd dealt with lawyers far more impressive than him.

"You tell *me*, Chief Anderson," he said, "why are you convinced that my client *did* take his daughter?"

I debated for a second. Normally, I wouldn't answer that, but...

While watching Silva's face carefully, I said, "Well, it's rather obvious that the Silvas are having marital problems. Maybe Mr. Silva here is planning to run off with the kids and figures getting Ashley first will make that easier. Then he can sneak out of the house with the baby one night."

Silva had been slowly smirking as I spoke. Now he scoffed. "Why would I do that. Ashley was my leverage. The prenup–"

The lawyer's hand flew out, firmly gripping Silva's arm. "My client has no intention of leaving his wife."

"This prenuptial agreement," I asked, "did you write it up, Counselor?"

"I can't answer that," he snapped, "and you know it. Attorney-client privilege."

I shrugged. "I wouldn't think that a simple yes/no question would be privileged." I paused. "But it doesn't matter."

I rose from my chair. "You may go, Mr. Silva. But I would suggest you not leave the city until your daughter is found."

Now the lawyer smirked. "Really, Chief. The old don't-leave-town thing. You know that won't hold up legally."

"It's not an order. It's a reminder that his leaving town would be highly suspicious," I hardened my voice, "and we would track him down and bring him back for questioning."

Especially if he heads for an international airport.

I swept from the room.

"Well, that was a big fat nothing," Barnes said as she exited the observation room.

"Maybe, maybe not," I said, pulling out my phone as we walked back toward my office.

Annie answered on the first ring. "Did you find him?"

"Uh..." Belatedly I realized I should have let her know we had, so she could stop worrying. "Yes, but I'm afraid we delayed him a bit. We had a few more questions for him."

She heaved a sigh that sounded like it ended on a sob. My chest tightened with guilt. I really should've called her sooner.

"Um, he mentioned a prenuptial agreement," I said. "What was in it?"

A half-beat of silence. "Why do you want to know?" Her voice was now wary.

"Um, just curious. Did the same lawyer write that up, the one who did your adoption?"

"Yes, he's a friend of my father's. And I'm afraid I have to agree with my husband now." Her tone was crisp. "Why are you wasting time investigating him, when you should be pulling out all the stops to find our child?"

I paused in the middle of the bullpen, trying to figure out how to answer that. I hated to tell her that I thought Silva was planning to leave her. And it really wasn't my place to get in the middle like that. Plus, now was not the best time for their marital problems to come to a head, when their daughter was missing.

The baby wailed in the background. "Look, I've gotta go," she said. "Cara had to leave and..."

"Sure, okay. I, uh..." But I was talking to dead air. She'd disconnected.

Barnes had stopped beside me and was looking expectantly up at me.

I held up a finger and punched the speed-dial number for Bradley.

"What's happening with the airports search?" I asked without preamble.

"The FBI is handling that," Bradley said. "They have agents from the local field offices talking to the airlines' people at each international gate where a toddler, girl or boy—the abductor could've changed her appearance—has been on an outgoing flight manifest since Saturday evening. Ashley's too young to be allowed to fly alone, so in addition to flashing her picture, they're asking about any young child who seemed ill at ease with the adults accompanying them."

"That's going to take forever," I said.

"Close to it, and then they're going to go to the domestic gates, in case someone took her to another state first, and on to Brazil from there, or elsewhere."

"Thanks." I disconnected and pivoted back toward the bullpen's entrance. "Come on. We're going to talk to that lawyer again."

Barnes scurried to catch up with my long strides. "The one who did the adoption. Why?"

"I've got a hunch."

I had no idea if the prenup agreement had anything to do with Ashley's disappearance.

But I did know that my hunches usually had some basis in reality. I'd learned the hard way not to ignore them.

And I wanted to chat some more with Herbert Campbell, Esquire, about his concerns regarding Gabe Silva's "rich and diverse Brazilian heritage."

In my passenger seat, Barnes fiddled with her phone. I was beginning to wonder if she was playing video games, when she abruptly said, "Aha."

"Aha what?"

"Diabetics can get cold easily. It affects their circulation."

"Thus Silva's long-sleeved shirts," I said, "and complaining about aggressive air conditioning."

She nodded, beaming, obviously pleased with herself.

But I wasn't all that sure this particular tidbit would be useful, other than establishing that he probably wore long sleeves most, if not all, of the time.

The lawyer's waiting room was occupied by three people. Two seemed to be together, although the stiffness of their body language said they weren't necessarily pleased about that. I didn't think Campbell handled divorces. Maybe siblings here to discuss a parent's estate?

A single woman sat across the room from the other two, leafing through a magazine. She glanced up, as I walked past her, and gave me a weak smile.

I approached Jannie Campbell's desk. "I'm sorry but we need to see Mr. Campbell. We'll only take a few minutes."

She frowned. "He's already running behind schedule. He, uh, had an unexpected request for an emergency appointment."

"With one or both of the Silvas, by any chance?" Although I couldn't think why. It just seemed suspicious that the lawyer was having an emergency session with someone right now.

She shook her head. "I don't know. He didn't say. And there's a private entrance to his office. Some clients ask to come and go that way, for discretion."

"And this one did that?"

She nodded.

The faint sound of a file cabinet drawer sliding closed with a click, then a muted roaring noise and a rat-a-tat-tat.

And the sound of a door closing.

I glanced over my shoulder. The file cabinet ten feet from Jannie's desk was closed with no one near it, and the door to the hallway was also closed, with the same three people sitting in the waiting area, now joined by Barnes.

I mentally shrugged and turned back to Jannie. "I know it's a major inconvenience but I need five minutes after that client leaves. A little girl's safety is at stake."

She blanched and whispered, "Ashley?"

I nodded, my lips pressed together.

"Please have a seat," she said.

Barnes had taken a seat two chairs over from the woman with the magazine. I sat in one of the vacant chairs, noting that the magazine was *People*.

It only took five minutes for my patience to begin wearing thin. I reminded myself that I was butting into the man's schedule.

My phone buzzed, indicating a text. Barnes glanced over from where she was fiddling with her own phone.

And Jannie had looked up from the papers on her desk, but the others were meticulously keeping their eyes down. The Age of Technology etiquette.

I pulled out the offending phone and checked the message. It was from Skip Canfield. I met Barnes's gaze and shook my head slightly, indicating it was not case-related.

The text read, *Young woman didn't have much info this morning. But I was packing to leave, and she called. Wants to meet again after work. Says she now has more to tell me.*

She didn't give you anything useful? I texted back.

Not this morning. She asked a lot of questions about your family. I think maybe she wanted to check on me, find out if I was a legit PI.

Makes sense, I texted.

I'll call this evening, after I meet with her.

Okay, thanks.

I checked my watch. Another two minutes had gone by.

The woman with the *People* magazine came to the last page. She offered it to me.

I shook my head with a fake smile. She gave me an understanding nod back.

I crossed my legs and swung my foot. A metronome, marking the seconds.

Jannie Campbell glanced nervously at the closed door to her husband's office.

I tried to think of something to occupy my brain, to keep me from becoming even more impatient. And of course, my cousin's face popped into my mind's eye.

I resolutely pushed that image aside, only to have it replaced with the photo of Ashley in her little pink sunglasses.

I swung my foot again. I was *literally* cooling my heels, waiting for this attorney, while she was out there somewhere... I ground my teeth.

Movement in my peripheral vision. I turned my head.

Jannie was beckoning me over.

I stood and hurried to her desk, avoiding eye contact with those who'd been waiting longer.

Jannie leaned forward and whispered, "It's been over a half hour now, since he said he had to take this unscheduled meeting." She glanced nervously at the closed office door again. "I'm...I guess I'm a little worried..." she trailed off.

"Do you know who the client is?" I asked.

"No, he talked to them directly. They called his private line."

An important client then, which would make it even more awkward if we interrupted.

I hesitated for a couple of seconds. This woman knew her husband, and she was worried. That told me something was off.

I beckoned for her to follow me and walked to the attorney's door.

Barnes was watching me, now perched on the edge of her seat. Again, I gave her a small head shake. Best not to have a whole crowd invade the meeting.

She sat back some, but kept her gaze on us.

I tried the knob, expecting it to be locked. But it turned.

I nudged the door open and took a step forward, my mouth opening to apologize for the interruption.

An all-too-familiar coppery smell hit me in the face. I jolted to a stop.

My arm flew out to block Jannie. But it was too late.

CHAPTER SIXTEEN

Jannie Campbell stepped around me, looking at the empty desk. "Herb?"

She half turned toward me. "Where...?" She froze, her face paling.

She'd seen the body—by the other door across the room—his chest bright red and blood pooled around him.

Jannie let out a scream and fainted.

A vise had clamped around my own chest, making it hard to breathe. I'd been sitting in the goddamn waiting room, while this man bled out. I mind-wrestled with the guilt. I couldn't have known. Then I pulled myself together.

Watching carefully where I put my feet, so as not to step on any evidence, I approached the body and felt his neck for a pulse. I didn't expect to find one since his eyes were glazed over, staring at the ceiling, and his chest wasn't moving.

His dress shirt front was saturated. I swallowed hard and looked away, breathing through my mouth. I'd recently realized that I'd inherited a mild case of fainting at the sight of blood that ran in my family. Both my Aunt Jean and my grandfather had the full-blown version. I'd always wondered why years of dealing with bloody corpses hadn't made me immune to their effects, but the disorder was genetic, not something one could overcome by exposure.

And it was damned inconvenient at times like this.

All those thoughts took about a nanosecond.

Barnes was now in the open doorway, her gun in her hand down at her side, her eyes wide as she stared at the corpse.

I stopped searching for the nonexistent pulse and slowly backed away, my eyes scanning the floor for anything useful. Like shell casings, or a dropped gun. That would be really helpful.

No such luck.

Jannie was sitting up, shaking her head. She looked across the office and burst into tears.

I yanked my phone out of my pocket and called 3MB, while helping her up with my other hand.

"Sergeant Johnson."

"Sarge, I need two uniforms, one detective and the dynamic duo out here asap." Normally, we'd dispatch several uniforms and at least two detectives to a murder scene, but we were stretched thin. I would pinch hit as the second detective.

"Uh, where's here, Chief?" Johnson asked.

"Sorry, uh..." My mind had gone blank. I turned to Jannie Campbell. "What's the address here?"

She stuttered a little as she got it out.

I started to repeat it into the phone.

"I got it, Chief," Johnson said. "Our people are on their way, minus the detective. They're all out in the field. What's going on?"

"It's an attorney's office." I paused, organizing my thoughts. "He might've had info on Ashley. And I was sitting in his fuh...uh, damn waiting room when somebody killed him!" I'd barely caught myself before I'd said the f- word, in front of a new widow no less.

But my words still triggered more sobs from Jannie, and fresh tears rolled down her cheeks.

I wrapped an arm around her shaking shoulders and steered her out of the room.

———◆———

The uniforms had gotten statements and contact info from the people in the waiting room and sent them on their way. The statements were short since none of them had any idea who might want to kill their lawyer in the middle of a work day, nor any clue why.

Johnson had texted me that there was still no detective available. Did I want one of them pulled from the Silva girl's disappearance?

No, I'd texted back.

I'd taken Jannie into the small conference room behind her work area. It also seemed to serve as a storage space and lunchroom. Glass walled on two sides and cement block making up the other two, white file boxes lined the farthest block wall. Nearby squatted a small fridge, like one might find in a motel room, with a microwave on top of it.

Barnes headed for a corner and discreetly took out her pad as she leaned her butt against the boxes.

I'd nabbed a box of tissues from Jannie's desk as we'd gone by it. Now I handed several to her, and we sat down. "Jannie, Mrs. Campbell, I hate to have to do this, but time is of the essence."

She waved a hand in the air, dabbing at her eyes with the other tissue-filled one. "Jan, call me Jan. Herb's the only one who calls me...called me..." She tried and failed to stifle another sob.

"Jan, do you have any idea who might've wanted your husband, uh, gone?" I opted against the word *dead*. It would probably trigger yet more fresh tears.

She shook her head. "He's well liked by every-one—friends, colleagues, clients. *Everybody* likes him."

"Okay, but maybe someone had a more practical reason for doing this, even though they liked him? Think about his recent cases. Anything tricky there?"

She began to shake her head again, then froze in her chair. "The person he was meeting with, I don't know who it was."

I opened my mouth, but she continued, "We record those sessions, though, in case something weird happens related to them."

I would think a bullet in his chest would qualify as weird.

"And I..." her face pinked, "well, sometimes I listen in during them, you know, in case..."

Hunh? What was she trying to say?

Then I got it. In case he was having an affair.

"Has he strayed before?" I asked gently.

This time her head shake was rather vehemently. "Nothing happened, but this young thing," her lip curled slightly, "she tried to seduce him. She works at the courthouse, as a clerk. They had lunch together a few times, before he figured out she was a gold-digger and sent her packing. And confessed to me."

As marital transgressions went, it was mild. I wasn't ready to put this widow at the top of our suspect list. But the "young thing" was a different story.

"Do you know the woman's name?"

She nodded, and I glanced at Barnes, who scribbled in her pad while Jan gave the name and an address here in Starling.

"You have her address memorized?" I asked.

Her blush deepened. "I, um, drove past there a few times to make sure his car wasn't there."

I wondered how many times was a few, but I didn't go there. Instead, I asked, "How long ago was this?"

"Three years, one month, and two weeks," she said, her voice firm.

Her tone and the precision of the length of time had me mentally popping her back up the suspect list some. But then again, she was out in the waiting room when he...but was she? She could've killed him and left him in there, pretending he had an emergency meeting with some mystery client.

Or the jilted woman, the "young thing" as Jan had called her, might have taken her revenge. But three plus years was a long time to wait for satisfaction.

"Is that woman the reason you all receive your personal mail through a mailbox service?"

Jan gave me a startled look.

"We were trying to find a home address yesterday," I said.

She nodded slightly. "Actually we started that long before *she* came along. A couple of times we had pregnant women, who were involved in cases, showing up on our doorstep. They'd be after more money for some supposed expense. Herb would explain that he'd have to submit the request to the adopting parents. But the incidents were kinda creepy. So he decided to make our home harder to find. We got an unlisted phone number and began using the mail service. We give out their address rather than our own."

We would need to check out those two women, but I put off asking for their info just yet. The next topic I needed to bring up might turn out to be a touchy one.

"When I met with your husband, he said that he always represented the pregnant woman, even though the adoptive parents were footing the bill." I wasn't even sure if that was ethical for a lawyer to do, but I wasn't the bar association. I had another reason for asking.

"His eyes got kind of shiny when he said that, which made me wonder if he had some personal reason for doing it that way."

Jan was already nodding. "He had a younger sister, who got pregnant while she was in college, when Herb was away at law school. A lawyer who arranged private adoptions had an ad in the paper. She answered it and thought he was such a great guy.

He was going to see that all her expenses were paid while she carried the baby."

She paused, took a deep breath. "This was before he and I met, but Herb has told me the story, several times. It still haunts him."

Haunted him, I thought, but didn't correct her use of the present tense.

"To make a long story short," Jan said, "after the baby was born, Lori—that was his sister's name—she changed her mind. But the lawyer turned nasty on her, told her she had to give the baby up, that she'd signed a contract. Then he pointed out that the adoptive parents were rich and powerful."

Jan grimaced. "Lori called Herb in a panic, and he told her to wait until the weekend and he'd come home and help her sort it out. But she didn't wait. She went to the adoptive parents' house and confronted them. And they threw her out on her ear."

I braced myself, suspecting where this was going.

"She went home and killed herself," Jan said, staring down at her hands on the table.

We sat in silence for a beat. Then I asked, "Is there any way that whole incident might have led to this? Anyone who was involved in his sister's situation who might want to harm your husband now, maybe keep him quiet about something?"

"I can't imagine who or why," Jan said. "That was over twenty-five years ago."

I had a niggling thought, hovering out of reach. I struggled for a moment and finally lassoed it and dragged it out into the light.

"How about Herb's cases, has there ever been one where the woman backed out after the child's birth, and Herb backed her against the parents?"

Jan sat up a little straighter. "Only twice. But in each of those cases, Herb found another pregnant girl and got them a baby, eventually."

"After they'd paid twice for both girls' expenses," I said.

Jan nodded. "Yeah."

I needed those case files as well, but still I didn't ask for them. I didn't want to alienate Jan and have her shut down on me. Not until I'd exhausted all my questions.

"You said you record the private sessions. Show me, please."

Jan rose and led the way back to her desk. Inside her top desk drawer was a small black box, an electronic gizmo that apparently received input from a transmitter in the lawyer's office and recorded it.

She started to reach for it, but I held up a hand. I used my phone to snap several pics of it *in situ*, then nodded. No point in making her put on gloves. Her prints would already be all over the thing.

She lifted it from the desk and punched a couple of buttons. Loud knocking came from the gizmo. The sound of a door opening, then road noise, metal clanging against metal, probably from the construction site across the street, and the rat-a-tat-tat of jackhammers.

"Ah, there you are." The lawyer's voice, fake jovial and loud to be heard over all that. "Come on in."

I strained to hear, but the client apparently wasn't saying anything. The background noise intensified, a loud engine roaring, maybe a passing truck. Then the sound of the door closing.

And silence.

Jan and I exchanged a look. Why wasn't anyone talking?

The rustle of papers and another sound I'd heard recently—that of a file drawer sliding. More rustling, then the sliding sound again and the click as the drawer closed.

That sequence repeated itself, file drawer opening, rustling, drawer closing.

The third time, after the drawer closed, came the sound of a door opening, a couple seconds of the road and construction noise, and the click of the door closing.

Silence for about thirty seconds, then a different clicking noise.

"Is the recording time stamped?" I asked.

"Yes." Jan checked the gizmo. "Two-fifty-eight to three-o-six. It's noise-activated so it only records when there are sounds."

Barnes was scribbling on her pad. "What time did we arrive?" I asked her.

"Three minutes after three, Chief."

That's what I'd thought. The faint sounds I'd heard while standing at Jan's desk—the file drawer sliding and a door opening and closing—had been the killer leaving, after they'd found what they'd been looking for. And the lawyer hadn't been killed while I waited, but a few minutes before we'd entered the offices of Herbert Campbell, Esquire.

"Play it again," I said to Jan.

This time I strained to listen, trying to detect any sounds hiding under the roar of the background noise when the door was opened. Was that the crack of a gun or only more construction noise? The gun had to have a suppressor. A full-blown gunshot would have aroused Jan's suspicions, even with the noise in the background.

If we'd gotten here a few minutes sooner, would *I* have recognized that as a gunshot, with the volume turned down and muffled from inside Jan's desk? If we'd gotten to Campbell right away, could we have saved him?

I shook my head slightly to clear it of those futile questions, and gestured Jan toward her desk chair. I pulled on a blue nitrile glove and took the black box from her. "I'll be right back."

After rapping a knuckle against the lawyer's door, I opened it. The ME's assistant, a middle-aged male pathologist I'd never met before, scowled at me from behind the visor he wore. His white, spaceman-like protective gear rustled.

Without entering the crime scene, I gestured to Bert. He came over, his own white coveralls slowing him down some.

"Got an evidence bag handy?" I asked.

"Sure." His voice was muffled coming through the clear plastic panel in the hood of his protective suit. He extracted an evidence bag from a pocket, took the box from me with his gloved hand, and lowered it into the bag.

"I'll label it," I said, taking the bag back. "Check that file cabinet for prints extra carefully. And note if anything looks disturbed, especially in or around his desk. Someone was searching in here for something, right after he was killed."

Bert's black bushy eyebrows—reminiscent of the Muppet character who shared his name—rose halfway up his forehead. But he didn't ask any questions, only nodded and went back to work.

Back out in the waiting area, I asked Jan Campbell, "Is there anyone I can call for you?"

She shook her head. "I just called a close friend. She's on her way. I'm in no shape to drive home."

I gave her a small smile. I liked this woman. She was practical and level-headed—obviously upset, but she was maintaining control. I hoped she would be just as practical about my next request. "We're going to need the files for his recent cases, and for those two women who showed up at your house, and the cases where the women backed out after their babies were born."

But she was already shaking her head. "I can't give you those, I'm sorry. Client-attorney confidentiality."

I thought for a moment. Maybe I could get a warrant, but I doubted it. I didn't want to push her though, not yet.

Maybe if she has time to think about it... In the meantime, I'd rule out another possibility.

I nodded. "We'll be in touch."

Barnes followed me out into the building's corridor. I stopped and sucked in air, then blew it out in a long sigh.

I'd come here searching for answers regarding Ashley's adoption and disappearance. And ended up with a new case, a homicide that might or might not be related.

I fumbled in a pocket for my pen and labeled the evidence bag I was holding. Then I turned to where Barnes stood behind me. I handed her the bag and the pen.

She gave me an odd look. But when I pointed to the spot on the bag where she was to acknowledge receiving the evidence, she signed her name.

"I need you to work this case," I said, "for now."

Her eyes lit up and the ends of her mouth twitched. She was trying not to smile.

I debated if I should point out that I *wasn't* giving her a field promotion to detective. But I let it go. Ignoring her glee, I continued, "Hang out in there, see what Bert and Ernie find and what the ME guy is willing to tell you up front."

She snorted. "If anything."

"Emphasize that you are the chief's assistant, and anything he can give us would be really, really helpful."

"What are you gonna be doing?" she asked.

"I'm going to track down the young woman the wife claims tried to seduce him three years ago."

Maybe that *non*-affair was more than Jan Campbell thought it had been, and maybe it hadn't ended when she believed it did.

CHAPTER SEVENTEEN

I had no problem finding Eleanor Jenkins's high-rise apartment building in Starlingville, the oldest and one of the nicest sections of town. The challenge was finding a parking space nearby.

Apparently, lots of people wanted to live in this area, but the old streets were narrow and public parking lots were few and far between. I finally parked partway into a crosswalk area, figuring people could go around the front of my car single file. I pulled out my white cardboard *Chief of Police* sign and placed it on top of my dashboard. Then I headed for the building.

Her apartment was on the third floor and had a nice view of a nearby park. After introductions, she led me to a white leather sofa across from the big picture window. She perched on the edge of a matching armchair across from me. There was no rug, no coffee table between us. Only polished hardwood flooring and a chrome floor lamp.

Ms. Jenkins was a minimalist perhaps. Then again, the furnishings looked expensive. Maybe she wasn't willing to buy things until she could afford the best. On a court clerk's salary—Florida was on the low end of the range for most government jobs—that probably took some serious saving strategies.

"What's this about, Chief Anderson?" she asked.

I leaned forward, trying to maintain some dignity as the couch attempted to swallow me up. "Ms. Jenkins, you know the lawyer Herbert Campbell, correct?"

"Ellie, please," she gave me a small smile, "and yes, I know him, from work. I'm a clerk at the courthouse."

I didn't bother to tell her I already knew that. Instead, I said, "I understand that you were a bit closer than acquaintances for a while, a few years ago."

"We went to lunch a few times. Lawyers are so busy, the only place they can really cultivate friendships is at the courthouse."

"How about their own staff?" I asked out of curiosity, to see how far she would go with the pretense that they were just friends.

"That gets complicated fast, since they're the bosses."

"I see." Personally, I'd known several lawyers who were friends with some members of their staff, and with lots of other people, such as their neighbors. And one who was very close to my psychologist friend Kate and her PI husband, Skip Canfield.

"So, how did this friendship get started?" I asked.

She held up a hand. "Before we go any further, why are you asking about Herbie? Is his wife finally divorcing him?" She tried to make her expression mournful, but didn't quite pull it off. Her mouth curved up a little on the end.

And she called him Herbie? *Ho boy!*

"Not that I know of," I said out loud, keeping my voice pleasant. "Why would you think that from my asking questions? The police don't investigate divorce cases."

"No, of course not," she quickly said. "I was only wondering..." She trailed off.

And I'm wondering why you're ducking my question. But I kept that thought to myself for now. Instead, I let the silence stretch out.

"Wait, where are my manners?" She began to stand. "Can I get you anything, coffee, tea, water?"

I signaled with my hand that she should sit again. "No, I'm fine. Please answer the question. How did you two go from casual acquaintances to going out to lunch together?"

"Well," she sat back some in her chair, "the first time, we ran into each other as we were both leaving the courthouse for lunch. And we decided to go to the deli together."

I sat quietly, waiting.

"Then we ran into each other again, at the Chinese carryout down the street. We ended up eating in the park."

Can we say stalker, *boys and girls?*

"Soon after that, I, uh, realized his birthday was coming up, so I invited him out for a nicer lunch, at an Italian place."

I nodded. That was enough background. It gave me the picture of a young woman methodically setting a honey trap for an older, well-to-do man. But what had her end game been?

"And you became friends. What did you two talk about?"

"Oh, all kinds of things. Movies we'd seen, books we'd read, places we'd been."

"Did he ever talk about his cases?"

She shook her head. "Not that I recall."

"And why did this friendship end?" I asked.

"Oh, I wouldn't say it ended, but we stopped going out to lunch. His wife found out we were doing that, and she thought there was more to it than there was. She made him stop. After that we only saw each other at the courthouse."

"Were you mad at his wife for doing that?"

She shrugged. "A little, because it was stupid. But it's not like I don't have other friends. And I still saw him now and then..." She trailed off yet again.

A convenient device if one wants to avoid elaborating.

"Only at the courthouse?" I cocked one eyebrow at her.

"Well, yes. I mean we walked to the deli at the same time a couple of times, but we didn't eat together. He was afraid someone would report back to his wife and he'd be in trouble."

"That didn't piss you off?"

Another shrug. "Why would it? I just thought she was controlling, and he was letting her get away with it." She'd managed to keep her tone light, but there was fire in her eyes.

Yeah, she's pissed.

"So you had no desire to go to his office and confront either him or his wife?"

"No, of course not. Did she say I did that?"

"Why would she say that if you didn't do it?"

She sat up straighter in her chair and made a harumph sound. "I have no idea, and I think maybe I don't want to answer any more questions."

"I only have one more." I leaned forward again. "Do you know if anyone had reason to shoot Herbert Campbell?"

Her face paled. "Shoot him?" she squeaked out.

"Yes, someone shot him, a couple of hours ago."

Her mouth fell open and tears pooled in her eyes. "Is he...is he okay?"

"No," I softened my voice, "unfortunately he's not. He's dead."

She burst into tears and buried her face in her hands.

Either she was a very good actress or she wasn't our killer. But I didn't believe for a New York minute that *Herbie* Campbell meant little to her, was only a casual friend.

It took her a few moments to gain control of herself. Then she raised her head from her hands. Her eyes were red-rimmed, but her cheeks weren't all that wet. Still a toss-up between good actress and truly shocked and grieving.

"Who, why?" Her bottom lip trembled. Then her mouth curled into a sneer. "Did that bitch of a wife do it?"

"I don't believe so, but it's early on in the investigation."

"Well, she's the super jealous type. I'd take a long, hard look at her, if I were you."

"Are you sure you don't know of anyone else who might want to kill him?"

She shook her head.

"And he never discussed cases with you?"

She began to shake her head again but stopped. "Wait, there was this one case. He seemed preoccupied one time when we went out to lunch. I asked him what was wrong, and he said he had an adoption case that was getting sticky."

When she didn't elaborate, I prompted, "That's the word he used, *sticky*?"

"Yes. I asked how so, and he said something vague, but I got the impression that the client wanted to do something that wasn't totally legal."

"What did he say exactly?"

She closed her eyes, and her face pinched in concentration. I didn't think this expression was feigned, although it could be.

She finally opened her eyes. "I can't remember, but that was the impression I got."

"That the client wanted to do something illegal, or that they wanted *him* to do something illegal?"

She stared at the ceiling for a beat. "I'm not sure. I guess it could've been either of those, but it obviously bothered him."

"When did this happen?"

"Around three years ago," she said without hesitation.

Hmm, too long ago to be Ashley's adoption.

"You seem pretty sure about that timing," I said.

"It was the last time we had lunch together, for my birthday."

"One last question," I said. "Where were you today between two-thirty and three-fifteen?"

She looked confused, as if she wasn't sure why I was asking that. "At work until three, and then driving home. Oh, was that when he was–" She stopped abruptly and sniffled a little.

But her eyes were dry now.

"Do you have a boyfriend, Ms. Jenkins?"

She bristled. "Why is that any of your business?"

I shrugged. "Just curious."

"As a matter of fact," her tone was now huffy, "I'm engaged."

"Congratulations. Who's the lucky man?"

"I, uh," she glanced away, "I'd rather not say. It's complicated."

Ah, because he's already married, perhaps?

I opted to drop that line of questioning for now. I'd check her alibi, and perhaps the folks at her office would know who her mystery man was.

I stood and thanked her for her time.

Once out on the sidewalk, I called Bradley. We gave each other quick updates on the two cases. Then I said, "I want to bring Silva in again. There may have been something hinky about the adoption agreement they had with Ashley's biological mother." And I still wanted to know what was in that prenuptial agreement.

I paused, took a deep breath. "And by the way, I have your sister working the Campbell homicide case with me."

"What? As a detective?"

"More or less. Sorry, I should've run it past you first, but we're spread so thin."

"Oookaay." He dragged the word out, leaving me wondering if it really was okay.

I was in my car, on my way back to 3MB, when my phone rang. *Skip Canfield* appeared on my Bluetooth screen.

I considered not answering, but decided that was the chicken approach. Or maybe an ostrich. Hide my head in the sand and...

And what? Why did I want to avoid talking to him?

The phone rang again.

Ignoring the butterflies in my stomach, I hit the button to answer it. "Hey Canfield, how's it going?"

"Okay. I'm going to be meeting this young woman again in a few hours. I changed my flight to this evening, but I may need to stay over here again, if she gives me anything new that I need to check out."

"What makes you think she's going to give you anything useful?" My tone was crisp.

What's the matter with me? Why was I asking that? Was I hoping he wouldn't get any new leads?

"Because she was hemming and hawing a lot this morning," Canfield said, his own tone slightly annoyed—but at her or at me?

"And when I asked certain questions," he continued, "she'd change the subject, or answer with her own question, sometimes one that wasn't the least bit related to what I'd asked."

"Such as?" I snapped, then guilt tightened my chest. Whatever was going on with me, it wasn't Canfield's fault. "I'm sorry. I–"

"Yeah, I know," Canfield said, his voice softening considerably. "You're dealing with a priority case, a missing child, Kate said."

"A toddler."

A beat of silence. I imagined Canfield's face—still handsome in his fifties—wincing.

"That's the toughest," he said.

"So, what kind of questions was she asking?"

"Where was her mother from? Was she unhappy at home, did she run away? Things like that. Because *she* was obviously not being very open, I felt uncomfortable giving her too much."

"Why?"

"It crossed my mind," Canfield said, "that this could be some kind of scam. Somebody trying to hook up with a rich family and pretend they're the offspring of some long lost relative."

"Well, if that's the case, she didn't do her homework. We're hardly rich. And how would she get her hands on DNA that was a mitochondrial match?"

"I don't know. She was just acting squirrely."

"Okay, I trust your instincts. What did you tell her?"

"I did say that her mother was from Maryland, and that she wasn't a runaway. But I ducked most of her other questions. And then we ran out of time. She had to get to work. She said she'd call me after she'd had a chance to quote, 'process' what I'd told her."

"Okay. Yes, you have my permission to stay another night to check out whatever she tells you."

"Thanks, and Judith..."

"Yes?"

"Take care of yourself. Being in charge isn't as easy as it looks."

I snorted. "Never thought it would be easy." I paused, then admitted, "But I didn't realize how hard it *could get* sometimes."

"Yeah." He paused. "I'll let you know what I find out."

"Okay. Uh, Skip..." I stumbled some over his first name, "thanks...for everything."

"You're welcome." He disconnected.

I breathed out a sigh and tried to sort out the jumble of sensations in my body. A tightness in my chest, my stomach roiling. But the most pronounced was my throat closing at thought of what this young woman might have to tell Skip.

Was it a scam? Or at least a dead end?

Maybe, but... What if we did find Meredith, and she blamed us, her family, for her abduction?

CHAPTER EIGHTEEN

Silva's attorney had beat his client to 3MB. He was cooling his heels in the waiting area out front as I exited the elevator. I signaled for him to follow me.

"You got here fast," I commented.

"I was just finishing up with something over at the court-house..." he trailed off, maybe realizing he was having a downright civil exchange with me.

Was this yet another legacy from my predecessor, John Black—animosity from all the attorneys in town?

I gave the attorney a big smile. "I don't think Lieutenant Bradley and your client are here yet. Would you like some coffee while you wait, from my personal stash?"

He stiffened a little, but then seemed to force himself to relax. "Sure, sounds good."

I led him to one of the interview rooms, ushered him in, but left the door open as I left.

Barnes was at her desk. "Nothing we didn't already know from the ME. Campbell was shot at point-blank range. Bullet went all the way through and lodged in the wall across the room. But the residue around the wound was less than expected, so maybe a suppressor was used."

"I already suspected that," I said. "Even with all that noise coming for the outside, a gun without one would have made enough noise to be recognizable as a gunshot. Anything from Bert and Ernie yet?"

She shook her head.

"Okay, I need you to check Eleanor Jenkins's alibi. She says she left her job at the courthouse at three and was driving home when Campbell was shot. Check with her coworkers, and see if any of them know who her current romantic interest is. He may very well be married."

I glanced at my watch. "On second thought, that can wait until tomorrow. Her coworkers may not even be there now."

"Okay."

"You wanna observe? I'm talking to Silva again."

She grimaced. "I need to get this report done on the murder case."

I hid a smile. Barnes might not be so eager to take on the detective role, now that she was getting a taste of the endless paperwork involved.

When I returned to the interview room, two cups of coffee in my hands, Silva's attorney was reading from a file folder he'd opened in front of him.

He quickly closed the folder and took one of the cups.

"Creamer or sugar?" I asked. I had some of both in one jacket pocket.

He shook his head, took a sip, then smiled up at me. "This is great."

I sat down across from him. "It is when I make it. If my assistant ever offers you coffee, politely decline."

He actually chuckled.

"I want you to know, Counselor," I said, "I'm not trying to pin anything on your client. But he's been less than helpful, downright evasive at times. He keeps railing that we should be searching for his daughter, not harassing him. But we have to pursue all leads. And the longer it takes to rule him out, the longer it takes us to find who really snatched her."

The attorney's sole reaction to this rather long speech was a nod and another sip of his coffee.

We sat in somewhat awkward silence for a few minutes, finishing our coffees.

Then Gabe Silva came through the interview room door, Bradley on his heels.

"Well, isn't this cozy?" Silva said, a sneer on his face.

Ignoring his obnoxiousness, I smiled. "We were having a caffeine pick-me-up. Would you like some, Mr. Silva?"

Before he could answer, I called Barnes on my cell phone. "Hey, can you bring a coffee, from my office, to Interview Room 2 for Mr. Silva?"

"Um, sure," she said. A rustling noise. "Uh, I'm in your office now, and the pot is almost empty. Should I make some fresh?"

I gave the phone a big smile. "Yes, that would be great."

By the time Bradley had run through the preliminaries—turning on the equipment, identifying for the recording who was present, and such—Barnes had arrived with a coffee cup in hand. She set it down in front of Silva, who was now sitting beside his lawyer and across from Bradley and myself. Then she left the room.

Silva took a sip and made a face.

I tried to feel guilty about being so petty, and failed. The man just rubbed me the wrong way.

"Mr. Silva, as I mentioned to your attorney, I'm not trying to make trouble for you. I'm only doing my job, following all leads. And we are pursuing multiple avenues. But I need to eliminate you as a suspect so we can focus on the other possibilities."

Silva scowled, but his attorney was nodding.

He leaned forward slightly. "Tell me, Chief, what has led you to suspect my client, other than he's the child's parent?"

I sat back in my chair, debating for moment. "Right before your wife screamed, Mr. Silva, a witness in the crowd saw

Ashley standing by herself. Then someone, an adult, took the child's hand, and she acted like she knew them."

"How good a look did this witness get of this someone?" the lawyer asked.

"Mostly they got a good look at the person's arm. They were wearing a long-sleeved shirt, color gray." I paused, letting that sink in.

Silva pulled nervously at the ends of his current long-sleeved tee shirt, this one medium blue.

"So, let me ask again, Mr. Silva, were you anywhere near the riverwalk at any time Saturday?"

He shook his head. "I most certainly was not."

"But you can see now why we would wonder." I pointed to his long shirt sleeve. "Why are you wearing long sleeves in August, *in Florida*?"

"Because Pen keeps her apartment too bloody cold."

"For the record, you're referring to Ms. Penelope Atkins?" He nodded.

I pointed to the recording equipment.

"Yes," he said.

"But you also wore a long-sleeved dress shirt to your office Saturday morning." I raised my eyebrows, turning the statement into a question.

"Mrs. Nelson, the office manager, I think she's menopausal or something. She keeps the AC cranked up as well."

That was *not* the explanation he'd given me earlier. Which could be significant, or mean nothing.

"Could you push your sleeves up, sir?" Bradley was asking.

"Why?" Silva asked, even as he complied.

There were no tattoos nor other distinguishing scars or marks.

"Again, just covering all the bases," I said. "Who else– "

"What else did your witness see?" the attorney interrupted.

"That was about it," I said. "The witness looked away, and when they looked back, the child and the other person were gone." I turned again to Silva. "Who else would Ashley recognize and let them lead her away without a fuss?"

"That nanny, Cara," he spat out.

"Anyone else?"

He shrugged. "Annie could answer that better."

I nodded. "Speaking of Annie, you mentioned a prenuptial agreement earlier, that her family's lawyer wrote up."

Both attorney and interviewee were stone-faced.

"Did you know that I was in that lawyer's waiting room a little while ago—to ask him about that prenup—when someone, in his private office, shot him?"

Silva's face registered shock. "What?"

"Herbert Campbell, Esquire, is dead," I said.

Both Silva's and his attorney's faces blanched.

I leaned forward. "What was in that prenup, Mr. Silva?"

"Nothing that has anything to do with all this," he snapped.

"Sir, I will have to be the judge of that. As I said, we need to eliminate you so we can focus all of our resources on other leads." I paused half a beat. "Or maybe there is something relevant in that prenup, and you were the one who went to Campbell's office, after our chat earlier, and shot him."

Silva threw up his hands. "That's ridiculous."

It actually was, since he'd been with us right before we'd left for the lawyer's office. I was mostly trying to rattle him.

Then again, he could've gotten there before us. It would've been tight, requiring that he break multiple speed limits. But he'd already shown earlier, in our own little version of the Indy 500, that he was willing to do just that.

I sat back. "I'll point out again that we need your full cooperation. You have been more forthcoming in this interview, but I feel you are withholding something. Maybe something related to 'leverage'," I made air quotes, "and that prenup."

His attorney put a hand on his arm, leaned over and whispered in his ear.

Silva gave a slight nod, shook off the hand and leaned forward. Linking his fingers together on the table in front of him, he said, "You have to promise not to let Annie find out about this."

"I won't have any reason to tell her," I said, "if it's truly unrelated to Ashley's disappearance."

"The prenup," he said, "keeps me from getting any of Annie's assets or alimony if I initiate a divorce, but if she initiates one, she can negotiate any settlement she wants."

He stopped, cleared his throat. "I was going to use Ashley as leverage. Annie adores her. Oh, she loves Teddy too, but not like she dotes on Ashley. If she initiates a divorce and gives me joint custody of Teddy, plus some money, she gets full custody of Ashley."

"How much money?" Bradley asked.

"A lump payment to help me get my own accounting firm started—a couple hundred thousand should do it. And two years of alimony. Then I'm on my own."

"And if she doesn't go along with that?"

"Well," he leaned back in his chair, trying to hide a smile. He wasn't entirely successful. "Then I'd sue her for full custody of both children, and child support, which isn't mentioned in the prenup. It should be substantial since it's based on the person's income. She gets ten thousand a month from her trust fund set up by her grandmother."

I frowned. They lived in a nice house, but not as nice as they could afford with that coming in, plus his salary.

"She insists on banking half of it, for the kids' future." He sneered. "She can give me half for two years instead. Or give me close to that in child support for eighteen years."

He was better at reading other people than I'd given him credit for, but he was still a son of a bitch.

"And how would you get custody of the kids? Courts rarely give fathers full custody of small children."

"But if the mother is unfit..." He trailed off and shrugged, then gave me a grin.

You trumped up that theft charge against Cara, so your wife would be overwhelmed.

I managed to keep that thought to myself. It wasn't immediately relevant to finding Ashley.

Too bad I can't arrest him for being a bastard.

"I think the point here," the attorney was saying, "is that my client had no reason to kidnap the child and every reason to have her safe and sound at home."

As a bargaining chip, I thought.

He rose. "I think we're done here." Silva rose as well.

"One more curiosity question," I said as I stood up. "Why do you want joint custody of Teddy?"

Bradley was already at the door. Silva strode in that direction, but he tossed back over his shoulder, "I want an heir, and Pen can't have children."

Bradley and I stepped out of the interview room behind him and his attorney. We watched as they walked down the hall to the elevators.

"Shame we can't arrest him for being an s.o.b.," Bradley said.

"Yeah." I gave him a crooked smile. "I had that same thought a few minutes ago."

Back in my office, I called Annie Silva again. "How are things going?" I asked first.

"Better. Teddy's down for a nap."

"I won't keep you long," I said. "I have a quick question. Whose idea was it to go to the Founders' Day celebration?"

"Gabe's, but then later he said he had to work." Her tone was angry. "And he said it right in front of Ashley. 'Sorry, dear, but we can't go after all.'"

"And she got upset," I said.

"Very. She threw a temper tantrum. And Gabe then says, all sweet and innocent, 'Why don't you take the kids anyway, darling?'"

I was tempted to ask if she suspected it was a set-up.

I certainly did. What a great way to prove Annie unfit, by having one of her children kidnapped from right under her nose.

But I resisted the temptation. No point in stirring that already boiling pot.

But I was definitely *not* taking her husband off our suspect list.

Before I'd even had a chance to sit down behind my desk, my private line rang. *Mayor's Office* appeared on the caller ID screen.

"Yes, Mayor Hayes," I answered.

"Chief, it's Carol. Um, the mayor would like you to come upstairs, if now is a good time."

I bit back the response that no time was good when I was looking for a missing child. "I'll be right up," I said instead, a lump of dread forming in my stomach.

Is he going to suspend me?

On the fifth floor, Mark Hayes was standing behind his desk, shuffling some papers around. "Come in, Chief. Have a seat."

I stopped in front of his desk, standing at parade rest. If he was about to toss me out on my ear, I wasn't going to delay the process by having to get up from a chair.

My eyes stung. Oh shit, I'm *not* going to cry!

I'd had very mixed emotions about this job the first few months, but in recent times, I'd come to love it...and the people I worked with. And Sam...

A lump grew in my throat. *Stop thinking about all that!*

"You wanted to see me, Mr. Mayor."

He glanced up from the pile of papers he was rifling through. "Yes." His eyes dropped to the pile again, then he sighed.

He made eye contact. ""I suppose you've heard about the sightings of John Black and his wife around the state."

I nodded.

"And certain items he's left behind in his hotel rooms?"

I nodded again.

"Chief, please tell me if you have had any contact with Black since he jumped bail last March."

"No, sir. I have not." I was a tad offended that he had to ask, but decided saying so out loud would not be helpful.

"And you have no idea how he got some objects that can definitely be linked to you?"

"Actually, yes I do have an idea. Those items were discarded in the dumpster behind my apartment building. There are now security cameras aimed at said dumpster." I was avoiding using Sam's name. No need to get him in trouble.

Hayes nodded. "Good idea. Unfortunately, the governor is concerned. He wants me to suspend you, with pay of course, while the whole thing is investigated."

I didn't mention that I already knew this from Dot Wilder. I also stifled the urge to say something snarky like, "Over a chewed-up cat toy and an empty wine bottle?" Couldn't Hayes—and the governor too, for that matter—realize this was a set-up?

And a sloppy one at that. I suspected that Black and/or his buddies in that gang just wanted to rattle me, keep me off balance. And damn it, they were succeeding.

I opted for raising my eyebrows to look surprised. "Now would be a really bad time to do that, sir. Ashley Silva's life would be further jeopardized if I were taken off the case."

"Surely, the FBI team could take over."

My stomach clenched. *What will I do without the job?*

"They don't have the local knowledge that my team has." Amazingly, my voice sounded normal. "We're pursuing multiple leads."

What would I be without the job?

"Lieutenant Bradley couldn't handle things?" Hayes asked.

"I'm sure he'd make a valiant effort to do so, sir." I paused, gathering my thoughts. I didn't want to sound like I didn't have confidence in Bradley. "But it would be unfair to dump this on him. He's still relatively new to his command position. No doubt, he would be successful, but..." I trailed off, unsure what else I could say.

"But he doesn't have your level of expertise." Hayes gave me a small smile. "I had no intention of suspending you, Chief. But I needed some input to have some good arguments ready, should the governor call again."

I returned the smile, relief washing through me and making my knees a bit wobbly. "Thank you, sir."

He waved a hand in the air. "Please stop *siring* me, Chief."

My smile widened, but then I sobered. "Mr. Mayor, may I ask about another matter?"

"Certainly."

"What were you doing at Mr. Campbell's law offices earlier this morning?"

"I told you," his voice had turned brusque, "some matters related to my wife's estate."

"Uh huh," was all I said. I waited patiently.

Hayes's cheeks pinked. "Look, it's none of your business, okay?"

I shook my head slightly. "Mr. Mayor, I hate to push, but Mr. Campbell was murdered this afternoon."

Hayes's mouth fell open and he stared at me. He flopped into his desk chair.

Now I sat down as well, but stayed perched on the front edge of his too-comfy leather visitors' chairs. "So it's important that I find out as much as I can about his recent cases."

Hayes sighed, and his gaze rose to the ceiling. Still examining the acoustic tiles there, he said, "You can't tell anyone about this. My son would be devastated if he found out."

I nodded and again remained silent, waiting.

He blew out air and lowered his gaze to make eye contact. "My wife had a baby out of wedlock, right before she and I met. When we wanted to get married, my mother insisted that no one could know that the baby was..." he paused, winced, "...illegitimate."

He continued, "I was outraged, but Karen said we should go along with her plan, for the sake of my future. A few months after we were married, we announced that Karen was pregnant. The baby was with Karen's mother at that point, in Georgia. At the stage where Karen would be showing, she was 'ordered' by her doctor," he made air quotes, "to stay in bed due to complications of the pregnancy. She stayed inside for the next few months, then went to a 'specialist' in Georgia for the delivery." Air quotes again.

"I wasn't in politics back then, so no one paid much attention to what the wife of a lawyer had to go through to have her child. We kept him well bundled up for the first few months, to hide the fact that he wasn't a newborn."

He shook his head and clasped his hands together on his desktop. "Our intention had been that I would adopt him, but we never got around to it. And then she died..."

I marveled at the irony of all this, since Hayes himself had fathered a child out of wedlock and was forced to give the child and the young woman up. By the same controlling mother who had orchestrated this whole plan.

But maybe it wasn't a coincidence or even all that iron-ic. Maybe Karen's plight had been part of her appeal. Hayes wasn't able to save his first love from the shame and the loss of her babe, but he'd help this woman salvage her honor and bring her child up in a two-parent household.

"Herb Campbell said he could handle the adoption discreetly." Hayes ran a hand through his carefully coifed hair, leaving it not so well coifed anymore. "That Brian wouldn't have to know. But as an adult, he had to sign that he agreed with the adoption. Herb said he'd disguise the papers, so Brian would think it was something related to his mother's estate."

Hmm, is that ethical? Apparently, as with client-attorney confidentiality, Campbell had been willing to bend some rules. Had he bent one too far and someone was pissed off enough to kill him over it?

All the more reason why we needed access to his client files. I needed to have another go at Mrs. Campbell about that.

Hayes was staring at me, waiting for a response.

"Then you weren't there to sign papers this morning," I said, "but to pick them up?"

Why go to all that trouble? I wondered, since the kid *is* now legally an adult.

Hayes nodded, his face sagging. "I'm not sure how Brian would take this. Would he feel betrayed by his mother? Or maybe think I wasn't really his father?"

He paused, then answered my unspoken question. "I wanted the adoption to be a done deal, should he ever find out. So he'd know that he was truly my son."

My chest ached. Hayes was a good man, and he'd had far more misery in his life than he deserved. "Mr. Mayor...Mark," I said, "your secret is safe with me. I'll do my best to keep you out of the investigation."

He gave me a feeble smile. "Thank you, Chief."

CHAPTER NINETEEN

Barnes was in the process of slipping her baton into her duty belt when I returned to the bullpen. "I was thinking it would be worthwhile to talk to Ashley's biological mother again," she said. "I'm wondering if she got pissed enough at Mr. Campbell for giving her child to irresponsible parents that she came gunning for him." She paused. "Wanna come with?"

The question brought me up short. She sounded so much like her brother, when he asked that question—did I want to come along to a crime scene or to interview a suspect/witness?

But in those instances, the cases were actually his. Did she think she was lead detective on the Campbell murder case?

"Uh, sure," I said. How was I going to disabuse her of that notion without hurting her feelings?

She gave me an odd look as pink tinged her cheeks, then she pivoted and headed for the bullpen's exit.

Out in the parking lot, Barnes slowed her pace. "Uh, could we take your car?"

I tilted my head at her.

"Mine's been acting up lately. I almost couldn't get it to start this morning."

"No problem." I shifted in the direction of my own car.

Once on the road, Barnes said, "I checked with the uniform who canvassed the building. One of the other tenants, an accountant, said he was driving back from a client meeting and saw someone outside Campbell's private entrance. The guy was just standing there, hands in his pockets. Then as he, the accountant, that is, was turning into the parking lot behind the building, he saw the guy knock on the door."

Ah, so there is a parking lot hidden back there. Out loud, I asked, "He's sure it was a guy?"

"No. He only got a glance or two at the person, but he said they were average height and stocky. And get this, they were wearing a hoodie and long pants, in *this heat.*"

I mentally fit the puzzle pieces together. They stood there, hands in pockets, maybe to hide the gun they were carrying? And then, when the road and construction noise was extra loud, they knocked on the door. And shot Campbell.

"We need to follow up with that witness," I said.

"Um, I already did, by phone."

I glanced her way. Her face was neutral, looking straight ahead out the windshield.

Was she only being efficient, or did she really believe she'd been unofficially promoted to detective?

At some point, we needed to have a conversation about the difference between taking the initiative and overstepping one's boundaries.

But I wasn't going to rein her in just yet. We were spread too thin, and I needed her "initiative" with the Campbell case.

And I needed the lawyer's files.

I instructed my Bluetooth to call Campbell's office. I got voice mail at the office. "We're sorry but the office is closed temporarily..."

I ended the call and tried the home number. It rang five times. I figured I was about to get voicemail again, when I heard a click and "Hello?" Jan Campbell's voice was tentative.

I forced myself to go through the niceties, asking how she was holding up and such.

She said she was doing okay, but she sounded almost feeble, as if reality was setting in.

I asked about the files, pushing gently.

"I shouldn't, Chief," she said.

"Well, think about it, okay? It would help a lot with the investigation. You want whoever did this caught, don't you?"

"Yes, of course." A pause. "Okay, I'll think about it."

We disconnected, and I wondered if she was just saying that to get rid of me.

A few minutes later, we stood outside Emma Blackstone's apartment door. Barnes's first knock got no response. She knocked again, and I held my badge up to the peephole.

The door opened. Emma Blackstone gave us an exasperated look. "I did *not* kidnap that child," she said, her tone emphatic.

I opened my mouth, but before I could speak, Barnes said, "We're not accusing you of anything. May we come in?"

With a pronounced huff, the woman stepped back and gestured toward her living room. It was sparsely furnished with an old sofa that sagged in the middle and one armchair, a coffee table and a floor lamp. A beige room-sized rug, with an indistinct pattern in faded black, made it somewhat less stark.

Barnes led the way. Blackstone stomped after her. I brought up the rear, studying the young woman's body language.

She was obviously angry, but about what? Was it simply because we'd showed up at her door?

Blackstone gestured toward her sofa, and Barnes sank down on it. It tried to swallow her.

I stifled a smile as she struggled to get back to the edge and firmly planted her feet on the floor in front of her.

First lesson in interviewing suspects in their homes, check out the seat before you sit down.

I balanced on the edge of the armchair. The young woman remained standing, her arms crossed. She wore a yellow tank top and khaki shorts, and her long blonde hair was pulled back in a loose ponytail. The room was stuffy, but not insufferable. I suspected she kept her air conditioning thermostat set high to save money.

"Ms. Blackstone," Barnes said, "when Lieutenant Bradley spoke to you earlier, you implied that you hadn't known exactly who adopted your child. Is that correct?"

Blackstone nodded, her lips a firm, straight line.

"So when did you figure out who the adoptive parents were?" Barnes asked.

"Not until this past weekend, when I saw the news about the missing child. I put two and two together."

"But how did you do that?" Barnes persisted. "I mean there are lots of toddlers in this city. The missing child could've been any of them. They never said on the news that she was adopted, did they?"

"Well, no." A hand wandered up and tugged on her ponytail. The other arm remained clutched around her middle.

"So how did you figure it out?" Barnes asked again.

Blackstone shrugged. "I don't remember exactly."

"You don't remember," Barnes echoed, with an exaggerated expression of confusion. "When did you first see it on the news?"

"Sunday morning."

"Um," Barnes said, "that was only yesterday."

Blackstone remained quiet, still fidgeting with her hair.

"So, do you recall what you were thinking when you saw the report?" Barnes asked.

Another shrug.

I considered jumping in, but decided that my assistant was doing the best she could with this situation. I'd let it play out.

"Where were you?" Barnes asked, "at the time that you saw the report, that is."

"Over there." Blackstone pointed to a small table with two chairs, in one corner of the room—her dining area, apparently.

An open double doorway led to a galley kitchen beyond it. "I was eating breakfast."

Barnes stood and walked to the TV that sat on a small table in the opposite corner. It was positioned so one could see it from either the table or the sofa. She patted the top of it. "And the news was on?"

"No, well, yeah. That Sunday morning show on the local channel. Then they interrupted it with a special report."

Blackstone fell silent.

After a few seconds, Barnes said, "What were you thinking as you watched the report?"

Hmmm, need to talk to her about letting silence happen. Often interviewees revealed something they hadn't intended to, when the discomfort of the silence got to them.

"I don't remember," Blackstone repeated. "I just suddenly realized that it had to be my baby."

"Uh, huh." Barnes's tone was thoughtful. She walked back toward the sofa. "But you waited until this morning to call Mr. Campbell, the lawyer who arranged the adoption."

"Yes. I kept watching the reports, hoping they would find her, but when they didn't..."

"And you told Lieutenant Bradley," Barnes said, "that you hadn't regretted putting the baby up for adoption before, but now you did."

Blackstone's gaze fell to the carpeting in front of Barnes, who'd remained standing next to the sofa. "Um, I knew she'd gone to a good home, or at least, that's what I thought." Her face twisted. "But then..." she spit out and stopped.

"But what?" Barnes said.

Too quick, Gloria. I kept my mouth shut.

Blackstone shook her head.

Barnes stared at her for a moment. "You said, you thought it was a good home. What made you think that?"

Good girl. She'd realized she was rushing things and had backtracked.

"Well, Campbell said it was. And they had that house..." she trailed off and her eyes flicked up, then back to the carpet.

Barnes raised her eyebrows. "You saw their house. Mr. Campbell took you there?"

Blackstone's face reddened. "Well, um, no. I followed him." She fell quiet.

This time, Barnes waited, but eventually prompted with, "When did you follow him?"

"The day I brought the baby to him. I waited outside and followed him and his wife when they took her to the...uh, her new home."

She swallowed hard. "It was so nice. I remember thinking that they could give her much more than I could. I felt better after that."

"Better about giving her up?" Barnes's voice was low and gentle.

Blackstone nodded. A tear trickled down her cheek. "That's how I knew the missing child was mine. The reporter was broadcasting from in front of the girl's house. It was that same house."

She sniffled and sank onto the sofa. "And they showed a picture of the girl. She looked a lot like my baby sister did at that age."

A beat of silence. We both watched the young woman, but she kept her face turned away from us.

Barnes asked, "Did you go out this afternoon?"

Blackstone's head jerked up. "No, why?"

"You've been here all day?" Barnes repeated.

"Yes. I sleep during the day and work nights, cleaning offices."

Barnes nodded. "Can anyone verify where you were between two-thirty and three-thirty today?"

"No." The woman now looked confused. "I'd just gotten up around then. I was drinking coffee." She poked her chin toward the little table in the corner.

"Thanks for your time." Barnes turned and headed for the door.

I rose from the armchair. "But you were up earlier than that on Sunday?"

She shrugged as she stood as well. "I tend to slide back toward a more normal sleep schedule on the weekends. I usually have to take something to make me sleep during the day on Mondays."

She pivoted toward Barnes. "Wait. Why did you want to know where I was today? Has something else happened?" her voice rose in pitch. "Did you find the child?"

I reached out and touched Blackstone's shoulder. "No, but Mr. Campbell was shot and killed, around three this afternoon."

She jerked back toward me, and her mouth fell open. She slid to her knees and covered her face. "Oh no! Now I'll never..."

We both stared at her for a beat, waiting to see if she would go on. Finally, I asked, "Never what?"

She looked up, her face tear-streaked now. "I'll never get her back. I was going to ask Mr. Campbell to help me *pro bono*." Her eyes hardened. "I figured he owed me that much, after giving my baby to those people."

In my car headed back to 3MB, we rehashed the interview. "She seemed genuinely surprised when you told her Campbell was shot," Barnes pointed out.

"True," I said, "but she wasn't as okay with the adoption as she pretended to be. There was some anger simmering under the surface."

"Yes," Barnes agreed, then paused. "Um, earlier, when I asked if you wanted to come with me, you..." She trailed off.

I mentally braced myself. "What about it?" My voice was a bit clipped.

She stared at my profile for a half beat. "Never mind. Um, thanks for letting me ask the questions."

"I figured it was time to let you try your wings a little." I glanced her way. "But don't let it go to your head."

She gave me a half smile that was also reminiscent of her brother.

I slowly let out the breath I'd been holding. We were back on an even keel, and she'd been reminded of her place.

And secretly I was pleased that she'd acquitted herself so well as the main interrogator. She'd make a good detective someday. But not quite yet.

As we entered the bullpen, the smell of hot pizza had both our stomachs growling.

Sam stood outside my office door, two large pizza boxes balanced on one palm, and a white plastic bag in his other hand. It looked a lot like the kitchen trash liners I used and it bulged some at the bottom.

"I apologize for bringing pizza for supper," he said, as we approached, "when you had it for lunch earlier, but–"

I grimaced. "I never got a chance to eat much of it."

Barnes's stomach growled again, loudly, and Sam grinned. He handed her the top box. "This one's for you, and anyone else who needs refueling."

He pointed his chin toward my office, waited while I unlocked it and followed me in. The pizza box landed on my desk, the bag on the floor.

Barnes appeared in the open doorway, a piece of pizza already dangling in one hand.

"Later, Gloria," Sam said and closed the door in her face.

I gave him a hard look, part curious, part censoring.

"Yeah, I know," he said, "that was kinda rude. But I don't want her DNA anywhere near this box."

I shifted to completely curious, but he opened the box and nudged it toward me. The fragrance of garlic and tomatoes wafted over me, and I figured my curiosity could wait awhile.

A few minutes later, I tossed the crust from my third piece back in the box and reached for another.

Sam nodded. "That should do it, but feel free to keep eating."

"Do it for what?" I mumbled around a big bite of pizza.

Instead of answering me, he picked up another slice himself and took a bite. Then he fumbled one-handed in his shirt pocket and took out a small USB drive. He held it out toward me.

"What's that?" I demanded, getting a bit annoyed.

He slid it across my desk toward me.

I lowered my half-eaten pizza to my napkin and plugged the drive into my computer. A grainy image appeared on my monitor.

It was the back of my building, a big blue dumpster centered in the frame. A flicker of movement, off to the side, as a teenaged boy came into view. He was tall and skinny, somewhere between fifteen and seventeen, with light brown skin and close-cropped dark hair.

He opened the lid of the dumpster, climbed up on one end and stuck his head inside.

I huffed. "I see they're still recruiting brown and black kids to do their dirty work." The core gang members were white supremacists, but they coerced minority kids into joining so they could give them the risky tasks.

"You agree with me then," Sam said, "that it's most likely that gang?"

"Maybe. Probably. Or it could be John Black getting his revenge."

Sam shook his head. He'd put his piece of pizza down as well. "John's not that smart, nor organized enough to pull off something like this from afar. This smacks of that gang leader."

A shiver slithered down my spine. "That gang leader" had come close to killing me.

"I thought he was in solitary confinement."

"Yes, but it's not that hard to get word to his people. Slip a crooked guard a note and a bribe."

"Black could be in on it though," I said. "I'm sure it galls him that he was brought down by a woman...two women actually, me and Dot Wilder."

"Hey, what am I?" Sam protested. "Chopped liver."

I chuckled. "Two women and one persistent male sheriff."

The guy in the video pulled his head back out of the dumpster, jumped down and walked away. He was trying to look nonchalant but the nervous glances over his shoulder belied that.

"Not surprised he didn't find anything," I said. "The dumpster's emptied on Monday mornings, and again on Thursdays."

"I'm hoping he tries again later. So he can find this." Sam held up the trash bag.

Then he pulled out a wine bottle, dark green, with a label I didn't recognize.

"Sorry, I can't indulge just yet," I said. "I may need to be alert if anything new comes up."

"You and I would never drink this swill. I bought it for the bottle." He twisted open the screw top, stood and went into my small bathroom. A gurgling sound.

He came back and handed the bottle to me. I examined the label. It was a vintage I'd never heard of before. A sour odor emanated from its open top.

"That should do," Sam said as he reached for the bottle again, this time taking it by the neck. "Both our fingerprints on it."

He dropped it back into the bag, then pointed to the pizza box. "You done?"

I took the last piece and added it to my napkin. "You've got the dumpster under surveillance?"

"Better still." He grabbed the box, containing a few gnawed crusts, and inserted it in the bag. That's why he'd brought pizza again, rather than something else. He wanted to make sure our DNA was on those crusts. And I noted that his last name was on the outside of the box, in big black letters.

"I've got a deputy watching the kid," he said. "I identified him with facial recognition. One of the other cameras got a good shot of his face as he was looking back. He's got a record, petty stuff, but he's in the system."

I smiled. "As was a current address for him, apparently."

"Yup." He lifted the bag as if toasting me with it. "Later, Chief. Watch your back."

"You too, Sheriff."

"Love you," he mouthed and opened the office door.

"Evening, Sheriff." Bradley's voice.

I was glad Sam hadn't said the L word out loud. My door was soundproof, theoretically, but Bradley had excellent hearing.

CHAPTER TWENTY

Bradley slipped into my office. I gestured toward the visitor's chair that Sam had vacated.

"I checked on Ms. Dexter, our Goth girl from the park," he said, as I settled into my desk chair. "Campbell was not the lawyer who arranged her babies' adoptions. It was a nonprofit charity organization."

"So unlikely she's related to his death," I said.

Bradley nodded, as his phone rang. He slipped it from the pocket of his navy blazer, which did not look as dapper as it had yesterday. Had he gone home last night to get some rest, as I'd told him and everyone else to do? He might've just crashed on the small sofa in his office.

He glanced at the phone's screen and tapped it. "Hey Sarge, what's up?" he said in its general direction.

"Our pervert's on the move again," Sergeant Johnson said.

"Stop calling him that," I said.

"Oops, sorry, Chief. I didn't realize..." he trailed off.

I swallowed a chuckle. I'd been thinking of him as "our pervert" myself lately.

"Where to?" I asked.

"Same warehouse," the sarge said.

"Bradley and I will head over there." We both stood.

The lieutenant pocketed his phone and said, "I'll meet you there, after I get a warrant. The judge said he'd grant one if the group congregated again, but we have to make sure first that it's not a twelve-step meeting."

Barnes rose as we stopped at her desk.

"Peter Richards is on his way to that warehouse again," I told her.

Her eyes lit up. "Peter Dick?"

"Don't call him that," I said in a mock stern tone. "At least, not in front of anyone else."

Bradley was chuckling as he walked away, headed for his office to call the judge for the warrant.

She leaned down and yanked on something under her desk. Her Kevlar vest emerged from the back of the knee hole.

Aha, one of Barnes's mysteries solved. I'd wondered where she kept that thing. It always seemed to magically appear when needed.

As we exited the building into the stifling August heat, I handed Barnes my keys.

"I need to make a call." I walked around to the passenger side of my car.

She nodded.

The call was to our new K-9 officer. "Can you and King come meet us at that warehouse? Or are you in the middle of something?"

"Nope," Officer Terry said. "I'm on standby if anyone needs a building or alley cleared. We're on our way."

"No siren, and stop a couple of blocks away and walk in."

"You got it, Chief."

I texted him the address.

At the warehouse, I grabbed my own Kevlar vest from my trunk. And again we slipped into Armstrong's backseat, Barnes now wearing her vest over her uniform shirt.

We encountered the same scenario as before. Several people went in the side door. This time, two women, one white and one Latina, and three men—four counting Richards, who'd already arrived. A couple of the faces seemed familiar.

I wondered how much the warehouse owner was charging them for his little peep show. I doubted it was cheap. How could these guys afford to keep coming? Richards, and probably at least some of these other people, worked low-paying jobs. It's hard to get something better when one is an ex-con, and especially when one's crime was sexual abuse of children.

Then the most interesting tidbit registered. It dawned on me, as one of them went through the door, that he was the second of the bunch who was wearing a long-sleeved gray tee shirt.

One person—in August, in Florida—whose blood ran so cold they needed long sleeves, that I *might* buy. But two?

"What's with the long-sleeved tee shirts?" I said out loud.

"Good question," Barnes said.

Armstrong shrugged. "Cover up gang tattoos?"

"You know that or you're guessing?" I asked.

"Guessing."

"Okay, when we're done here," I said, "no matter what else goes down, I want those two brought in for questioning about Ashley."

I pulled out my phone and texted Derek. He was trying to track down the identities of the people from yesterday's visit to the warehouse. I asked if he'd had any luck.

He called rather than texting back. "I've got most of them identified."

"Hang on, let me put you on speaker. We're in Armstrong's cruiser watching the warehouse. Another group has gathered today." I tapped the button for speaker.

"Two of the men are on the sex offenders' registry," Derek continued, "but they're listed as living in other states."

"So they've either moved," I said, "without reporting their new addresses, or they're visiting."

"Most likely the former. I'm working on getting current addresses. The woman is also on the registry but she lives in southern Georgia. Maybe a day trip?"

"Maybe, but she's back today. There's also another woman and a new man in today's group. We'll send you pics."

"On it, Chief. I'll send you what I have on the ones I've identified so far."

"Thanks." I disconnected as one of the gray tee-shirted men exited the building.

"That was fast," Barnes muttered beside me.

I quickly checked the info that Derek had just attached to a text. This guy was one of the ones from another state, and he was still on parole.

Yes! I resisted the urge to pump my fist in the air. "Officer Peters..."

She looked at me over the seat back, and I showed her the report on my phone. "Follow him," I ordered. "Once he's out of sight and earshot of the building, arrest him for the parole violation. Associating with other felons."

The officer, again in plain-clothes today, began to exit the car before I'd finished speaking. I grabbed her shoulder. "Explore the idea with him that it was a twelve-step meeting, but don't plant any seeds."

She nodded, climbed out and took off at a trot, on an angle to intercept the guy.

I called Bradley. "We got that search warrant yet?"

"Yup. You need me there."

I thought for a half-beat. Bradley no doubt had better things to do. "Four of us and the K-9 unit, I think we can handle it. You can send a uniform with the warrant."

"You got it, Chief."

Armstrong's radio crackled. A female voice spoke for several seconds, but I couldn't make out the words. "Got it," he said into the radio.

Over his shoulder, he reported, "Peters says the guy was kicked out because he couldn't pay for a full session. He was trying to negotiate for a shorter session, but no dice. When she asked what kind of session, he clammed up. She started out asking what kind of meeting was going on in the warehouse. He just gave her a confused look."

I snorted. "Okay, I'm saying that we ruled out a twelve-step meeting, as the judge requested." It wasn't definitive, but I was willing to take the chance.

The next fifteen minutes involved one of the more tedious parts of police work—staring at a building you are surveilling. Officer Terry had checked in to tell us they had arrived in the industrial park. He and King were behind the next building over.

I instructed him to hold his position for now, and we went back to watching the warehouse.

I jolted when the passenger door opened. Peters climbed into the front seat.

I put my hand over my pounding heart. I must've been drifting off to be that startled.

Peters handed me a piece of paper over the back of the seat. "Search warrant. I exchanged my prisoner for it." A broad grin lit up her face. "Thompson's taking him back to book him."

I nodded, my chest warming a bit at the thought of Officer Thompson. We'd come too close to losing him last spring when a perp gave him a bad concussion with a gun butt. It wasn't bad enough to be fatal, but the doctors were worried for a while that he would have brain damage.

He didn't. And Armstrong, who was in charge of supervising the rookies, pointed out that Thompson's skull was way too thick for that. He and Thompson had laughed at the time, but I had only managed a fake chuckle.

Now, I smiled at the memory.

The department I had inherited had been riddled with corruption and discord. John Black had encouraged the latter by favoring some officers and giving others an unnecessary hard time. But I was well on the way to clearing out the last of the corruption. And the department was becoming more cohesive every day.

Another boring forty minutes had ticked by before the warehouse's side door opened again. Two men came out, one of them the other gray tee-shirt wearer.

"Go get 'em, you two," I said.

Armstrong and Peters slid out of the car and took off to intercept them.

Now there were only the women, "our pervert," and the warehouse owner in there.

"We going in now?" Barnes asked.

"Yeah, I think it's time." I picked my phone up off my lap and called Terry. "I'll take the front and Barnes will take the back, in case anyone tries going out a window or out through the loading dock door. You and King take the side door."

"Is it unlocked?"

"Unlikely, but we have a search warrant. I don't really want to give them much warning, though." I believed it was a long shot that Ashley was in that warehouse, but if she was, I didn't want anything happening to her.

But I wasn't convinced that one of these perverts didn't have her stashed wherever they were staying. I didn't want any of them slipping past us.

"I've got a crowbar in my car," Terry offered.

"Get it. One knock, give them twenty seconds, then get that door open."

Despite the bulk of her Kevlar vest, my assistant was out of the car in a flash. She took off, staying low, and heading around the building to the back.

I climbed out of the car, dumped my jacket on the seat and struggled into my own vest.

My heart rate kicked up several notches as adrenaline zinged through my system. I jogged down to a pile of old wooden crates about twenty feet from the front of the building. They provided some cover for keeping out of sight, but wouldn't be much help in a gunfight.

I was far enough back to see around the corner to the side door. Armstrong had arrived to help Terry, no doubt having left Peters with the task of taking the other two culprits into the station.

The sound of the officers knocking was faint, but a few beats later, I heard the distinct screech of the door being forced open. I leaned out a little and saw the wooden side door hanging on an angle from its hinges.

Armstrong was behind the door.

"King, guns. *Such*," Terry yelled, from the other side of the door's opening. The command sounded like *zoo*. I assumed it was German for *search*.

A few seconds went by, and a sharp bark emanated from inside the warehouse.

"*Fass*," Terry yelled.

I knew that command from watching them train a couple of times. *Attack.*

"Someone's armed in there, Chief," Armstrong yelled, stating the obvious. Then he and Terry bolted into the building.

Glock in hand and staying low, I scrambled across the space to the corner of the building. There I could see the front if anyone tried to escape that way.

And a dirty window near the corner gave me a view of most of the scene inside. In the middle of the floor, stood the owner of the building. King had the guy's arm in his teeth. A pistol dangled from the man's hand and he was struggling to get loose and/or turn it to fire at the dog.

"*Hält*," Terry yelled. Another one I knew, *Hold*.

The man screamed as the dog clamped down. The gun fell from his now limp hand, clattering on the cement floor. Armstrong scooped it up.

Peter Richards came out of a side room. His zipper was undone but thank goodness his junk wasn't hanging out. He froze, mouth slack. Then he shot toward the side door.

I stepped into the opening and raised my gun. "Nope, you're not going anywhere."

He scrambled to a stop, eyes wide in his pale face. Half a beat and he raised his hands in the air. I stepped inside and he backed up.

"*Aus.*" The dog let go of the warehouse owner's arm, and Terry and Armstrong wrestled him to the floor.

Barnes came in the door behind me, her hand clasped firmly around the upper arm of the Latina woman, whose clothes were grubby, probably from climbing out of one of the filthy windows. The other woman was standing against a wall near the far end of the large room, her hands in the air.

Armstrong was cuffing the warehouse owner—ignoring the blood that seeped from teeth marks on his forearm—while Terry kept a knee on the man's shoulder. But the dog had apparently taken the fight out of the guy.

The two officers stood, and Armstrong dragged him to his feet.

"*Komm, sitz.*" King immediately trotted over and sat beside Terry. He clicked on the big dog's leash, then gave him a treat from his pocket.

Meanwhile, I was taking deep breaths, trying to quiet my racing heart, and also trying to hide a grin.

My guilty secret was that I lived for these adrenaline-laced moments.

Bradley and Cruthers were interviewing "the perverts." I'd given up on getting my people to call them something else and had settled for an admonishment that they not call them that when their lawyers were in earshot.

And Collins and Wellbourne had gone to get search warrants signed so they could begin searching their residences, some of which were rooms in cheap motels.

The detectives weren't getting much out of these people. Some even tried to refuse to give their addresses. But their lawyers—most of them from the public defender's office—informed their clients that this information was not considered private when it came to the police. We already had parole violations to hold over the heads of some of them—failure to register new addresses and associating with known felons.

And once Derek was finished digging through the laptops we'd confiscated from the warehouse owner, we'd have plenty of other charges too.

Cruthers stepped out of the interview room, and I exited the observation area next door.

"I don't think we're gonna get much cooperation here," the detective said.

Bradley came out of the other interview room and joined us. He was looking almost as rumpled as Cruthers. He simply shook his head, a frustrated frown on his face.

"Call the ADA," I said to him, "and tell her what we've got. Ask her if we can offer a deal to the first one who flips on the rest and tells us what was going on in that warehouse."

He nodded. I left him to it and headed back to my office.

Halfway there, my phone rang, and *Skip Canfield* came up on the screen.

I picked up speed, power walking past Barnes at her desk and ignoring her curious look.

With my door closed, I answered the call.

"Hey Judith. How's it going?"

"Could be better," I said.

"Still haven't found the child?"

"No. What have you got?" It came out sharper than I'd intended. "Sorry, my frustration isn't with you," I added.

"I know. Okay, here's what our young lady had to say. All she'd been told initially by her adoptive parents—and then only when she was older and she pushed them for info—was that she'd been brought as a baby to a major hospital in Des Moines. Like every state, Iowa has a safe haven law, so once the baby was examined and was declared healthy, the guy who brought her in was allowed to leave without giving any info. Our gal—her name's Joy Harrington, by the way—she did some digging and found a retired nurse, who was there at the hospital when she was brought in. The nurse said the guy was a big black man with a beard. She thought he was in his forties, and he was wearing a business suit that looked expensive to her. At the time, she wondered if maybe he was a lawyer."

A short pause. "I'm thinking, though," Canfield added, "that he might've been a pimp."

My gut twisted. "Why do you say that?"

"Well, we're pretty sure that Meredith is still alive," he said. "And at the time that Joy was born she would've been twenty. I mean, it's certainly possible that her abductor just cut her loose when she reached a certain age."

I swallowed hard. Canfield was being careful how he phrased things, but he was assuming my cousin had been abducted by a sexual predator. It was the most likely scenario...I knew that, but...

"And it could've been a case of her getting pregnant by a boyfriend, or a husband even, and she couldn't take care of the child. But then we would expect either a young woman—Meredith herself—or a young man around her age to bring the baby in. But an older, well-dressed man, well..." he trailed off.

My cop brain finally cut through the emotions and kicked into gear. "You're thinking she was still under the control of a pimp and was being trafficked."

"Yes. Either by the original abductor, or he sold her to somebody."

"Or he cut her loose, and a pimp stepped into the void and took over controlling her."

"Or, if this guy was a lawyer," Canfield said, "he might've been the pimp's lawyer."

"What do you want to do?" I asked.

"Stay here for at least another day, maybe more. I'd like to talk to that nurse myself and try to find some local detective who was on the force back then. I'm gonna send you a photo of Joy. Can you take a look?"

My phone pinged. I clicked over to the text, and my mouth fell open.

My Aunt Jean was staring up at me. Not as she was today, a woman in her eighties, but the way she looked as a young woman, when I was that six-year-old kid.

CHAPTER TWENTY-ONE

A commotion out in the bullpen brought me out of my reverie. I'd been staring into space ever since I'd disconnected from the call with Skip Canfield, after giving him permission to take as long as he needed in Iowa to find out what he could.

It was now mid-evening and no one was around. Some folks, like the department's clerk, had gone home. And I'd sent Barnes home to get some rest. But most of our people were out searching for Ashley, or any clues as to where she might be.

By now, the detectives would be finishing up searching the homes of the people we'd arrested at the warehouse. Was this one or more of them coming back?

Hands on my desk, I shoved myself to a stand and walked over to open my door.

Sam stood on the other side of it, his fist in the air, about to knock. A young black man sat at a desk, arms cuffed behind him, head hanging down.

"He's our dumpster diver," Sam said. "I brought him here, rather than my jail."

Unfortunately, John Black's corruption had extended to the Clover County jail, which served both the county and city, but was under the county sheriff's supervision. Last winter, we'd discovered that some of the jail's staff were on the take when a witness against Black, who'd taken a plea deal on a corruption charge himself, was attacked right under a guard's nose. Sam still wasn't sure he'd rooted out all the bad apples there.

"But," he frowned, "I discovered that you've got all your holding cells occupied."

"And then some. We've got them stacked three and four deep in there." I gave him a brief summary of the warehouse raid.

"You gonna be keeping all your guests overnight?" he asked when I'd finished.

"Probably not." I looked at his prisoner. He was a kid really, no older than late teens, if that. "I can't put him in the same cell with any of them though. He wouldn't be safe. And no interview rooms either," I added, "but you can use the small conference room."

"Is the table bolted down in there?" he asked with a grin.

"Yeah." I gave him a small smile back. Last fall, during another case with multiple suspects, we'd been using the conference rooms as additional interview rooms. A suspect, despite being cuffed to a chair, managed to flip the big wooden table over on Sam's foot. No long-term injury, but he'd limped for a few days.

"Okay," Sam said, "I'll take him in there."

I opened my mouth to suggest I sit in on the interview, but then thought better of it. The kid might be more forthcoming with a man.

I woke with a crick in my neck and drool on my desk. My watch said it was four minutes to midnight. Absolute silence out in the bullpen.

I stood, intending to go check in with the night watch commander, when I saw a note stuck under the edge of my computer's keyboard.

It was folded over once and it was from Sam.

Kid doesn't know who hired him. Just some "white dude." I'm taking him out to the sheriff's department and will babysit him there. Tomorrow he's taking the pizza box to the guy, and I'll be following him. Watch your back, Chief.

"You watch yours, Sheriff," I whispered. It was a little ritual we'd developed, when we were working tricky cases. It could be said in front of others which made it preferable to "I love you." And it was more respectful than "Be careful," which implied that the other couldn't handle themselves. But it served as a reminder that someone cared, and we should each make sure that we came home in one piece.

Suddenly, my throat closed and my eyes stung. I ground my teeth. Why was I getting all emotional?

Cut yourself some slack. My friend Kate's voice in my head.

My shoulders sagged. It *had* been a very long day...and a very emotional one.

I gathered up jacket, laptop case and Glock and trudged across the bullpen. Time to go home to my cat.

———

Sunlight sliced between my bedroom curtains and danced across my face, waking me from a sound sleep. I yawned and stretched.

Pipsqueak, curled at my feet, followed suit, stretching out her white furry limbs at both ends of her lean body and opening her mouth wide to expose a pink tongue and tiny sharp teeth.

Had I really slept through the night without dreaming? Had exhaustion trumped nightmares for once?

Then it hit me, like a fist to my solar plexus. I gasped. *Ashley!* The child whose abduction had most recently triggered the nightmares.

For a few blessed seconds of early-morning mental fog, I'd forgotten about the poor kid.

This was Day Three. I shuddered.

I glanced at my alarm clock, which I rarely needed and apparently had forgotten to set last night. I generally woke on my own by no later than six. The clock said seven-ten.

Ashley was taken at eight-fifteen Saturday evening. We were thirteen hours from the end of the crucial first seventy-two hours.

They were considered crucial for some very good reasons. During those three days, the witnesses' memories were the clearest, the evidence was more easily found and less likely to be contaminated, and the leads were easier to develop.

And sure enough at sixty hours in, as predicted, the leads were drying up. The odds of finding little Ashley alive were diminishing rapidly.

I threw back the covers and practically ran for the bathroom. No morning exercises for me today.

Fifteen minutes later, I was showered, dressed and in my car, pointing it toward the municipal building. My phone rang. *Bert* popped up on my dashboard screen.

"Hey Chief," he said when I'd answered. "I tried your office but nobody picked up."

Nobody? Where's Barnes?

"I'm afraid I have some, uh, awkward news," Bert continued. "It's some fingerprints I found on that lawyer's file cabinet and on some of the file folders themselves. No hits initially from the criminal databases, but when I dug further..."

A beat of silence. "So," I said, "don't keep me in suspense." *I'm not in the mood*, I added inside my head.

"Um, they belong to Mayor Hayes."

Say what? I managed to keep that response internal as well. Out loud, I said, "Thanks, Bert." I disconnected and mulled over the implications.

Why would Mark Hayes be touching the lawyer's file cabinet, and some of his confidential files as well? Files that, even in her grief, Jan Campbell was quick to point out should not be opened. The forensic folks had only dusted the outside of them for prints.

I couldn't think of a good explanation. Only a bad one came to mind, that Hayes was the one in the dead lawyer's office rooting through his file cabinet.

But did he kill Campbell? I absolutely could not see mild-mannered Mark Hayes killing anyone, especially not his own lawyer. He knew the secret regarding his son's parentage would be safe. The lawyer had to keep it confidential.

But Campbell wasn't perfect in that department. He'd given in pretty easily and talked about several things he probably shouldn't have, including discussing his concerns about Silva being from Brazil.

Then again, he'd been talking about his own speculations in that instance, not anything Silva had told him.

Shaking my head in confusion, I instructed my Bluetooth to call Barnes.

"Chief," she answered on the first ring, sounding a bit out of breath, "I was about to call *you*. My car just died. I stopped to get donuts and when I came back out, the damn thing wouldn't start."

"Why did you get donuts?" I asked. Normally the detectives took turns doing the morning donut run. But all that had gone by the wayside the last few days, since none of us were keeping regular hours.

"I, uh, figured it would be a nice gesture."

I shook my head slightly. She was bound and determined to step into the detective role in whatever way she could.

"Don't worry," she said. "I'll call an Uber and be in soon."

"Don't bother." I flipped on my left turn signal as I approached the next intersection. "I'm in my car. I'll backtrack and get you."

She spluttered a little and thanked me. I made a U-turn and headed down the block toward the only bakery in downtown Starling.

No Barnes in sight as I pulled into the only available space in front of the bakery—a bus stop. I waited impatiently for a couple of minutes, then started reaching blindly under my seat for my *Chief of Police* sign. Feeling around, I couldn't find it, and my light bubble had somehow been shoved forward, where the sign usually rested.

I glanced at the top of my dashboard and realized I'd never taken the sign down the last time I'd used it.

My hand was on my door handle when Barnes exited the bakery, a big pink box in her hands.

I leaned over and pulled on the passenger door's handle—one of the advantages of a compact car, almost everything is within reach of the driver's seat. I shoved the door open. "Get in," I snapped.

"Sorry," she said, sticking her head partway into the opening. "The bear claws were calling to me. I went back for a few of them. Let me put these in the back."

Her head disappeared, followed by the back passenger door opening. She leaned in.

A half beat of nothing happening. "So, get in already," I said as I shifted around some to look over my shoulder.

Her face stark white, she'd frozen in the act of putting the pink box on the backseat. "Chief," her voice shook, "undo your seatbelt, gently."

"What? Why?"

"There's a bomb under your seat."

CHAPTER TWENTY-TWO

My heart raced even as my mind was still processing my assistant's words. My fingers fumbled with the seatbelt latch. It clicked open.

Barnes's face had disappeared from the back. It reappeared in the opening of the front passenger door. She grabbed my arm and yanked, dragging me across the console and the passenger seat and out the door.

We staggered a few steps, clinging to each other for balance. Then she planted her feet firmly, grabbed my upper arms and stood me up straight.

"You okay?"

Intense pain shot from my shoulder up the side of my neck. I wanted to scream but I ground my teeth. "Yeah," I managed to get out.

She let go, turned away from me and started shooing people away from the cars. They weren't paying her much attention, just moving a few feet toward the buildings and continuing along their way.

"Move, people," I shouted. "There's a bomb in that car!"

The pedestrians scattered, horror on their faces.

I ran into the bakery. "Everyone, get down!" People stared, open-mouthed.

Jeez Louise. "Bomb!" I yelled. They dove for cover.

It crossed my mind that this would be quite embarrassing if Barnes turned out to be wrong. I pivoted, planning to go next door to the nail salon.

Instead, I froze as I watched my car morph into a ball of fire.

———————— ·◆· ————————

Ears still ringing, I stood on the blackened sidewalk, surveying the damage. My car was a grey and black shell, smoke drifting upward from it. The car in front and the one in back of the bus stop were both semi-obliterated as well. I recognized the pale blue back fender of the car behind—the paint was blistered.

It was Barnes's car. *Well, at least she won't have to worry about getting it fixed.*

And she was okay. She'd ran past me a few minutes ago, yelling over her shoulder that she was going to check the businesses farther down the block.

My insides twisted again at the thought of that terrible moment when I'd believed she was dead.

But surprisingly, there had only been one serious injury. The receptionist at the nail salon had suffered a major concussion, and she had cuts, most of them tiny but a few more serious, all over her face and arms, from the shattered plate-glass window that had fronted the shop.

The paramedics were working on her. One had told me she would probably be fine.

I didn't care for that word *probably*.

Someone touched my shoulder. I winced and jerked away.

"You okay?" It was Sam, his face twisted with worry.

I could barely make out his words. Had the explosion damaged my eardrums?

"What happened to your shoulder?" he asked, his voice sounding distant and wobbly, like we were underwater. "Did something hit you?"

"No. It's from Barnes yanking me out of the car. I think she dislocated my shoulder."

Movement in my peripheral vision and I jumped. A gurney rolled past, the receptionist strapped down for her ride to the hospital. The two paramedics were on either end of it.

It bothered me that I hadn't heard them coming.

They loaded the gurney into the back of their ambulance, parked in the middle of the road about a hundred feet from the blast zone. Then the paramedic I'd talked to earlier slapped his partner on the shoulder and walked toward us. The partner went to the driver's door, and a few seconds later, the ambulance pulled away, lights and sirens going. Although the latter sounded like whimpy little wails to me.

The paramedic arrived at my side and gently took my right forearm. I bit my lip, suppressing a scream as pain shot from my shoulder to my brain.

"I think it's dislocated," I pushed past gritted teeth. I'd been cradling my arm in the other hand, and as long as I'd kept it perfectly still it only ached some. And tingled, like it was going numb.

The paramedic had stopped moving it, but it still hurt where he was touching the shoulder itself. "It's not hurting right now?" he asked, raising his voice.

"Only where you're touching it."

He shifted his feet and pain shot through me again, my knees threatening to buckle. "Please, let go."

He did and I went back to cradling it in the other hand.

He came in close and examined my face, moving his head around to cover every inch. "Some dirt, but no cuts."

My cheeks heated, as if it were somehow shameful to be cut-free when others weren't. "I, uh, was on the floor, my arms covering my neck and ears." I mimicked that pose with my good arm, but winced even at that small movement.

What amazed me was that there'd only been a nanosecond for me to react, before the blast wave reached me. I didn't remember diving to the floor but I must have.

The paramedic pulled some instrument out of his breast pocket and poked it into my ear. "It looks like your eardrums are intact."

"I'm not hearing too well."

"Ringing and it sounds like everybody's under water?"

"Yes."

"That'll pass. Let's get you into this. It will help a lot with your arm." He held up a piece of white cloth.

"What is it?"

"A sling."

"Can't you pop my shoulder back into its socket."

"No, because it's not a total dislocation. If it were you'd be in nonstop intense pain. It's a subluxation, a partial dislocation."

I've had root canals that were more fun than struggling to get my arm into that sling. But once it was there, it did feel better, as long as I moved carefully.

"You really need to go to the hospital and get a doc to take care of that," the paramedic said, once our short wrestling match was over.

"I'll go later."

The paramedic glanced at Sam, who rolled his eyes. "I'll get her there, somehow."

The paramedic gave him a look that said *good luck with that*, and he turned away.

"Thanks," I called after him.

Barnes popped up next to me. I startled, but at least she was on the side of my good arm.

"What'd you see?" I asked. "How'd you know there was a bomb?"

"I just finished telling all this to the bomb squad."

I gave her a hard stare.

"I didn't think that would get me out of going over it again." She let out a small sigh. "There was something, some kind of black box, tucked partway under your seat, and it had lit-up red numbers on it, counting down. It said 2:48 and then 2:47, and I realized what it was." She paused, sucked in air. "The bomb squad's going to extract the remnants of the bomb from the car, before it's towed to our yard. They'll take the bomb to the FDLE lab, once they've made sure it's stable."

It registered that her uniform was filthy, and half her hair had fallen out of its bun. "Where's your hat? Are you hurt?"

"Lost it somewhere, and no, I'm fine. My ears have even stopped ringing. I was inside the dry cleaners on the other side of the bakery. The couple who owns it barely speak English, so I just grabbed them by their shoulders and pushed them to the floor, then I lost my balance and fell on top of them."

"You're getting good," Sam said, a half smile on his face, "at shoving people around by their shoulders."

Barnes turned back to me, her eyes taking in the sling. They went wide. "I'm so sorry, Chief..."

I held up my good hand. "It's fine. Your quick thinking saved my life, and some other people's as well."

Her face blanched, not the reaction I'd expected. "What if my car hadn't broken down? What if I hadn't decided to get donuts?"

I began to shake my head, about to tell her to not go there.

But Sam jumped in. "The car would've blown up around the time you got to the municipal building's lot."

I felt the blood drain from my own face. "They were hoping to take out more than just me."

Sam nodded grimly. "Some other cops perhaps, or city workers, or maybe they'd get lucky and get the mayor."

I swallowed hard as I realized that I'd almost gotten out of the car to go find Barnes. If I'd done that, we probably would've been on the sidewalk, me chewing her out, when the bomb went off. Or maybe opening the doors to get in.

There would've been little or no warning, and lots of people would've been injured, or worse.

And Barnes and I would be dead.

A shudder ran through my body.

"So, what brought you to town this morning?" I asked Sam. "Surely you didn't hear the blast all the way out in Clover County."

We were sitting in the ER of Starling-Shands Hospital, waiting for a doctor to take a look at my shoulder.

I had tried to resist, but Barnes and Sam had ganged up on me. The best argument, the one that finally swayed me, came from Sam. "It's your right arm. What if you can't fire a gun anymore, because it didn't heal properly?"

So here we sat, while my people were processing the scene and looking for leads to yet another case.

I ground my teeth.

Sam had been watching my face, a slightly bemused expression on his own. Apparently I wasn't masking my impatience all that well.

He finally answered my question. "That young man I caught last night, I had him call his contact and set up a meet. Then I put him safely back in a holding cell, with a personal guard I know I can trust, and I took the meet instead. I left the pizza box on the bench in Holly Park, as he'd been instructed to do."

He paused, shook his head. "But it was another kid who picked it up, on a skateboard. I followed him, but he got away from me when he darted across a street between moving cars. I had to stop and wait for the traffic to clear. By then, he was long gone."

"You sure he didn't think it was a real pizza, and he was hungry?" I'd tried for a light tone in my voice but wasn't totally successful.

Sam offered a small grin as a reward for my efforts. "Nah, he kept looking back over his shoulder. He was plenty nervous. I'm pretty sure he was the gang's courier."

"Okay, so we know who was dumpster diving, but we can't definitively connect them to the gang."

"Not yet. But I called Dot Wilder and told her the whole story. She's going to contact the mayor and the governor and tell them she considers you cleared of any connection to all this. It's clearly some kind of set-up."

A couple of the knots in my stomach unwound. I hadn't even realized how tense I was getting as we talked.

A nurse approached. "Chief, we have an exam room ready now."

I stood. "And does that mean you have a doctor to go with the room?"

She smiled. "Soon. We know you've got things to do, but we had to triage the folks who were hurt in the bombing first."

"I know. Sorry," I said, feeling chagrined.

"No need to apologize. We need you to catch whoever did this." She stopped at an open doorway and made an after-you gesture.

"Oh, don't worry," I said, as I walked past her, "I will."

"*We* will," Sam said and followed me into the room.

At 3MB, I tossed the prescription the doc had given me for painkillers and the referral for physical therapy into my top desk drawer.

Sam looked on, frowning. "He told you if you didn't do the physical therapy, and rest that shoulder as much as possible, you could end up needing surgery."

"Yes, I was there. I heard him."

Sam shook his head and sat down in the visitor's chair.

I went into my small bathroom and washed my face one-handed. Then I stared at the fresh clothes on their hangers behind the door.

This week has been hard on my wardrobe. And it was only Tuesday morning.

It felt like way too much effort to change, and I wasn't at all sure how I'd even get my current sleeveless blouse off, without further damaging my shoulder.

I settled for brushing off the smudges of dirt and soot as best I could. Then I grabbed the fresh jacket—the one I'd left my apartment with this morning had been lying on my backseat. Now it was ashes. I went out to my desk and draped the jacket on my chair back.

As I lowered myself carefully into that chair, Cruthers stuck his head in my door. "You okay, Chief?"

"Yes, I'm fine."

He lingered.

"Go!" I waved my good hand in the air. "Do something constructive."

Collins's head replaced his. "Chief, you al–?"

"I'm fine," I cut him off and waved my hand again.

Bradley appeared next.

"Grr, I'm fine!" I practically yelled.

"Good to know," Bradley said, his tone easygoing. "What the hell happened?"

I waved him in. "Close the door."

He did so and perched on the edge of one of the uncomfortable chairs. I gave him a short synopsis of my harrowing morning.

When I'd finished, Sam leaned forward. "I just thought of something. How did the gang know so quickly that their efforts to discredit you with the cat toy and wine bottle hadn't completely worked?"

Bradley looked from him to me, confusion on his face.

"It's a long story," I said. "And not anything you could've done anything about. The FDLE was already investigating it."

"But whatever it is," Bradley said, sounding a bit annoyed, "it's somehow related to someone trying to blow you up. So *now* I'd say that maybe I should be told what's going on."

I sighed and gave him yet another synopsis of the new mess created by John Black and the gang that he was possibly involved with.

Then I shifted the focus back to Ashley, where it needed to be. "What have you got for me this morning?"

"Nothing useful from the warehouse raid yet," Bradley said. "At least, not helpful to finding the child. We've got a pretty solid case against the owner for possession of child pornography. Several of the perverts are behind bars already, due to parole violations, and awaiting new charges. A couple others, who weren't on parole and had no prior convictions, did get bail, sadly."

"Grrr," Sam said under his breath.

"Yeah," Bradley agreed. "Wish we had the manpower to put them under surveillance."

"Nobody flipped on the warehouse owner?" I asked.

Bradley shook his head. "I put the ADA's offer out there. Not sure it's enough to tempt them though. She's only offering shorter sentences, no immunity for possession of child porn."

I frowned. "Can't say that I blame her. These creeps don't deserve a break. Anything from the searches of their residences?"

"Not really. No signs that any of them had anything to do with Ashley's disappearance."

"Other than those strange long-sleeved gray tee shirts."

"One of them claimed he gets cold easy in air-conditioned buildings in the summertime. The other had prison tattoos on his arms, which I don't think he got willingly."

"What are they?"

"The word *pervert* on the outside of each arm."

I winced, trying not to imagine what the man had encountered in prison. Convicts were not kind to child abusers, but I had trouble feeling too sorry for them. "Why hasn't he gotten them removed?"

"I asked that. He said no money. He can't get a job with his record. Bert and Ernie are going to go over some of their residences again, searching for trace evidence and DNA, but I honestly don't think any of these clowns took Ashley."

Bradley shook his head slowly. "And the hotline has been humming with crazies, but only a few semi-credible leads. They haven't panned out though."

"Such as?" I asked.

"The most credible one was from a man who said he saw an older woman dragging a child that matched Ashley's description across one of the public parking lots near the riverwalk. The child was screaming and fighting her. This was shortly after Ashley was taken and we'd stopped the boat parade."

I sat up straighter in my chair.

"But," Bradley let out a short chuckle, "turns out the woman *is* the child's grandmother. Collins tracked her down and he also interviewed the child's mother and met the kid. He said the little girl did match Ashley's description, blue-eyed and blonde. But the mother verified that her mom had permission to take the toddler to the parade, and she's prone to temper tantrums when she has to leave someplace where she's having fun."

I blew out air. "Okay, I–" A soft knock on my door.

I nodded to Bradley and he jumped up and opened the door.

SAC Dennis Trager was on the other side. "I hope you don't mind, Chief. I took the liberty of rerouting the bomb remnants and your car to the nearest FBI lab. They're already working on them."

"Uh, sure. That's fine."

"We should have some preliminary results for you in a few hours."

"But the bombing probably isn't related to Ashley's case," I blurted out.

He gave me a small smile. "No way of knowing that until the lab examines everything, now is there?" He turned and walked away.

Bradley chuckled. "Sure doesn't hurt to have an FBI agent or two stashed in the back room."

I'd waited for Bradley to leave my office before I asked Sam, "Does this mean we have a mole somewhere?"

Looking grim, Sam nodded. "Most likely. How else would they know so soon that their efforts to discredit you weren't working?"

We tried to hash out who it might be, but came up blank. "It doesn't even have to be someone in our departments," Sam said. "It could be someone at the FDLE."

I sighed. "Maybe the lab results will give us a thread to pull on."

Sam sighed as well and stood. "I'm gonna go to the deli and get us some egg sandwiches, okay?"

"Sounds good." My tone was lackluster.

I heard Sam say hi to Barnes as he left, then she appeared in my open doorway. She'd donned a fresh uniform—she kept one stashed in her locker—and straightened her bun.

"How ya doing, Chief?"

"I'm fine," I was trying hard not to snap at her, but I was getting super tired of being asked that. However, it's not nice to be cranky with the person who just saved your life.

A commotion behind her had Barnes turning around. "Mrs. Campbell?" she said.

I stood and followed Barnes out of my office.

The lawyer's widow stood next to Barnes's desk, holding a white file box. A uniformed officer behind her had two more boxes stacked in his arms.

He grimaced from the weight, and Barnes gestured for him to put them on her desk. He did so, with considerable relief on his face. I nodded my thanks and he turned away.

"I did what you asked, Chief," Jan Campbell said, as she deposited her own box next to the others. "I thought about it. And I decided the *hell* with ethics." Her tone was sharp, angry. "They can't disbar *me*. I'm not a lawyer. These are my husband's current and most recent clients, plus those others you asked about."

Bradley walked over, his eyebrows in the air again.

"Would you like to come into my office?" I asked Mrs. Campbell.

She shook her head. "I have a hundred things to do, between the practice and...other arrangements. Herb mostly did private adoptions, but you can't make a living off of that. So he did other related work, usually with the same families he'd arranged adoptions for at one time. Trusts and wills, uncontested divorces. He wasn't willing to go to court and get into the nasty stuff, though. I'm not sure if these will help, but..." She tapped the box she'd been carrying. "Current files and those special cases. And those are from the last ten years." She pointed to the other boxes.

"Let me know if you need more or I can do anything else to help." She turned and headed back across the bullpen.

"I take it that was the lawyer's widow," Bradley said.

I nodded. Then I raised my own eyebrows in a question and gave his sister a pointed look. She had her head down, examining the outside of the boxes.

He nodded once, an almost imperceptible up and down of his head.

"Why don't you go through them, Gloria," I said. "See what you can find that might be useful."

Barnes looked up, her eyes wide. She began to grin but caught herself. Then she actually rubbed her hands together. "I'll start on them right now."

We'll see how long that *enthusiasm lasts.*

Bradley gave me a knowing look. I suspected he was thinking something similar.

"Wait," I said, and took the lid off the nearest box. I awkwardly rummaged through it one-handed but didn't find what I was searching for.

Bradley took a step forward. "Here, I'll help. What–?"

I shook my head and opened another box. Halfway through that one, I saw the tab, *Mark Hayes*.

I pulled that file out. "Now you can go through them," I said to Barnes and turned toward my office.

I closed my door and picked up my desk phone. "Carol," I said to the mayor's assistant when she answered, "I need to see him. Right away."

CHAPTER
TWENTY-THREE

Mark Hayes spluttered, "I have no idea what you're talking about."

Unable to think of a diplomatic way to introduce the issue, I'd just blurted out the question. And I'd remained standing, a signal that this was not a friendly visit.

I'd wanted to throw him off balance, but a part of me felt bad for him. We'd trusted each other, become a well-oiled team, running the city and keeping it safe.

I should know better than to trust a politician.

Hayes had risen to his feet as well, was standing behind his desk. Now he sighed, raised his gaze to the ceiling for a beat, then gestured again for me to take a seat in one of the leather armchairs in front of his desk.

I waited until he'd slumped into his own chair before I sat, perching on the edge of the seat.

Hayes stared into space for another beat, then cleared his throat. "I may know how it happened."

I leaned forward a bit but said nothing.

"I was there for a meeting, in Herb's office. He was carrying some files from his desk over to the cabinet, and he tripped. He caught himself, didn't fall, but everything in his hands went flying. I stooped down and helped him gather up the papers and file folders. He said to put them on top of the file cabinet and he'd have Jannie sort them out later, after our meeting."

It was a plausible story, and Hayes told it well.

"Convenient that the only one who can confirm it is dead."

"Well, I didn't make it up," Hayes snapped.

Oops, I hadn't meant to say that out loud. Despite getting a fairly decent night's sleep, I felt exhausted.

I guess almost getting blown up saps your energy.

But I wasn't ready to cut Hayes too much slack yet. "Please forgive my skepticism, Mr. Mayor." My tone was crisp. "Occupational hazard."

He shrugged, but his expression looked a little hurt. "If you don't know by now that I'm an honest man..."

"Oh, I do know that. But you've been hiding a whopping secret all these years. Even honest men will tell fibs to protect those they love."

He said nothing, just stared off in space.

My limbs felt heavy as I pushed myself to a stand with my good hand. "Thank you for your time, Mr. Mayor."

In the elevator, I began to shake. By the time the bell dinged for the third floor, I wasn't sure I could walk.

What's going on? Was there something physically wrong with me, some injury from the explosion that had gone undetected?

Surely this wasn't a reaction to confronting the mayor, who was my boss and could fire me. But I knew he wouldn't. He was too honorable to do that. Still, the last few minutes had not been fun.

Somehow I managed to get past the reception area without falling on my face—the clerk was away from her desk and the watch sergeant was on the phone. And then through the bullpen. It was mostly deserted. Everyone was out in the field, working the three major cases we now had on our plates.

My office door was open. I thought I'd locked it. And where was Barnes? The file boxes sat, unopened, on her desk.

I stopped in the doorway, trembling.

Sam sat in my visitor's chair, an egg sandwich unwrapped in front of him. "Hey, Judith. Barnes is in the... You okay?"

The scent of bacon had hit me, making my stomach roil. I clamped a hand over my mouth and stumbled into the room.

Sam was out of his chair, holding me up by my left arm, and closing the door behind me. "What's wrong?"

I collapsed against him. He wrapped his arms around me, loosening the circle when I winced.

"I...I don't know," I said, my voice sounding shaky in my own ears.

Sam led me to his chair and sat me down, then knelt in front of me. He swiped a finger across my cheek. "You're crying."

"I am not!"

"Okay, your eyes are leaking. What's going on?"

I shook my head, and wished I hadn't. A throbbing pain had invaded my right temple and was migrating across my scalp. "I don't know what's going on," I wailed.

An image flashed across my brain, an orange ball of fire. "Maybe I've got a head injury."

"Do you want to go back to the hospital? The ER doc looked you over pretty good. He said you were only mildly concussed, that diving to the ground and covering your head like that was exactly the right thing to do."

"But I don't remember doing that."

"It was instinctive, I guess," Sam said.

Another flash of memory—turning away, my knees giving out, the pain in my chest so intense it was almost unbearable.

My face heated. The turning away was probably instinctive, and covering the back of my head with my arms, maybe. But...

"I didn't dive to the floor," I said. "I fell. I collapsed. I might've even fainted for a few seconds."

"Dove or fell," Sam said, "not sure it matters." Somewhere along the way, he'd taken my left hand between his two. The gentle pressure had stopped the trembling.

"Either way, it was a good thing you were down low, or you could've been killed."

My heart squeezed in my chest and it was suddenly hard to breathe. "I thought Barnes was dead," I whispered, "and that I was going to die too."

I shook my head. The throbbing intensified. I ignored it. "I mean, I didn't have time to think all that in words. It was just this gut feeling, that she was gone and..."

I ground my teeth. "I was being a wimp, worrying about all that when I should've been getting more people to safety."

"You got plenty of people to safety."

"Not that girl in the nail salon," I protested.

"Yeah, right," Sam scoffed. "In the nanosecond between seeing the explosion and feeling the blast, you could've run next door and thrown her to the floor. Besides," he let go of my hand and used his thumbs to swipe under my eyes again, "Barnes got a call while you were upstairs. From the hospital. The young woman is still listed as serious, but she's stable."

He stood, his knees making creaky noises, and sat beside me in one of the uncomfortable chairs. "As for you being a wimp, nothing could be farther from the truth. You're the bravest, strongest woman I've ever known. And, between the female cops and the criminals I've crossed paths with, I've known some pretty tough women in my life."

A tentative tapping on my door.

I turned my face toward Sam. "Do I look okay?"

He nodded.

"Come in," I called out.

Barnes stuck her head in. "There are some people out at the watch desk who want to see you, Chief."

I stood, slowly. The arm in a sling was throwing me slightly off balance, and my legs were still a bit shaky. "Where were you a few minutes ago?"

"Ladies' room," she said, falling into step beside me as I crossed the bullpen. She had a funny look on her face, like she was trying to hide a smirk.

"Well, you shouldn't have left those file boxes untended. They could be evidence."

An exaggerated throat clearing came from Sam, following behind us.

Okay, message received.

I stopped at the entrance to the bullpen and turned to Barnes. "And by the way, thanks for saving my life by hauling me out of that car, and for the others you got to safety. I'm putting a commendation in your file."

She beamed.

I noticed that Sam had turned around and gone back to her desk. He was putting the boxes in my office.

Sheez, I'm snapping at her, and I just did the same thing. I was definitely not at my best today.

I walked to the watch desk.

Where I was greeted by two young people, grinning from ear to ear. On the sarge's desk was the biggest bouquet of flowers I'd ever seen. It covered half the desktop.

"Everybody who was in the bakery, they all pitched in," the young woman bubbled.

"And we volunteered to bring it to you," the young man said.

"This couple is barely back from their honeymoon," Barnes said from behind me. "Been married three weeks total. They were sitting at a little table right by the window in the bakery."

"Perfect timing, folks," Sam muttered *sotto voce*. He'd caught up with us again, after locking the files in my office.

I gave him a mock scowl over my shoulder.

The young woman pointed to my sling. "You were hurt." She sounded on the verge of tears.

"Yes, but not in the blast," I said. "This was from my assistant here hauling me out of that car, exactly two minutes and forty-seven seconds before it blew."

"Oh," the man turned to Barnes, "we should've gotten you something too. If you hadn't saved her, we–"

"Don't worry," she said, letting a small smirk surface, "these'll end up on my desk anyway." She pointed to the flowers.

We all exchanged multiple expressions of gratitude, and the young couple finally headed for the elevators.

Sergeant Armstrong leaned toward me. In a low voice, he said, "Should I call Terry and have him bring King in to sniff it for a bomb?"

I started to chuckle, then sobered. "Might not be a bad idea."

※

By early afternoon, I had regained my emotional equilibrium, for the most part. My hand still trembled as I tried to type on my keyboard one-handed.

Barnes had gotten through a third of the lawyer's files. In the recent cases box, she found one file that she felt worthy of bringing to my attention.

Campbell had handled the rewriting of the last will and testament of an old man who died a few months later. He'd changed his will shortly before that and had left half of his considerable estate to the woman he was living with, who was *not* the mother of his biological children. Their mother had died years before, and originally the man's will had divided everything three ways between the children. But then the man had met this new woman, a good bit younger than himself, and she had a twelve-year-old daughter. He'd wanted to adopt the daughter—which is how he ended up consulting Herb

Campbell originally—as well as marry the woman. But she'd refused, saying she'd been burned so badly in her first marriage that she wasn't willing to go there again.

All that had occurred two years before he'd changed his will and then died. The new will also divided the remaining half of the estate four ways, including the woman's daughter.

"The kids claimed undue influence from Campbell," Barnes said, "whose sister happens to be the woman who inherited."

"Oh ho," I said. "The plot thickens."

She nodded. "When the case went to court, the will stood, and Campbell was exonerated of any wrongdoing after he showed the judge a letter from his client indicating the whole idea was the old man's."

"So, you're thinking one or more of the kids might be mad enough to kill Campbell?"

Barnes shrugged. "I figured it's worth checking out."

"It is–"

Movement in my peripheral vision. A uniformed arm had reached out to knock on my open door.

"Come in," I said.

Officer Terry stepped into the doorway. King's snout poked past his knee.

Barnes grinned at the sight. I held out a restraining hand to remind her that the police dog was not a pet.

"Chief," Terry said, "I've been told I'm your new driver."

"Told by whom?" I snapped.

"Sergeant Armstrong. Unfortunately, there's only room for one passenger in my cruiser, with the back end set up for King. If Officer Barnes is going with you somewhere, she could follow in another car. But..." he held up a finger, "only after King examines both vehicles for explosives."

I'd been preparing a no-way-in-hell response, until he got to the last part.

"Oh, and I brought the flowers back," he added. "They're out here on Barnes's desk."

I nodded at him, and he withdrew from the doorway.

"Set up meetings with the three biological children," I told Barnes. "I'm going to call Campbell's sister."

That turned out to be one of the most awkward calls I'd ever made. The woman was grieving for her brother, murdered only yesterday, and I was asking nosy questions about her family's dynamics and a fiercely contested will. But the end result was that she didn't think her late lover's kids would have gone after her brother. "Now, if they tried to kill me," she concluded, in an acerbic tone, "I wouldn't be the least bit surprised. But not Herb. That wouldn't get them anywhere."

I was gathering my things to go with Barnes to interview the grown children, when my cell phone pinged and *Skip Canfield* appeared on its screen.

Call me when you have a couple minutes. I've got a lot of news. Some bad, but mostly good.

I reread the text. *Boy, talk about intriguing.*

Barnes appeared in my doorway. "Ready, Chief?"

"Not quite. I need to make a call first. Close the door, please."

CHAPTER TWENTY-FOUR

"Hey, Lieutenant, I mean, Chief," Skip's voice sounded tinny and like he was in a wind tunnel, but I could still hear the sarcastic edge to his voice. I suspected he kept forgetting my current title on purpose, just to yank my chain.

I ground my teeth. I wasn't in the mood at the moment.

"Your money has been well spent," he was saying. "I've had a very productive day."

"We've got a terrible connection, Canfield."

"It's the cheap Bluetooth in my rental. Here, let me pull over. I've got plenty of time." A couple of seconds ticked by. "There, at least we won't be fighting the road noise. Better?"

"Yes." He still sounded tinny, but clearer and louder.

"I'm on my way to the airport to fly home, but I've got a couple of hours before my flight. So the bad news first?"

"Okay."

"I don't know your cousin's current whereabouts, nor am I sure what name she's using now."

"That's a lot of bad news," I said.

"Yes, but progress is being made. I caught up with that nurse last night. She remembered the baby. It was the only time she was personally involved in a safe haven drop-off. And she remembered something else that was really helpful. The name of the police detective who came around asking questions.

"They didn't officially report safe-haven babies to the police, but the hospital informally let the local precinct know. In case they found a woman passed out somewhere, they'd have a clue what was going on and wouldn't assume she was a drunk or an addict. The day after this baby was left by the man in an expensive suit, a detective shows up and is asking questions about him, and whether he had any women with him."

"And the nurse remembers his name, after all these years?" I said.

"Yes, because it was John Smith. She thought maybe it was a fake name. But there *was* a John Smith in that precinct's Vice Unit. And he's now retired. I tracked him down this morning. I showed him Joy Harrington's photo and he recognized it. Only he thought it was of her mother, a hooker named Trixie. He'd seen her multiple times with a local pimp—the same guy who dropped off the baby. He had a pic of said pimp—he'd apparently made a copy of Trixie's file before he retired and kept it. I borrowed the pic and took it back to the nurse. She confirmed he was the man who brought the baby in."

"Wait, lemme see if I've got the players straight here. Mr. Nice Suit is a pimp, confirmed by this retired detective and recognized by the nurse as the man who dropped off Joy as a baby. And the detective recognized the pic of her as a grown-up, thinking it was one of that pimp's hookers, Trixie."

"Exactly. Smith, the detective—he thought this hooker didn't seem quite right. She was quiet, always kept her head down, whenever Vice ran a sting and she got arrested. The other hookers would be making a fuss, yelling to be let out of the holding cell, and she'd be sitting quietly in a corner of the cell. And with the other hookers in that pimp's stable, he'd send a bail bondsman or one of his henchmen around to spring them. But when this gal was arrested, he'd show up in person and physically escort her out of the PD."

"Physically escort her?" I repeated.

"Yeah, I asked the same question. As in, take her by the upper arm and lead her away. Smith suspected maybe she'd been trafficked and was not a willing participant in the whole process."

Skip paused, cleared his throat. "Smith said that's why he copied the file. It kinda haunted him that he'd never done anything more definitive about Trixie. And within a month of the baby being abandoned, she disappeared. He confronted the pimp, who pretended he'd never seen the young woman before."

"Nothing came up when Smith ran the prints?" I asked.

A beat of silence. Then Skip said, "Her fingerprints had been altered, with chemicals. She gave the police some story about having an accident in her high school chemistry class."

I winced, and my stomach churned as my brain registered on a deeper level that this was most likely my cousin we were talking about.

"Smith has a copy of her rap sheet and mug shot," he continued. "She was using the last name of Graham, Trixie Graham. And she definitely looks a lot like Joy Harrington."

I blew out air, struggling a little to process it all. "And Joy looks a lot like my Aunt Jean when she was in her thirties."

"So now we have the name Meredith was using in the early 1990s, and her new fingerprints. But I can't find any trace of her in Iowa after 1992."

"And they wouldn't have been collecting DNA from hookers back then," I said.

"Sadly, no, not until the late 1990s. Oh, and since Joy was more forthcoming, I told her some more about you and your aunt and cousin. But I didn't give her your contact info. Not without asking you first."

My stomach knotted. I wasn't sure how I felt about meeting this girl—well, young woman. Was I prepared to embrace her as family? I wasn't one to readily let people in as it was.

"Leave that for now," I said. "What's your next step?"

"Not sure. I need to go home and kiss my wife," his voice had that flippant edge again, "get a good night's sleep, and then think that through."

"Okay, thanks." There was a slight quiver in my voice.

"I know it's a lot to digest." Skip's voice had dropped an octave and lost the flippancy. "How's your case going?"

"It's not. And we have two more major cases now, a murder that may be related, and a..." I hesitated. I didn't want Kate to know about the bomb. She'd worry.

"A what?" he asked. "I didn't catch that."

"Um, another attempted...murder." I stumbled a little over the word *murder*. I swallowed hard. My *own* death had been the desired outcome. "Look, I gotta go. I'm late for an appointment. Thanks again."

"You're welcome. And Judith...take care of yourself."

Once in the passenger seat of Officer Terry's SUV, I attempted to make conversation by asking, "Why is it that police dogs are not trained in search and rescue?"

What I didn't say out loud was that it would be a handy skill for King to have.

"King has been trained as a patrol dog," Terry said, "for officer protection, clearing buildings, and tracking and apprehending suspects. He's also been dual-trained in detecting explosives and guns. That's a lot for one dog. If they're trained in too many tasks, their expertise gets diluted. While doing one thing, they may get distracted by something else."

I nodded, but he went on. I suspected he'd given this explanation more than once.

"And search and rescue of a victim is quite different from apprehending suspects. With the latter, his job, to put it crudely, is to chomp down on the nearest limb and hang on. He's not expected to be gentle or worry about hurting the person."

I winced at the mental image of King—who probably outweighed the toddler by fifty pounds—*apprehending* little Ashley. "I see your point," I said, as we pulled up in front of a McMansion in Starlingville, the classiest section of town.

I climbed out of the SUV, as Barnes exited the cruiser the sarge had assigned to her. "Hopefully this won't take long," I said back over my shoulder to Terry.

As a lead in Herb Campbell's murder, the heirs of Everett Purdue, Sr. were a bust.

The three adult children—Everett, Jr. and his two younger sisters—had congregated at the son's house. And they were not happy that we'd kept them waiting a few minutes past our appointed interview time.

They all struck me as obnoxious enough and entitled enough to be potential killers. But their late father's "paramour," as Everett Jr. kept calling her, had been right. They were furious with her and with their dead father, but they'd already pretty much forgotten about the lawyer. He'd only been a handy instrument for contesting the will.

And they all had alibis for yesterday morning. Everett Jr. and his eldest sister had been at work. He now ran the business his father had started decades before. And Sis was an interior decorator.

The other sister, who described herself as "happy and content to be a wife and mother," was having a mani-pedi at her favorite nail salon at the time.

"More like *pampered* and *spoiled*," Barnes had muttered as we'd let ourselves out.

I concurred, then sent her on her way to check their alibis. It came in handy that she'd had to drive separately.

Officer Terry, King and I returned to 3MB.

————◆————

Sam was leaning his butt against the edge of Barnes's desk, his arms crossed over his chest and his head tilted down. And he looked damn fine, even though his khaki uniform was a bit rumpled.

Did he get any sleep at all last night?

I intentionally made noise, scraping my feet, as I approached. He lifted his head.

I smiled. "Good, you're awake. I thought you might be literally asleep on your feet."

"Nah, just thinking. What's happening?"

"Not much, I'm afraid," I said as I walked past him and unlocked my office door. I gestured for him to proceed me.

Two of the file boxes were piled on one of the uncomfortable chairs, with the one Barnes had already gone through underneath it. "We were checking out a lead based on one of the lawyer's recent cases," I said. "But it's looking like a dead end. Barnes is verifying alibis, to cross the t's and all that."

"Nothing new on Ashley, I assume."

I shook my head.

A throat clearing behind me.

I pivoted in my doorway. I'd forgotten that Officer Terry and King were now my shadows.

"The sarge has an abandoned building he needs us to check out," Terry said. "It's near the residence of one of the guys we arrested at the warehouse yesterday."

"Wasn't it searched already?" I had thought my people, with the help of the volunteers and the agents from FDLE and the FBI, had searched every square inch of the city. At least, that's what Bradley had reported earlier.

"Yes, but the sarge has got the patrol officers searching again, near where all those...people live."

"Okay, go. I don't have any plans to leave here just now."

I entered my office and headed for my desk chair. "What brings you back into town?"

"Oh, I was nearby," Sam said. "At the jail."

Which was in the county, but barely over the boundary line. Not really all that nearby.

Frowning, I sat and faced him across my desk. "So you thought you'd stop by and check on me, make sure I hadn't fallen apart completely?"

Sam frowned back. "There's no shame in falling apart a little now and then, especially when someone tries to blow you up."

"Speaking of which," came a male voice through the open doorway. SAC Denny Trager appeared and leaned a shoulder against one side of the door jamb. "I have a tentative report from our lab on the bomb."

I stared at him. "Already?"

He nodded. "I put a rush on it. It was definitely an IED with a pressure plate switch."

"I thought they only had IEDs in war zones," I said.

"Improvised explosive devices can be anywhere. IED merely means it's homemade. Which this one was, but by someone who knew what they were doing. There were two triggers. The pressure plate being suppressed started a timer, which controlled the actual trigger."

I looked at Sam. "As you speculated earlier, they wanted me to be in or near the municipal building's parking lot, to take out more cops."

"Very likely," Trager said, "since the only fingerprints on the entire thing were from someone that you and your department have a history with, Chief."

"One of the members of that gang we took down last winter?" I asked.

Trager shook his head and opened his mouth.

But Sam beat him to it. "No. John Black."

CHAPTER TWENTY-FIVE

I realized my mouth was hanging open. I closed it as I looked back and forth between Sam and Denny Trager. "John Black?"

"Yeah," Sam said. "That's really why I came back into town, to tell you I'd remembered something. Black was a demolition expert during the Vietnam War. He used to brag about some of his exploits there."

Of course, Sam didn't need to come in person to tell me that. He could've called, but I didn't point that out.

And it dawned on me that, while Black had left me a mess to clean up, at least I hadn't had to deal with him day in and day out like Sam had for years.

I almost blurted out, *How could you stand the man?* But instead, I said, "I'm surprised that Black didn't wear gloves when handling the bomb."

"It's delicate work," Trager pointed out. "You can't really do it with gloves on. I'm sure he thought he'd wiped it clean, but there were a couple of prints on the pressure plate—which survived in one piece, relatively speaking. Its edges were jagged, but the majority of the plate itself had blown forward into the engine area."

I grimaced, trying *not* to imagine what would have happened to me had I still been sitting on it at that point.

"So now we have solid evidence," Sam said, his voice grim, "that will keep Black locked up for the rest of his miserable life. That is, once the FDLE finds him."

"Actually the FBI has offered our help. Not my unit, but the local field office. He's apparently crossed state lines, playing this game where he's leaving stuff lying around to set you up, Chief. And an attack on a law enforcement officer, a chief of police no less." Trager shook his head. "My boss told SAC Wilder that our resources are at her disposal."

"I still don't believe Black would risk getting caught," Sam said, "by letting himself be spotted like that at various hotels. I think it's someone pretending to be him, maybe from that gang. They are good at disguises."

Trager looked confused, so Sam gave him a brief summary of that case. "They even had one of their leaders going around town with various women, pretending to be me, to make Judith jealous and keep her off kilter."

"Jealous?" Trager glanced my way, one eyebrow raised. "Are you two...?"

"Yup," Sam said, as my cheeks heated.

Sam was grinning.

I glared at him. "Getting back to Black, you think he's hired a couple of people to pretend to be him and his wife. But didn't they find one of his fingerprints in that first hotel room?"

"Yeah, on a lamp," Sam said. "Easy enough, though, to sneak in a lamp that looks like the ones that hotel uses."

"Do you really think Black's that bright?" I asked.

"Well, as my dad used to say, he's 'dumb like a fox.'" Sam paused. "Not super intelligent, but cunning. And those guys who were running the gang, they are definitely smart enough to come up with all this."

"Hmm," Trager said, "I think we need to find out who's been in contact with them in prison."

Sam nodded. "Good place to start. I've got the kid who was stealing stuff from Judith's dumpster out at my department. So far, he's refused to say who hired him, claims it was done anonymously. You want to have a go at him?"

"Not me," Trager said, "but I'll send the local agent out to take him off your hands, if you don't mind."

"Not at all," Sam said, a look of relief on his face.

I had a pretty good idea what he was thinking. Better to turn him over to the feds, since the county jail might not be the safest place for the kid.

How long will it be before we're sure we've rooted out all of Black's corrupt tendrils from both our departments?

Trager shifted in my direction. "My team is tracking down the last of the semi-plausible hotline leads. I'm not optimistic, and the calls have fallen off some. Mostly crazies now."

I sighed. "Thanks again for all your help."

"You're welcome. We'll keep the hotline going for a while, though."

I nodded, and Trager left my office.

Sam stood up. "Guess I better get out there, so I can turn the kid over to them." He groaned. "There will be paperwork involved...And, uh, I didn't mean to embarrass you that way. Sorry."

"No, you didn't mean to," I aimed a mock glare at him, "but you were enjoying it nonetheless."

He gave me a half smirk. "Maybe a little."

"How did you stand being around Black all those years?" I asked.

Sam snorted. "I stayed away from him as much as I could." Another half smirk. "After all, the scenery at the SPD wasn't nearly as attractive back then as it is now."

I repeated the mock glare as he went out my door, but there was a warm glow spreading through my chest.

I sat at my desk, trying to come up with a new course of action to find Ashley Silva. Leads were few and far between now, and they were drying up almost as soon as we pursued them.

I texted Bradley. *Are you near 3MB?*

Just got back, he replied. *Headed for the elevator.*

Come to my office. I have a couple ideas.

Will do.

"Lame ideas," I muttered to myself, "but ideas."

As Bradley entered my office a few minutes later, his sister let out a soft moan at her desk.

"What's the matter with her?" he asked in a low voice, while settling into the comfy visitor's chair.

"She's going through the lawyer's files a second time," I said, also in a low voice. "Her idea, to make sure she didn't miss anything. But I think the tedium of trying to decipher legalese is getting to her."

He shook his head and smiled. "She's always been an overachiever. She had this math teacher—in seventh grade, I think it was—who sent home extra credit questions along with the homework. Gloria got straight As in math, but she still did those extra credit questions every night. Our mother used to laugh at her and ask her why. Gloria's answer was always, 'Just in case.'" He mimicked his sister's voice.

I chuckled softly as Bradley, in his regular voice, began his report. Sadly it was very short.

"Nothing so far from Bert's forensics sweep of the, uh, residences of the people arrested at the warehouse. And Sarge had the uniforms and wannabe cops re-search the neighborhoods around them. Nada there so far either."

"Lola Dexter? What's she been up to?"

"Not much. She goes to work and comes back home. She's avoiding the park now, which is probably a good thing, psychologically speaking. And the FBI has finished checking the airlines for any toddlers who were flown out of the area in the last couple of days. Nothing suspicious there."

"Okay, time to get creative," I said. "I want to do three lineups. Bring back in all the people we arrested at the warehouse. Divide them into two groups and add in some fillers. Our auxiliary folks might be able to help with that. Then bring in Annie Silva and the nanny, Cara, to take a look at them. Ask them to point out anyone that they've seen around town."

"And the third line-up?"

"The two guys from the warehouse who were wearing long-sleeved gray tee-shirts, in those tee-shirts, and Gabe Silva in the dress shirt he was wearing Saturday. Plus some male fillers, also in long-sleeved gray dress shirts or gray tee-shirts."

"You're going to have that lady, Gardner, look at them?"

"Yup. I know it's a long shot–"

"And would never hold up in court," Bradley added.

"But it may show us what direction to go. At this point, I'm more concerned about finding the child than prosecuting her abductor. If we don't find her soon…"

"But then the kidnapper will be free to do it again," he protested.

"Not if Mrs. Gardner identifies Gabe Silva's sleeve in that lineup. I doubt he's into kidnapping random children, only his own."

Bradley's mouth twisted in a grimace. "I'll get started organizing all that."

Two hours later, we'd completed the lineups with Annie Silva and Cara. They had to take turns, one in the observation area while the other took care of baby Teddy. Cara said the same thing with both groups, that she'd never seen any of those people before.

Annie's reply was similar to Cara's with the first group, but with the second one, she did identify a man and a woman whom she said she'd seen before on her street. Unfortunately, they were fillers—auxiliary folks who'd been involved in the search of the Silvas' neighborhood on Sunday.

As I was escorting Annie and Cara to the reception area, one of the auxiliary guys, an older man in a light blue tee shirt and cargo shorts, stepped past us. "Excuse me," he muttered.

Annie froze and wrinkled her nose. A second later I knew why, as the odor hit my own nose. The man reeked of alcohol.

I glanced at my watch. I couldn't fault him. It was almost five o'clock and he was most likely a retiree from the looks of him.

"Wait," Annie said, grabbing my arm.

"Sir," I called out to stop the man.

He pivoted. "Yes, Chief?"

I turned to Annie. "What?"

"I remembered something," she said. "Right before Ashley pulled away from me, I smelled what I thought was a diabetic with ketoacidosis. But then I realized it was most likely somebody's beer breath."

The older man was rubbing self-consciously at a pale purplish stain on his tee shirt. "Sorry, I'd just spilled some wine, when the lieutenant called. He said he needed people right away, so I didn't take the time to change." His eyes were wide when he made eye contact. "Honest, I hadn't had any of the wine yet."

I waved a hand at him. "You're not in trouble. Thanks for your help." He nodded and quickly walked away.

To Annie, I said, "You thought of ketoacidosis because of Gabe?"

"Yes. It's how he smells when he's forgotten to take his insulin. The ketones build up in his blood and–"

I nodded to indicate I knew what ketoacidosis was. "Does he do that often, forget his insulin?"

She rolled her eyes. "Way too often. But of course, lots of people in that crowd had been drinking."

"Of course," I said, while thinking, *Not court-worthy evidence, but another small sign pointing toward Silva.*

"Sarge, would you get someone to take Mrs. Silva and Ms. Hidalgo home?" I handed the two women off to the watch commander.

Bradley joined me in my office a few minutes later. "Time to do the third lineup?" His voice still sounded skeptical.

I told him about Annie smelling either alcohol on someone's breath or a diabetic person in ketoacidosis, right before Ashley pulled loose from her hand.

His face grim, he nodded, not so skeptical now.

CHAPTER TWENTY-SIX

"I'll pick up Gabe Silva," Bradley said. "Do you want to go get Mrs. Gardner, since you have a rapport with her?"

I opened my mouth to say yes, then remembered I didn't have a car. And Officer Terry had not returned. Maybe the sarge had him doing something else with King.

I could ride with Bradley... My chest tightened. I'd be putting him at risk from whoever was trying to take me out. And what would that accomplish? We'd still only be able to pick up one of them at a time.

Grrr.

Out loud, I said, "I have no vehicle. Bring in Silva first. I don't mind wasting his time. Then fetch Mrs. Gardner."

A faint groan from Barnes's desk.

"And take your sister as backup with Silva, in case he gives you a hard time. She could use a break."

And I can use a break from her sound effects.

I interrupted Bradley in mid-eyeroll by yelling, "Barnes."

In less than a second, she popped into my open doorway, an eager expression on her face. "Yes, Chief."

"We need to bring Mrs. Gardner in for a lineup, but she has her two grandchildren staying with her. Would you mind going over there with the lieutenant and, if she doesn't have anyone else she can call, maybe babysit while she comes in? Or you all can bring the kids back with you and watch them here."

"The lineup shouldn't take long," Bradley said, as my desk phone rang.

"No, it shouldn't," I said, "and normally I wouldn't ask a sworn officer to babysit, but time is of the essence here."

"No problem, Chief," Barnes said. "I like kids."

I didn't mention that these two might be a handful. Especially the younger one, who had sounded like a bit of a hellion.

My phone rang again. I glanced at the caller ID screen. *Mayor Hayes*, on my private line.

I made a shooing motion. "I gotta get this."

They left, and I dropped into my desk chair before picking up my desk phone's receiver. "What can I do for you, Mayor Hayes?"

"Do you have any good leads on that little girl?" he asked, his voice anxious.

"Some leads, not sure I'd call them good." I gave him a quick update on Ashley's case, leaving out the long-shot line-up we were about to try with Mrs. Gardner.

That seemed to be all he wanted, an update on the delicate case. Neither of us mentioned the other sensitive topic that hung in the air between us—his own involvement with a now dead lawyer.

We signed off, and I sat at my desk, trying to decide if we should be considering Hayes a serious suspect in the lawyer's murder.

"This is why you get paid the big bucks," I muttered, then snorted. My salary was barely higher than what I'd been making as a lieutenant in the Baltimore County PD. And despite the fact that it stretched farther here in Florida—where the cost of living was lower—I had frequent moments when I felt it was inadequate compensation for this job.

This was definitely one of those moments.

A frisson of anxiety ran through me, as I realized that was the second time, in just a few hours, that I'd been talking to myself. "I should ask Kate if that really does mean you're going crazy."

Damn, I'm doing it again. I smacked myself lightly on the forehead. But it was still enough to bring back my earlier headache, although not as intense.

I ground my teeth and, feeling restless, got up to take the lawyer's files to the evidence room, so I didn't have to worry about keeping an eye on them. I waved over a passing uniform and asked him to carry the two boxes Barnes had already gone through a second time.

Then I tried to pick up the third box one-handed. It was too heavy. I blew out air. Sometimes maintaining the chain of evidence was a royal pain.

As is dealing with a damaged limb. I glared down at my sling.

Silently, the officer put his two boxes back down and put the third one on top. He strained a little, leaning backwards some, as he carried them down the hall.

As I followed him, my mind returned to thoughts of Campbell and Hayes. Had the lawyer tried to blackmail the mayor perhaps?

Campbell hadn't struck me as the dishonest type, but I'd only interacted with him once.

Maybe he hadn't gone for money. Maybe he'd used his knowledge of Hayes's secret to try to manipulate the mayor politically. *That* would make Mark Hayes far angrier than demanding money would.

The evidence room was manned by a rotation of part-timers, most of whom were retired cops from states with cold winters. I'd met today's protector of the realm a few times before, but was grateful for the name tag pinned to his uniform shirt.

"Hey Phil, you can put those two away." I pointed to the boxes at the bottom of the pile the officer had just wrestled onto the counter. "The top one keep handy. Barnes will be looking for it later." I thanked the uniform, filled out the paperwork for the evidence transfer, and went back to my office.

Once there, I pulled out my bottom desk drawer to retrieve the lawyer's file for Hayes's case. A faint ping came from my leather laptop bag beneath it.

I removed the laptop bag instead of the file and fished out my personal phone.

A text from Kate. *Wondering how things are going? No need to reply if you're too busy. I just can't stop worrying about that little girl.*

"You and me both," I muttered as I called Kate's number.

After a quick exchange of amenities, I said, "To answer your question, things are not going well, and we haven't found the child yet. Indeed, we're getting kinda desperate." I told her about the plan to do a lineup of shirt sleeves, including the girl's father as one of the possibilities.

"Will that stand up in court?" Kate asked.

"Never. But it may tell us where to concentrate our investigation. Hey, lemme ask you something. Would it help if I asked Mrs. Gardner to close her eyes and visualize what she saw, the little girl and the arm, to refresh her memory?"

"Let me think about that." A pause. "No, probably not a good idea. She might not visualize it accurately. And I'd suggest telling her not to embellish on what she remembers, to only base her responses on what she truly saw on Saturday. Um, has the father been on TV?"

"He wasn't part of the official plea to the kidnapper, but the news media has caught candid shots of him. Hmm, I see what you're getting at. I should think of a way to block their faces so she only sees the sides of their bodies."

"I think that's a good idea," Kate said. "And then maybe let her see their faces, but straight on, and ask her if she–"

"Saw any of them in the crowd on Saturday," I finished her sentence.

"Uh, actually I was going to say, ask if she's seen any of them *anywhere* before. If you get too specific, that could act as a suggestion and her subconscious may produce a prevarication."

"Isn't that a fancy word for a *lie*?"

Kate chuckled.

I smiled. "You psychologists do love your fancy words."

"Well, I'd better let you go." The chuckle was still there in Kate's voice.

"Okay, I'll keep you posted." I disconnected and placed the phone on my desk.

My good elbow on the polished wood surface, I rested my chin in that hand and stared across my office. But I wasn't seeing the books on my bookcase. My mind was turned inward, replaying the scene in Penelope Atkins's living room.

Was it significant that Gabe Silva was color-blind, or that he was diabetic? Or were those just random factoids about him?

And how likely was it that he'd spirited Ashley off to his family in Brazil? All signs indicated that he wasn't all that interested in the little girl.

It dawned on me that I could contact the chief of police in whatever Brazilian city Silva was from, and find out if his parents now had a granddaughter staying with them. I resisted the urge to smack myself on the forehead again. I should've thought of that sooner.

SAC Trager—Denny—would've thought of that. But I hadn't even told the FBI agents about the Brazilian angle. I'd mostly had little to do with them, leaving that liaison task to Bradley.

Damn, I should've been making better use of their resources.

But would the Brazilian police chief even give me the time of day, since his country's *de facto* policy was lack of cooperation regarding international child custody laws? Well, he could at least tell me if the child was there, so we could stop wasting our resources searching for her here.

I reached for my desk phone's receiver to call over to the conference room. Maybe Denny Trager could get that info faster than I could. The request to the Brazilian police chief would have more oomph behind it if it came from the FBI.

The phone rang under my hand, making me startle slightly. I took a deep breath and answered it. "Chief Anderson."

"Chief, this is Jan Campbell. I, um, wasn't sure if I should call or not. I remembered something."

"What's that?"

"Herb has a secret compartment in one his desk drawers. I don't think he's put anything in it for years. But I went to check, and it's jammed. I can't get it open. I didn't want to force it and maybe damage something in it, if there *is* anything there."

My heart rate kicked up a notch. "Good thinking. I'll be there as soon as I can."

I hung up and pulled my Glock from my top desk drawer, thinking I probably had enough time to get there and back before Bradley had the lineup ready to go. "Damn," I muttered. "No car."

The lack of a vehicle was so frustrating. It left me feeling kind of trapped, and that was a feeling I did *not* like one bit.

With my left hand I awkwardly maneuvered my gun into its small-of-the-back holster, then draped my pantsuit jacket over my shoulders to hide it.

Out at the watch desk, I asked, "Sarge, where's Officer Terry?"

"He's clearing another warehouse near where one of the per–" Sergeant Johnson caught himself. "Uh, one of the detainees lives."

"Where's the cruiser Barnes was using earlier?"

"In the lot beside the building."

Hmm, King had checked it out earlier, and it had been sitting in the open lot in broad daylight ever since. Unlikely that anyone had messed with it.

I held out my hand.

Sarge stared at it for a half-beat, sighed and produced the keys.

While on the way, my phone rang. *Bradley* appeared on the cruiser's Bluetooth screen. I was a little surprised that it had automatically synced with my phone.

"Accept call," I said.

Nothing happened.

Crap. The Bluetooth wasn't as sophisticated as I'd thought it was. Indeed, the cruiser seemed to be an older model, no doubt kept in reserve in case one of our newer vehicles broke down.

I had to pull over to answer the call, since I was driving one-handed. I made a mental note to make sure vehicles we ordered in the future had the latest and best version of Bluetooth, completely audio-controlled.

"Silva's not home, *again*," Bradley said, his tone disgusted. "We're headed for the girlfriend's place."

"Okay. If he's not there, put out a BOLO." I was tired of messing with this guy. I hit the button to disconnect, actually glad for the extra time to deal with Campbell's secret drawer.

At the office building, I found the entrance to the small parking lot behind it. Most of the spaces were occupied. I parked in Herb Campbell's spot.

His wife must have been hovering near the outer office door because it opened immediately when I knocked. "This way," she said without preamble. She seemed nervous.

In her husband's office, Jan waved toward the desk. "I might have the wrong drawer."

I pulled a blue nitrile glove out of my jacket pocket and, in the process, dislodged the jacket from my good shoulder. My attempt to pull the glove onto my left hand had the jacket slithering to the floor. And my shoulder was screaming at me, objecting to even that small movement of my right hand.

Grrr. I resisted the urge to kick the jacket and left it lying on the floor.

Jan grabbed the glove, then tugged it onto my good hand for me.

My cheeks burning, I turned away to examine the drawer she'd pointed out.

"It's supposed to have a spring release," Jan said, as she picked up my jacket and brushed it off. "You push down on the right side and it opens."

I tried that but there was no give in either edge of the drawer bottom. I found a small ruler in amongst the pens and detritus she'd dumped from the drawer onto the desk. Measuring the outside and inside of the drawer, there was three-eighths of an inch difference.

"You've got the right drawer," I said, then pressed my lips together. *How did Bert and Ernie miss this?*

I rapped on the wood bottom. A dull thud, not the hollow echo of a hidden compartment.

That's how...

"Do you have an Exacto knife or letter opener?"

"The latter." She fetched it from her own desk, and I gently inserted the tip between the edge of the thin wooden bottom and the drawer's side.

Nothing.

My cell pinged. I dropped the letter opener and reached for my pants pocket. The glove made it difficult but I managed to extract the phone with two fingers.

A text from Bradley read, *Not at girlfriend's either. Put out BOLO and swinging by Gardner's to give her a heads-up that we'll probably need her to come in soon.*

My stomach clenched. Was all that hooey about using Ashley as leverage just BS, and Silva was on the run? That would prove his guilt, but it might not help us find the child.

Blowing out air, I pocketed my phone and picked up the letter opener again. Jan leaned forward and watched as I tried several places along the right edge of the drawer bottom.

Finally, the thin piece of wood sprang open. Jan jumped a little, dropping my jacket again.

Under the false bottom was the reason it hadn't opened before, and had produced a dull thud when I'd rapped knuckles against it.

An overstuffed manila envelope that was so fat it filled the entire space and then some. Hand-printed on the envelope was *OPEN IN THE EVENT OF MY DEATH.*

CHAPTER
TWENTY-SEVEN

My heart raced as I used my phone to take several photos of the envelope in the drawer. Then I wiggled it loose from its tight resting place, put it on the desk and slit the top with the letter opener.

I glanced up at Jan. Her face had paled. She grabbed for the edge of the desk to steady herself.

I reached into the envelope and pulled out a clump of papers. The top sheet was a typed note, addressed to his wife.

I skimmed the first paragraph. He was telling her to take this "packet of proof" to the police. My eyes snagged on the name at the beginning of the next paragraph.

Bea Gardner needs to be stopped.

I swallowed hard, having trouble believing my eyes.

She's kidnapped five children in the last thirteen years. But this time, she's fouled her own nest, by taking a child right here in Starling.

Fouled her own nest... Where had I heard those words before? I flashed to the lawyer's outer office, Mrs. Gardner waiting, and Campbell behind me muttering. I'd thought at the time he'd said, "fooled the rest this time." But it had been "fouled her nest this time."

Heart now pounding double-time, I dropped the papers and yanked out my phone again. I called SPD and got put through to the evidence room. "Phil, I need you to go through those boxes I just brought in, quickly. Look for a file marked Gardner."

I set the phone down and put it on speaker, then picked up the lawyer's note again.

It ran on for a page and a half. Damn lawyers, always so wordy. I skimmed it.

The gist was that Gardner had lost a granddaughter at age eighteen months. She'd drowned when the child's mother had fallen asleep while the toddler was napping. The little one had woken up, figured out how to get out of the house and had fallen into their backyard pool.

I believed her, Campbell had written, *when she said the first girl was a distant relative she wanted to adopt. She had a birth certificate and death certificates for the parents. They'd died in a car accident, supposedly. I took care of the adoption for her, not realizing those certificates were forged.*

After that, she had me over a barrel. If I didn't help her, she'd see that I was disbarred, maybe imprisoned as an accomplice.

I rummaged through some of the additional papers from the envelope. They appeared to be copies of legal briefs and adoption certificates.

A duplicate of Gardner's file!

"Chief?" Phil's voice coming from my phone and sounding a bit breathless. "Couldn't find it, sorry."

"I wasn't expecting you to. Thanks." I disconnected and turned to Jan.

She had fire in her eyes. "She stole it," she spit out, "after she murdered my husband."

I thought fast. This woman looked like she was ready to go after Gardner with her bare hands.

"Jan," I said, "I need you to stay here and guard this envelope. It's crucial evidence and we have to be able to testify that it was never out of our sight."

Wait, a defense attorney could argue that she'd tampered with the papers in my absence.

I called Bradley. The call went to voicemail.

"Don't go into Gardner's house," I yelled into the phone. "She's our kidnapper, and she probably killed Campbell."

Damn! I had no choice. I had to get to Gardner's house and stop Bradley and Barnes from innocently walking in there. And I didn't want to take the time to bag the envelope. I wasn't even sure if there were any evidence bags in the cruiser.

Not to mention needing to keep Jan Campbell out of harm's way.

"I really, really need you to stay here," I told her. "That is the best way you can help us nail this woman."

Lips pinched into a thin line, she nodded. "I'll stay and guard it."

I ran out of the office, calling the watch desk as I went.

"Sergeant Johns–"

"Get the address off of Bea Gardner's witness statement and send backup to that address."

"How much backup?" the sarge asked. "We're spread pretty thin."

"Everybody!" I yelled into the phone.

In the back lot, I jumped into the cruiser, started it and hit the lights and siren controls. I raced out of the lot and only slowed slightly before pulling out onto the busy main road.

Tires squealed behind me, but no sound of crunching metal. I kept going.

I instructed the Bluetooth to call Bradley again. It went to voicemail. Again.

I told it to call Barnes. Same result.

My phone jangled, *Bradley* on the screen. I grabbed the bottom of the steering wheel with my right hand. My shoulder objected, strenuously. I gritted my teeth and used the left hand to hit the *accept* button.

"Bradley..." I said, my voice sounding strangled and faint. A vise around my chest was making it hard to breathe.

"Sorry, I hit the wrong button." Bradley's voice, loud and tense, talking over me.

"Just put it down!" Bea Gardner's voice, pissed off. "You too, girlie. And that radio of yours."

A couple of clunking sounds.

My mouth had fallen open. Bradley had somehow managed to speed-dial me as he'd handed over his cell phone.

Trying to hold the steering wheel steady with my knee this time, I used my good hand to turn off the siren. Gardner might hear it through the open line.

Reflections of red and blue glinted on my hood as the lights flashed. I hung a right and raced down a side street, a few blocks from Gardner's house.

Gardner was speaking again. "Get it tight, Allie," she instructed, her voice a bit harsh. "That's a girl," she added in a more soothing tone.

"Mom-mom, what are we doing?" A small child's voice.

"Playing cops and robbers," the woman said.

"But isn't he a cop?" the little girl questioned.

"No, he's only pretending to be one. They're the robbers."

"But she's wearing a uniform." The kid's voice was shrill. Poor tyke knew something was off. Smart kid.

"Allie, just tie her up," Gardner said, her tone terse. "She's a robber too."

A long pause, then, "Good girl." A wailing cry in the background. "Go find out what Allie two needs."

"Aw, Mom–" the girl's quick complaining response.

"Do it," Gardner snapped.

Something else I had misheard at the time. I'd thought it was Allie *too*, as in also Allie. But it was Allie *t-w-o*. She was calling both children by the same name. Good bet that had been her granddaughter's name.

My phone pinged. I prayed Gardner couldn't hear it and took my eyes off the road long enough to glance at the dashboard screen. *Backup on its way.*

Shit! I pulled to the curb so I could send a reply. *No sirens.*

Then I put the phone to my ear. The line was still open, I could hear someone breathing nearby. Maybe even hyperventilating.

I dropped the phone on the passenger seat and pulled back out onto the side street. *Having to do everything one-handed is getting old real fast.*

I had to slow for two intersections, before I pulled the cruiser to the curb a half block from Gardner's house and jumped out.

But then I just stood there, realizing that I needed to wait for backup. Storming into that house might get someone killed, maybe someone I cared about, and/or maybe a child. I reached behind me and touched the Glock in its holster. I regularly practiced shooting with my left hand, but it wasn't nearly as accurate as my right.

I tried to pull my right arm from the sling. Pain shot up my neck, making me clench my teeth.

I leaned into the car and grabbed the cell phone from the passenger seat. Holding my breath, I put it to my ear.

"What are you going to do to us?" Bradley was asking, trying to sound calm, but I could detect the tension in his voice.

"I haven't decided yet," Gardner said, her voice conversational now.

"Why are you doing this?" Barnes said, with definite tension in her voice.

A snort that sounded like it came from Gardner. "I knew y'all were onto me when that police chief came sniffing around, asking all those questions about the girls."

Shit! I'd been right there, with Ashley only a couple of rooms away.

"What are you talk–" Bradley's voice but Barnes interrupted him.

"We were only here to ask you to do a lineup." Barnes's voice was close to a wail.

"A lineup?" Gardner echoed.

"Yes," Bradley said, "of guys with gray long-sleeved shirts."

A pause, then Gardner laughed. "Oh my. I guess I jumped the gun, huh. No pun intended."

"But why?" Barnes asked again.

"Because, Officer," Bradley said, his voice firm, "that other little girl in the next room—Allie two, Mrs. Gardner called her—her real name is Ashley Silva."

A gasp from Barnes.

I noted that Bradley had called her Officer. *Good!* He wasn't letting on that there was any kind of personal relationship between them, which Gardner might try to use as leverage.

"I don't want to hurt you two," Gardner was saying, again in that conversational tone. "Not if I can help it. I'm not a violent person."

"But you killed Campbell, didn't you?" Barnes demanded.

"Well, yes. That was necessary. He was going to turn me in. And then what would've happened to Allie?"

"Which Allie?" Bradley asked, his voice calmer now that he had her talking.

Two cruisers pulled up behind mine. Four uniforms and the watch sergeant piled out.

"What do you mean?" Gardner said. "There's only one Allie, my sweet little toddler grandbaby." She was downright cooing.

I used my little finger to cover the mouthpiece of my phone and whispered to Johnson, "You and one officer in the back, and one on each side." I glanced at the other uniforms. "Thompson with me, out front. She's armed and has Bradley and Barnes tied up."

"So innocent and young," Gardner was saying, "not even talking all that much yet."

Johnson pulled a police radio from his pocket and tried to hand it to me.

"Turn it down some," I whispered, "and put it in my pocket." I cocked a hip toward him.

Eyes down, his ears turning red, the watch sergeant fumbled the radio into my pants pocket. Then he leaned in close to the ear not glued to the phone and whispered, "SWAT team's on its way."

I nodded, as a shrill child's voice yelled, "You're talking about Allie two, aren't you? What about me?"

"Shh, Shh, child," Gardner said. "It'll all be okay. I'll see that you're cared for."

The officers were moving into position, but I still wasn't sure what the hell was the best approach here. Two of my people—people I cared about—were in that house with a crazy woman. Not to mention two small children.

Even with all this manpower, we couldn't just storm the place.

A faint thud. "No, I'm your Allie," the child cried out.

Had she stomped her foot?

"I'm your sweet grandbaby," she yelled.

"Be quiet," Gardner said, her voice sharp. "Hey, come back here!"

The front door of the house flew open. A little girl ran out.

The crack of a gunshot. The child shrieked and fell to the ground.

The front door banged shut.

CHAPTER TWENTY-EIGHT

The child moved slightly, and whimpering reached my ears.

I lifted a foot to dash to her, then thought better of it. I wouldn't be able to carry her with my bum arm.

I held the phone away from my ear, but didn't bother to cover the mouthpiece. "Thompson!" I yelled.

He looked my way, and I pointed to the child. He nodded.

I mouthed. "I'll keep her distracted."

"Calling for an ambulance," someone called out from behind me.

"Hey!" Gardner's voice as I put the phone back to my ear. "What's this? You've had your phone on the whole time?" A screeching sound. "I should shoot you right now!" she yelled.

"You'd better not," I growled into the phone. "Or..."

I'd do what?

"I'll shoot Allie," I said.

"What? You'd never do that." Her voice was clearer now—she'd picked up the phone and brought it to her ear.

"I will. I'll come in there, guns blazing, if you hurt either of my people. And Allie may be caught in the crossfire." Of course I wouldn't do that, not unless I had to, and I'd try my damnedest to protect the child.

But I needed to keep this woman distracted.

And it was working. Thompson had reached the child on the ground. He gathered her up, and she cried out in pain.

I could see blood dripping from one dangling foot. And the leg of her navy-blue capris had turned purple.

Thompson huddled over her little body in his arms, protecting her as best he could as he ran for the cruisers.

"I'm glad you got her," Gardner's voice in my ear. "Is she okay?"

"Of course, she's not okay," I growled into the phone. "You *shot* her."

"I shouldn't have done that," she said. "I lost my temper."

A siren wailed as an ambulance approached. It grew louder, then ended with a squeal.

But I didn't look over. I kept my eyes on the outside of the house.

"Good, the paramedics will take care of her." The conversational voice was back. "My son was a paramedic. They are angels."

"Your son, Allie's father?" I asked, trying to make my voice sound normal. I figured my best bet was to keep her talking. One, to keep her calm so she didn't shoot anybody else. And two, to stall until the SWAT team got here.

By the time they arrived, I had more of the story. Gardner's daughter-in-law had felt ill one summer day, but there are no sick days for mothers. Once Allie—the girl's formal name was Alicia, but her grandmother's nickname for her was Allie—was down for a nap, mom gratefully fell into her own bed, and into a deep sleep. So deep that, despite the baby monitor, she didn't hear Allie get up and go searching for her mom. The child managed to open the back door and went to the pool, where she'd been playing in the shallow end earlier that morning.

The latch on the gate to the pool enclosure didn't always close properly, and the child got in there, and fell into the deep end.

And six months later, the mother, who'd "gone off the deep end herself"—Gardner's words—couldn't take the guilt anymore. She'd committed suicide, but not before taking her husband with her.

The pistol was found by her hand in the kitchen. Two shots had been fired.

The husband's body, Gardner's son, had been found in the bedroom. He'd apparently been asleep.

"Hopefully," Gardner said, her voice catching, "he never woke up to see his wife standing over him, about to pull the trigger."

I shuddered, then jumped several inches in the air as a hand came down on my good shoulder.

It was Sergeant Collins. Normally a plain-clothes detective, he was currently decked out in protective gear, in his occasional role as the head of SPD's SWAT team. Fortunately, we only needed a SWAT team occasionally.

I covered the mouthpiece of the phone.

"You're in touch with her?" he whispered.

I nodded.

He held out his hand for the phone.

"Bea," I said. "I'm going to turn you over to Sergeant Collins now. He's trained in how to figure out these kind of situations, so nobody gets hurt."

I handed him the phone, but not before I heard her saying, "Somebody's already been hurt." Her voice sounded sad. I hoped she was close to giving up.

I walked away from the cruiser, where I'd been huddled for what felt like a week, but it had been about ten minutes. My eyes were stinging so bad I could hardly see where I was going.

I swiped the back of my hand across a cheek. It came away damp.

I told myself it was sweat.

Ten minutes later, Collins was still on the phone, standing by the cruisers. Bea was quite the talker.

I stood behind a tree at the side of her property, my radio in my hand.

Armstrong had arrived and had supervised the evacuation of the houses on Gardner's street and the block behind her property. Civilians were now clustered behind sawhorses blocking the entrance to the cul-de-sac.

Collins lowered the phone to his side and spoke into his radio. "Bradley and Barnes are coming out. Don't know about the child yet. Can we get the K-9 team here?"

"Already on their way," Armstrong said from beside me, "but they were across town when I called them."

"Team, hold your positions." Collins's staticky voice through the radio. "We'll wait for the dog."

I breathed a little easier. That was the safest way to end this.

I prayed that Gardner wouldn't shoot the dog.

The front door opened, and Bradley came out, hands in the air. His sister was close behind, struggling to hold onto the squirming toddler in her arms.

I felt lightheaded with relief and resisted the urge to shout *Hallelujah*.

Armstrong ran to Barnes and hustled her and the child away from the house. Bradley trotted over and joined Collins by the cruisers.

The SWAT team tightened their perimeter, stealthily moving closer to the house.

"Try not to hurt her," I said into my radio. I wanted to add, *she's only a crazy old lady*. But that crazy old lady was also a killer.

"But if you or others are in danger, take your shot," I said instead, my mouth set in a grim line.

CHAPTER TWENTY-NINE

Less than five minutes later, the SUV, with *K-9 Unit* on its doors, pulled up at the end of the row of police vehicles and another ambulance we'd called, just in case. Officer Terry jumped out. He ran around to the back and opened it, but the dog stayed in the vehicle until he gestured with a downward motion.

I jogged over to them.

The dog jumped out, and Terry offered him a small bowl of water. The dog bounced around, ignoring it.

"Drink!" Terry commanded, then looked at me. "Sometimes he gets too excited to take care of himself."

"I know the feeling."

He gave me a thin smile, while pulling a dog-shaped Kevlar vest out of the SUV. He strapped it on King with swift and precise movements.

He said something that sounded like "foos"—German, I suspected—and the dog moved into place beside him. The officer clicked the lead on his collar.

"Is there a back door?" Terry asked me.

I nodded. "Simple wood, Armstrong said. Easy to breach. He's getting the ram."

I keyed my radio. "Bradley." I waited a second while Collins handed his radio to the lieutenant.

"Does she have any other weapons in the house?"

"Not that I saw," Bradley said. "Other than our two service weapons, that is."

"Has she fired on anyone out here?" Terry asked.

"Only the little girl who ran out of the house," I told him.

Terry winced. "Okay, to be on the safe side." He pulled a laminated card out of his pocket. Then he grabbed a bullhorn off his passenger seat. He handed both to me. "After I signal that we're in position, have Sergeant Collins call out this announcement, twice about thirty seconds apart."

"He can't just tell her over the phone?" I asked.

"No, we want all the officers and hopefully some of the neighbors to hear it as well."

He didn't have to explain why. We needed proof that Gardner had been warned about the dog.

I took the card and megaphone over to Collins, then trailed after the K-9 team, which was giving the side of the house a wide berth.

I hung back some, staying out of my people's way.

Armstrong was on one side of the back door, with the ram. Terry, his dog beside him, moved to the other side. He nodded to me.

"Now," I said into the radio.

Collins called out the first warning. The dog bounced a little on his paws and barked twice. Terry made what sounded like an R sound and a hissing noise. "*Ruhig,*" he hissed out a second time, and King settled down.

Collins's voice sounded again from the front of the house. "Last warning," he was ad-libbing some. "Come out with your hands where we can see them, or we'll send in the dog, and he *will* bite you."

Terry waited a few seconds, then unclipped King's lead and held him by the collar instead. He nodded to Armstrong, who lifted the ram.

But before he could step into position, the back door flew open. Bea Gardner surged past them and ran for her back fence, the long barrel of her gun and its suppressor dangling from one hand.

"Gun!" I yelled.

"*Fass!*" Terry shouted and let go of the dog. King bulleted across the yard.

Gardner was attempting to scale the wooden fence, but it was six foot and built for privacy, not climbing. She had little in the way of footholds.

Is she trying to commit suicide by cop?

"Drop the gun," Armstrong yelled. "Now."

Gardner ignored him and continued to scrabble her feet against the fence.

King grabbed an ankle and pulled backward. She tumbled to the ground.

"*Fass,*" Terry repeated. "Gun."

King let go of her leg and ran to her right side. He clamped down on her wrist, and she let out a scream.

Terry ran up and snatched the gun from her hand.

"Get him off of me. I'll sue," Gardner was yelling as I strode over.

"Go ahead," I said. "The whole neighborhood heard that you were warned."

"*Aus,*" Terry said, and King dropped her wrist, took two steps back, then sat.

Armstrong was on the woman in a nanosecond, cuffing her, and none too gently.

"Easy," I said quietly. No need to give her other reasons to sue.

"That damn dog bit me," Gardner ranted. "I'll have him put down."

"Just doing his job," I said, as I wondered where the sweet little old lady had gone.

She continued her tirade, but I ignored her, no longer willing to add fuel to the fire.

I turned to Terry. "May I pet the dog?"

"Later," he said, "when he's off duty."

"I only wanted to thank him. He probably saved lives today." I nodded toward Gardner. "Especially hers." Without the dog, one of the SWAT team would've been force to shoot her when she didn't drop the gun. Otherwise, she could've turned it on any of us in an instant and pulled the trigger.

Terry patted his pocket. "He's already been rewarded."

I caught the faint scent of meat and smiled. "Well, good work, both of you."

He grinned. "Just doing our jobs."

Bea Gardner gave us a tentative smile as we entered the interview room. Her eyes looked worried.

I suspected the little old lady routine was back.

Her right wrist was wrapped in a gauze bandage, as was her left ankle, dressings applied to the dog bites by a paramedic at the scene. But when she was asked if she wanted to go to the hospital, she'd declined.

Bradley identified those present for the recording and repeated the Miranda warning. Was that a note of joy in his voice? He was relishing this.

I couldn't blame him. How humiliating to be ambushed by this woman and her pistol, then tied up by a five-year-old.

I suspected that Barnes, in the observation area behind the one-way mirror, was also enjoying this. Armstrong was with her. After the threat to sue, I wanted as many witnesses as possible.

"Are you sure you don't want a lawyer, Mrs. Gardner?" Bradley said.

She shook her head.

Maybe because the one she trusted is dead.

"The court will provide one," the lieutenant said, "if you can't afford your own."

"No, I have no need for one. I didn't do anything wrong," her voice was syrupy. "I was only defending my home. We have stand-your-ground laws in this state, you know." She batted her eyelashes at him.

I resisted the urge to snort out loud, but let Bradley continue to take the lead.

He shook his head slowly. "My partner was in uniform and we both showed you police ID. And you invited us inside."

Gardner didn't say anything to that.

"I'm afraid the list of charges against you is lengthy," Bradley continued. "Assault of a police officer, two counts; attempted murder, one count; obstruction of justice–"

"Obstruction of justice?" Gardner protested.

"Giving false information to the police," I said.

"Harrumph, I was only trying to help. And that man deserves to go to jail. He's a horrible father."

I assumed she meant Silva, and she wasn't wrong. But being a crappy father was not against the law, unfortunately.

And thank you, Bea, for giving us proof of premeditation. Kidnapping Ashley had not been a spontaneous thing. She'd been watching the Silvas, probably for weeks.

"Endangerment of a child, at least two counts," Bradley continued. "Kidnapping of a minor, at least two counts; and more to come–"

Gardner waved her hand in the air. "I never kidnapped anyone."

"What do you call snatching Ashley Silva out from under her mother's nose?" I demanded. My voice sounded harsh to my ears. I decided I was okay with that. I'd happily play bad cop to Bradley's good one with this lady.

"Liberating her from neglectful parenting," Gardner said, "before something terrible happened."

Bradley cocked an eyebrow at her, which she ignored.

"And you've done that four times before Ashley," he said.

"Five, the first one wasn't as sweet as I thought she would be. The ungrateful thing ran away when she was five years old."

My heart clenched and sank into my stomach. There was yet another child who'd been torn away from her family?

"I couldn't call the police," Gardner was saying. "That's when I decided I needed to officially adopt them, so I could get assistance in a situation like that."

My chest ached. That child was out there somewhere—if she was even still alive. The lawyer's documents had only given the background information for five kids. We needed to find this sixth one, or rather the first, who would be a teenager now.

I turned and looked at the mirror behind me, a signal to Barnes, then I quickly turned back. I heard the faint sound of the observation booth's door opening and closing. She'd gotten the message and was starting the search.

"So you felt justified," Bradley was saying, "in taking these children because their parents were neglecting them?"

"Yes, terrible things can happen when you're not keeping a sharp eye on small children."

Bradley leaned forward. "We know about your granddaughter's drowning," he said, his voice gentle. "Weren't these girls replacements for her?"

"Well, yes, but that was only a positive side effect. I was protecting them, mainly."

"What about the things you left behind, the stuffed animals?" Bradley asked.

"They were a signal that the child was safe. To comfort the parents, and I didn't want police departments wasting their time searching for her."

Again, I struggled not to snort out loud. *As if a teddy bear would have us shrugging and going home. 'Oh well, no need to look for this child. She's in good hands.'*

Bradley sat back. "Let's talk about the shooting of your lawyer."

She nodded, almost eagerly. "He asked me to come to his office. I assumed it was about the adoption of Allie two."

"Or the adoption of the older Allie by someone else," I said, my voice now neutral. That had also been spelled out by the lawyer. Each time a child reached five, Gardner would instruct him to find a new family for her.

"Yes. After that first time, I knew I might not be able to handle an older child, but I always made sure they had a good home."

And then you could kidnap another cute little one. I managed to keep that thought to myself. But I wasn't sure I had completely stifled the sneer that came with it.

Gardner was blatantly ignoring me, though, focusing her gaze solely on Bradley. "You have to understand, Lieutenant, I meant Mr. Campbell no harm. But he pulled a gun on me, said he was turning me in. There was a scuffle and the gun went off. It was self defense."

I didn't tell her that we had an audio recording of her entire encounter with Campbell, which had little resemblance to her current story. Her defense lawyer would eventually get a copy under discovery. But for now, I wanted her to keep digging herself into a hole, which was getting bigger by the moment.

"His wife says he never owned a gun," I said. "He hated them."

"And I suspect the lab will tell us," Bradley's tone was mournful, "that the bullet in him was from the Sig Sauer you were holding when we apprehended you."

"Oh no, that was his gun. I took it with me."

I let the sneer show this time, with no restraints. "We currently have officers tracking down where you bought it."

Gardner glared at me, then quickly rearranged her face into her little old lady persona. She turned back to Bradley. "I'm getting rather tired."

Neither of us responded.

"I think I'll take you up on your earlier offer of a soda and some food."

Bradley glanced my way. I gave a slight nod.

He checked his watch. "Interview suspended at seventeen-twenty."

CHAPTER THIRTY

In the hallway outside the interview room, Bradley said, "She's a piece of work. What's next, Chief?"

"You go at her again, see if her answers change any," I said. "The rest of us have some evidence to gather."

"Like where did she really get that Sig Sauer and the suppressor?"

"Yes," I said, "and we need to contact the parents of those kidnapped kids, and their adoptive families."

Bradley's expression turned grim. "They're going to be devastated."

I shook my head. "Nobody's going to win here. Those kids will be ripped away from the only families they remember. And then their legal parents will have to deal with resentful kids who see them as strangers."

"Maybe, maybe not." A voice from behind me. I whirled around.

Jenny Coleman, from the Department of Children and Families, stood a few feet away. "We may be able to work something out."

I breathed out a sigh, my body relaxing some.

Bradley left us, in search of food and drink for our prisoner.

Jenny fell into step with me, as I headed for my office. "What do you mean?" I asked.

She sighed. "We'll try to work out some kind of joint custody, for a while at least. And the adoptive parents should get visitation indefinitely."

"What if the legal parents refuse?"

She shrugged. "It's my job to convince them that it's in their child's best interests. And theirs, if they want to bond with those children again. And we only have to deal with that with the first three kids. The two she still had, we only need to reunite them with their parents."

"How's the five-year-old doing?"

"She's okay physically. The bullet went through her calf, no permanent damage. Mentally, she's more than a little confused, but she's a survivor. She vaguely remembers her parents, but Gardner had told her they were dead. Hey, loop me in, please, once you've located the parents of the others—both sets."

"Will do." I opted not to get into the additional kidnapped child we'd just learned about. Not until we saw what Barnes could dig up.

She peeled off and headed for the elevators.

Back in my office, I read through the lawyer's missive again, taking notes this time of what we needed to follow up on. The dates when Bea Gardner had adopted each toddler were within a month or two of each kidnapping case. Those biological parents should be easy to find.

Locating the couples who had adopted those same children when they were older might be a bit tougher.

Campbell didn't mention the first child whom Gardner said had run away. He probably hadn't known about her.

But Barnes was hunched over her computer, her fingers flying on the keys. I knew she'd find that kidnapping case eventually.

I shook my head sadly, then turned my focus to Gardner's story of the lawyer's death versus what we knew. Had he called her and told her he was going to turn her in, and she asked to meet with him first?

Would he have been foolish enough to agree to that? Maybe. Her sweet little old lady act was pretty solid, most of the time.

But if that really happened, if Campbell had told her what he was going to do, that would make our case for premeditation stronger. I suspected her defense lawyer would figure that out and tell her to drop that nonsense. Especially after he heard the audio tape.

I hoped the tape would be admissible.

I sighed. If Campbell had turned Gardner in sooner, it would've saved more families from the worst kind of grief there is.

And the poor man would still be alive.

Then it dawned on me...maybe Campbell had bent some rules, secretly hoping he'd be disbarred, as a way to get out from under Gardner's thumb.

It took a full day of Barnes's research and another conversation with Bea Gardner before we got a lead on the first child the woman had kidnapped.

By that time, Gardner had consulted with a defense attorney. She waltzed around our questions and finally would only answer them "hypothetically." But she finally admitted that the first child *might* have been *rescued* in Athens, Georgia.

"The child's toy was left on the porch," she'd said, in that syrupy voice of hers, "and no one came after...um, pursued her. So it worked. The parents were reassured, and the police weren't all that invested in finding her."

I'd resisted the urge to confront her about that silliness—her attorney would have kept her from answering anyway. Did she really believe that a simple toy would be enough to stop a search for a missing child? Did she really believe that *I would believe* she was that naive...or crazy?

Maybe that was it. Maybe she was building a case for an insanity plea.

Sitting at my desk, I ground my teeth at the thought of her getting away with what she'd done. With what she'd put everyone through, what she'd put the Silvas through—although I had trouble feeling all that bad for Gabe Silva.

Annie had called yesterday to thank me, and had mentioned she was filing for divorce. "He doesn't even want visitation with Ashley," she'd said, disgust in her voice. "I can't think what I ever saw in that man."

I'd made what I hoped were sympathetic noises, resisting the urge to say something stronger like, "Good riddance."

But at least Barnes could now focus on old kidnapping cases in southern Georgia.

And I'd enlisted Jenny Coleman's help to see if a child had been found, in Georgia or Florida, around the time that first girl would have run away from Gardner.

Jenny had also mentioned contacting the National Center for Missing and Exploited Children. "Are you familiar with NCMEC?" she'd asked.

I'd given a humorless half-laugh. "Oh yes, I'm quite familiar with their excellent work."

My cell phone pinged, pulling me out of my reverie.

A text message from Kate Huntington. *Can you talk?*

I had texted her yesterday to tell her Ashley was safe, but we hadn't been able to connect since.

I responded by calling her.

She greeted me with a chuckle. "Well, once again, my friend, you've made it onto the national news."

I winced, not crazy about the notoriety. Then I gave Kate a summary of all that had happened in the last few days.

"There was something in the story about a car bomb," she said. "It didn't quite make sense how that was related to the missing child."

I sucked in a deep breath. "It isn't related. Um, it looks like my predecessor, John Black, is trying to either discredit me or, um, kill me."

"You mean it was your car?" Kate's voice rose some. "Are you okay?"

"Yeah, mostly. Barnes got me out in time, but I hurt my shoulder a little."

A long pause. "And you didn't tell me this *why*?"

"I, uh, didn't want you to worry."

"Good lord, Judith. You do remember what I did for a living, right? *Therapist*, and trauma specialist at that. I've heard it all. Not to mention the times I've ended up involved in criminal investigations, many of them yours—and some of them murder investigations. Do you really think I'm that fragile?"

"Well," I chuckled myself, "when you put it that way, I guess not."

I gasped as something dawned on me. Was this why I resisted friendships, especially with other women? Did I assume they would be fragile, like my suicidal mother had been?

"What?" Kate asked.

"Um..." But I couldn't force the words out to tell her my insight. I suddenly felt like the teenager I'd been—hiding in my room, listening when my dad came home, trying to assess his mood. Would he be angry tonight, would he get drunk, would he beat my mother? And maybe seriously hurt her this time?

I felt the old scared, trapped feelings, the vulnerability.

"Nothing," I said. "I, uh, just thought of something I need to do. Good talking to you, Kate, and thanks again for your help on this case."

"You're welcome."

We disconnected and I blew out a sigh of relief. But my insides were still churning.

By the end of the day, I'd calmed my frayed nerves—nothing like the dull routine of perusing incident reports to bore oneself into a semi-comatose state.

And Barnes had found what we thought was the kidnapping case in Georgia, seventeen years ago. But before we contacted that family and got their hopes up, I wanted to locate the girl herself.

At five-thirty, Barnes appeared in my office doorway, grinning from ear to ear. "Ms. Coleman found her, Chief. The girl was picked up wandering the streets of Jax, fourteen years ago. She told them she was five and her name was Allie, but she didn't seem to remember a last name. She was put in foster care, and aged out of the system last year. She's still living with her foster parents, though, going to community college."

"Phew." I matched her grin, suddenly feeling twenty pounds lighter.

"Ms. Coleman's working on reuniting her with her family."

I nodded.

"And I was looking into Bea Gardner's finances," Barnes said. "You're not gonna believe this. She won the Florida lottery fifteen years ago."

"I had wondered," I said, "how a cafeteria worker could retire early and still afford a lawyer like Campbell."

"And that property she owns, she's only been there for three years. She's moved every three to four years, sometimes here in Starling, sometimes in Jacksonville. I guess she didn't want her neighbors getting suspicious when her granddaughter suddenly disappeared, replaced by a younger version."

"Good work," I said.

Barnes's expression sobered. "I thought that was an urban myth, that criminals insert themselves into the police investigation. Why did she do that?"

"It happens," I said. "Although not nearly as often as cop shows on TV imply. But I've seen if before. Like Gardner, they may be trying to throw the investigation off track, and/or trying to find out what exactly the police know. Sometimes, they do it for kicks, to relive the crime, or to laugh at the cops behind their backs. Those clowns almost always get caught, though."

I shut down my computer and pushed myself to a stand with my good hand. "Time to go home." Sam had promised to cook me a celebratory dinner tonight, at my apartment, and I didn't want to be late.

Barnes grinned again and sketched me a salute before disappearing from my doorway.

I was debating whether or not to even bother taking my Glock home, when my desk phone rang. *Watch Desk* appeared on the caller ID.

"Yes, Sarge."

"Chief, there's a young woman out here who wants to see you. She refuses to say why. But she's been checked for weapons, and she seems harmless enough."

It occurred to me that it might be the mother of one of the kidnapped girls. Kate said the story had hit the national news.

"I'll be right out." I locked the pistol in my desk, draped my jacket around my shoulders and grabbed my laptop case handle. I'd deal with this woman and then go right out the door.

There were only two people sitting on the metal folding chairs in the makeshift waiting area. And only one of them was young and female. She had her head bent over a magazine.

I took a step in her direction and she lifted her head, turned it toward me.

I gasped.

She was the spitting image of my Aunt Jean in her youth. Shoulder-length, light brown hair curled around a fair, heart-shaped face.

The young woman made eye contact and smiled as she rose. We both stepped forward, stopping a few feet apart in the middle of the waiting area.

"I think you must be my Aunt Judy," she said.

Remarkably, I didn't tense up. For once, I didn't mind a bit being called Judy.

She took another step and opened her arms.

I stiffened. Nope, not ready for a hug from a stranger. Instead, I offered my left hand.

She took it between both of hers and squeezed slightly. "I'm so glad we've found each other."

I smiled despite myself, but resisted the urge to say, "Me too."

"How *did* you find me?" I asked instead, as I gently pulled my hand loose. I was buying time as my brain scrambled to process the jumble of feelings inside.

My stomach churned and my chest was tight, but it also felt full and warm.

She chuckled. "Google is my friend."

A shiver ran down my spine. The chuckle had sounded a lot like Aunt Jean's laugh.

"Your PI told me you were a police chief in Florida," she said. "There are only about a dozen chiefs and sheriffs—female ones, that is. I had it narrowed down to three, and then I saw the report on the news last night about the kidnapped girl your department had just found."

She paused, hooking a hank of hair behind her ear. "Mr. Canfield had mentioned you were involved in a kidnapping case."

I froze, staring.

"What?" She looked confused. "What's the matter?"

"Meredith," I whispered under my breath, then cleared my throat. "My cousin..." I faltered, immobilized by an internal argument. No, it was time to acknowledge reality.

"Your mother...she used to do that." I mimicked the gesture, even though my hair was almost too short to go behind my ear.

Her hands flew to her face, and she burst into tears. Then she threw her arms around me.

I winced and pulled my damaged right side away from her.

She let go of that arm, but continued to cling to my left arm and cry on that shoulder.

Again I stiffened, not sure what to do.

Movement out of the corner of my eye. The sergeant, who'd been standing by his desk out of earshot, was now moving toward us.

I held up my left hand, as best I could, in a stop gesture. He withdrew.

The young woman pulled away, her face flushed. "I'm sorry."

"No." I put my hand on her shoulder. "It's okay." The remaining tensions from the last few days drained away, and the warmth in my chest spread.

"It's okay," I said again.

And it was. Because she wasn't a stranger after all.

She was family.

———— ⋅◦⋅ ————

AUTHOR'S NOTES

If you enjoyed this book, please take a moment to leave a short review on the ebook retailer of your choice. Reviews help with sales and sales keep the stories coming. You can readily find the links to these retailers at the *misterio press* bookstore (https://misteriopress.com/bookstore/) .

This is Book 6 in this series; Book 1 is *Lethal Assumptions*, and Book 5 (the one just prior to this one) is *Malignant Memories*. (All of my series are listed in the front of this book.)

This book was proofread by multiple sets of eyes, but proofreaders are human. If you noticed any errors, please email me at kass@kassandralamb.com so I can have them corrected.

Heck, email me anyway. I love hearing from readers!

And you may want to sign up for my newsletter at https ://kassandralamb.com to get a heads up about new releases, plus special offers and bonuses for subscribers. You will receive a free novelette, *The Tell-Tale Bark*, the prequel to the Marcia Banks and Buddy cozy series, AND a free novella, *Sweet Sanctuary*, the prequel to my Kate Huntington Mysteries. The C.o.P. on the Scene Mysteries are a spinoff from this series. Judith is a secondary character in that series, first showing up in Book 4, and playing a more extensive role in most of the books after that.

Also, *misterio press* has a readers' group on Facebook (https://www.facebook.com/groups/misteriopressmys teries/) where we chat with readers and also offer giveaways, contests and other goodies. Please stop by and check it out!

If you're wondering why it's taken so long for this book to come out, that has mainly been due to some health issues I've had this year. Nothing life threatening, but things that have sapped my energy and taken up time for doctors' visits. The problem is partly that my mind still thinks I'm forty, while my body is solidly in its seventies. But I'm doing better now, and I hope to be a bit more productive this coming year.

Bear with me as I spread around some gratitude, and I'll give you an inside look at some of the research I had to do for this book, and some insights into some of the characters.

As I've said before, it takes a village to produce a book, and my village includes five wonderful ladies, the crew at *misterio press*. They have always been supportive of me and each other, but this year I appreciated that support more than ever. I especially want to thank Shannon Esposito and Kirsten Weiss who critiqued this manuscript and made it better (and in Kirsten's case, caught quite a few misplaced commas). And then, after I'd messed with it awhile, Kathy Owen gave it one more perusal to make sure everything still made sense. Thanks so much, Kathy. You're a gem.

And much gratitude to my long-suffering husband, who puts up with my crazy hours (sometimes you just have to get those words down, even if it's four o'clock in the morning) and who also does the final proofread of each book.

My village also includes two other awesome ladies. One is my cover designer, Melinda VanLone. She's been bringing my mental visions to life now for over a decade, and it has been great working with her. No matter how many covers we create together, I still get so excited as each project starts to gel and the image I had in my head actually evolves into a book cover.

The other awesome lady is my author's assistant and formatter, Joy Hampp. She takes care of many annoying business tasks for me, so I can spend more of my time and energy writing. And she does a great job of formatting each manuscript. She is very aptly named; she's a joy to work with.

And now on to the fun stuff...well, mostly fun.

It was really interesting researching police dogs so that I could introduce a K-9 unit to the Starling PD in this story. I was surprised that many police dogs in the US are actually trained in Germany and then imported. Thus the common use of German commands. And I also found it interesting that these dogs can only be trained in a few tasks, lest their training become diluted.

If you've read my Marcia Banks and Buddy mysteries, you'll know that I'm a dog lover. So it was great fun being able to add King to Judith's department.

My research into the sex offenders' registry in Florida was also more than a little surprising, and depressing. Why depressing? As of 2024, there were roughly 86,000 names in the Florida registry and only about 400 of them still lived in Florida. The population of Florida is currently estimated to be around 23,839,000. Eighty-six thousand is only one third of one percent of that population. That's a pathetic number of abusers who have been caught and registered; and trust me, there are far more than that out there, most of them hiding in plain sight. (And, as Lieutenant Bradley says, Florida is known to be more diligent than most states at maintaining this registry.)

I'm not sure why so many of them no longer live in Florida. One possibility is that many of those arrested here were tourists (we get a lot of them), and after they were processed through the Florida legal system (and hopefully spent some time incarcerated), they moved back to their home states. But it's also possible that abusers move away so that they can evade the authorities and disappear in another state.

Okay, on to a somewhat less grim subject—Improvised Explosive Devices. ;-)

Actually, this *is* kind of a funny story. For the car bomb in Judith's car, I wanted to use an IED with a pressure plate trigger. Usually these go off when pressure is applied to the trigger plate (such as when the person enters the car and sits down). But I wanted it to go off when she gets out of the car, i.e., when the pressure is removed.

So I googled "can a pressure plate explosive go off when pressure is released?" The answer that immediately popped up stated that I was asking how to build a bomb and that information would not be provided.

I was both relieved and frustrated by this news. I'm very glad Google is making it more difficult for crazies to build bombs, but...

I ended up having the pressure plate set off a secondary trigger (a timer) instead. I'm fairly confident it's possible to rig a bomb that way, but I wasn't about to research it online to find out for sure. I don't need the FBI showing up at my door!

I always enjoy revisiting Kate Huntington via these stories, but this time her private investigator husband also played a significant role. Skip Canfield has had a somewhat strange relationship with Judith through the years. For the most part, she viewed him as a nuisance because he would periodically stick his nose into her homicide investigations in Baltimore County. (And in one Kate story, Book 5 in the series, he's the prime suspect in a murder and Judith is actively trying to chase him down.) But she has begrudgingly developed a fair amount of respect for his investigative skills and his integrity.

Skip also has mixed feelings about Judith, and he believes she takes herself far too seriously. To defend against her negative attitude toward him, he tends to act like he's mildly amused by her, using a flip tone and doing little things to get under her skin, like pretending to forget her current title. But deep down he respects her, and in this story that comes through more, and he shows concern for her in her new high-pressure role.

If you'd like to understand the dynamics between them better, I'd suggest reading *Police Protection*, the last book in the Kate Huntington Mysteries. Judith begrudgingly asks for Skip's help in that story, when her old training officer is accused of shooting an unarmed child. That book, in a way, acts as a prequel to the C.o.P. on the Scene series, as Judith becomes disillusioned with the bureaucracy of a large police department.

Please stay tuned for the next installment in this series, a story set at Halloween (which I had planned to have out this Halloween, but that didn't happen). It is tentatively titled *The Night of the Living Bled,* and it revolves around the very real rivalry football game played each year between the University of Georgia Bulldogs and the University of Florida Gators. To avoid either team having the home-field advantage, it is played in Jacksonville at the Jaguars stadium. And almost every year, the revelry and the rivalry get out of hand and violence occurs.

And since Judith's fictitious city of Starling is right next door to Jacksonville, her town would naturally get considerable spillover of players and fans—staying in their motels, having rowdy parties, and bringing chaos to their streets.

ABOUT THE AUTHOR

Kassandra Lamb has never been able to decide which she loves more, psychology or writing. In college, she realized that writers need a day job in order to eat, so she studied psychology. After a career as a psychotherapist and college professor, she is now retired and can pursue her passion for writing.

She spends most of her time in an alternate universe with her characters. The portal to that universe, aka her computer, is located in Florida, where her husband and dog catch occasional glimpses of her.

Kass has completed the ten-book, traditional mystery series, The Kate Huntington Mysteries (set in her native Maryland, about a psychotherapist/amateur sleuth), plus four Kate on Vacation novellas (with the same main characters). She is also the author of the thirteen-book Marcia Banks and Buddy cozy mystery series, about a service dog trainer and her sidekick and mentor dog, Buddy, set in north central Florida.

And her current series are police procedurals, the C.o.P. on the Scene Mysteries, with Lieutenant Judith Anderson from the Kate Huntington series as the main character—only now she is the Chief of Police of a small Florida city.

To read and see more about Kassandra and her books, please go to https://kassandralamb.com. Be sure to sign up for the newsletter there to get a heads up about new releases, plus special offers and bonuses for subscribers (and free stories).

Kass's e-mail is kass@kassandralamb.com and she loves hearing from readers! She's also on Facebook and Goodreads and she blogs about psychological topics and other random things at https://misteriopress.com.

Kassandra also writes romantic suspense under the pen name of Jessica Dale .

~~

Please check out these other great *misterio press* series:
Karma's A Bitch: Pet Psychic Mysteries
by Shannon Esposito
Multiple Motives: Kate Huntington Mysteries
by Kassandra Lamb
The Metaphysical Detective: Riga Hayworth Paranormal Mysteries
by Kirsten Weiss
Dangerous and Unseemly: Concordia Wells Historical Mysteries
by K.B. Owen
Murder, Honey: Carol Sabala Mysteries
by Vinnie Hansen
Payback: Unintended Consequences Romantic Suspense
by Jessica Dale
Buried in the Dark: Frankie O'Farrell Mysteries
by Shannon Esposito
Her Little Secret: Detective Mila Harlow Mysteries
by Shannon Esposito
To Kill A Labrador: Marcia Banks and Buddy Cozy Mysteries
by Kassandra Lamb
Lethal Assumptions: C.o.P. on the Scene Mysteries
by Kassandra Lamb
Never Sleep: Chronicles of a Lady Detective Historical Mysteries
by K.B. Owen
Bound: Witches of Doyle Cozy Mysteries
by Kirsten Weiss
At Wits' End Doyle Cozy Mysteries

by Kirsten Weiss
<u>Steeped In Murder: Tea and Tarot Mysteries</u>
by Kirsten Weiss
<u>The Perfectly Proper Paranormal Museum Mysteries</u>
by Kirsten Weiss
<u>Big Shot: The Big Murder Mysteries</u>
by Kirsten Weiss
<u>Steam and Sensibility: Sensibility Grey Steampunk Mysteries</u>
by Kirsten Weiss
Plus even more great mysteries/thrillers in the *misterio press* bookstore .

www.ingramcontent.com/pod-product-compliance
Lightning Source LLC
Chambersburg PA
CBHW020225260626
47156CB00002B/547